PRAISE FOR

ATACAMA

"Jendia Gammon's *Atacama* masterfully weaves a gripping sci-fi mystery that blurs the line between reality and nightmare. With lyrical prose, Gammon builds an atmosphere thick with tension and dread as she takes you on a heart-pounding race for answers. What begins as a twisted mystery quickly spirals into a cosmic nightmare, unearthing surreal horrors lurking beneath the surface that will haunt you long after the final page. A mind-bending exploration of grief, love, and the unknown, *Atacama* is as unnerving as it is hopeful, and left me clawing for more as it pulled me deeper into its eerie world."

—Mallory Pearson, author of *Voice Like a Hyacinth* and *We Ate the Dark*

"*Atacama* is a devious blend of mystery and horror set against the unforgiving background of a remote and brutal desert. Chockful of relatable characters and unexpected twists. Jendia Gammon brings real game to this cross-genre thriller!"

—Jonathan Maberry, *NY Times* bestselling author of *NecroTek* and the *Joe Ledger Thrillers*

"An enthralling horror thriller from a masterful storyteller."

—Gareth L. Powell

"Jendia Gammon weaves lush description with ratcheting tension to deliver a story that is both chilling and compelling. *Atacama* is a book that will stay with the reader long after the last page."

—Helen Glynn Jones, author of *The Last Raven*

"Gripping and fast paced, Jendia Gammon's *Atacama* blends the horror elements of *The Thing* with the nightmarish complexity of Stephen King's *The Outsider*. Sharp prose, flawed characters, and a complex plot will appeal to horror and thriller readers alike. Highly recommended!"

—D.K. Stone, author of the *Edge of Wild* trilogy, and *Inescapable: A Ghost Story*

"Gammon's *Atacama* is a fast-paced thriller that showcases her strengths of strong heroines and divine prose. Whether transporting us to a lab full of chaos or the dry flats of the desert, when Gammon turns to the stars and the mysteries of the universe, that is when she shines and I'm in love."

—Rowan Hill, author of *Foxfire* and *No Fair Maidens From Earth to Mars*

ATACAMA

ATACAMA

JENDIA GAMMON

COVER ILLUSTRATION: CHRIS PANATIER

INTERIOR ILLUSTRATIONS: JENDIA GAMMON

ISBN: 978-1-957941-17-2

Cover illustration: Chris Panatier

Interior illustrations: Jendia Gammon

Cover design: Ranxvrus

Interior design: Dreadful Designs

First Edition

2025

For my children
For Gareth
And for all those in science who are nameless
but tireless in the goal of discovery

What matter, what hollow swan
plunges its naked agony into the sand
and hardens its slow liquid light?

—Pablo Neruda: *Atacama*

PROLOGUE

A spectacular crash of glass blasted through the hallway of the first floor of the Hansen Biology Building. Gale Thompson spilled her LB solution onto her lab coat, and it seeped onto her shoes. She scowled over its fetid reek, even as she trembled from the shock of the crashing glass. She craned her neck to see if Will had heard it, but he sat with headphones on, analyzing data on the lab computer. She sighed, set the solution down, and stepped out into the hall.

The hallway floor outside lab room 175 glistened with a pile of shattered glass. A tall man with dark, curly hair and stylish glasses emerged from the room, whistling, and walked with jaunty purpose all around the mess. Gale could see he brandished a shop broom like a rock star might hold a microphone at a concert. He swept and whistled, swept and whistled, his whistles and the clinking of glass echoed down the hallway from where she peered around the corner of her lab's door. It was late, 6:47 according to her phone, and 6:49

according to the fast analog clock wheeling its benign wand in a drab and economical circle perched on the wall opposite the door in the lab. Dr. Franks had left at 5:25 to go home; the grad students would drift in and out like the tide, but she, the lab tech, tended to stay late on Thursdays. She had little else to do except to go home to feed her birds and watch TV.

She stared at the mess and dithered over what to do. But the man saw her, and she jerked instinctively but did not reenter the lab.

He laughed. "It's all right," he called. "Just cleaning up my mess."

Gale emerged fully and tugged at her light brown ponytail. "Are—are you all right?"

He was whistling again as he shoved the quite spectacular pile of broken glass of all sizes into one position.

"Feeling great!" he said. "Are you the new tech of Franks?"

Gale nodded. She stood awkwardly in the hall. She decided to walk toward him.

"Yeah. I'm Gale. Do you need help?"

The man set the broom against the wall and approached her. He wore fine Italian boots, she noted, had artfully distressed jeans, a fancy belt buckle, and a crisp, dark brown shirt. His eyes were hazel, and he was indeed quite tall as he looked down at her.

"I might! I'm Jack. Jack Cordeiro." He extended his hand for her to shake.

She blushed. "Oh! Dr. Cordeiro! I'm sorry. I didn't know you were back."

"Please," he said. "Call me Jack. Come in, if you have a moment?"

Gale could tell he caught a whiff of the spilled LB on her lab coat. Embarrassed, she quickly dashed back to her lab, doffed the coat, and returned. She followed Jack into Room 175. She found a chaotic scene inside, with piles of plastic zip bags spread out across the black lab benches. No one else was in the lab; the PI, Dr. Sykes, had taken the day off after receiving some bad news (so she had heard from Dr. Franks).

Jack gestured to a lab stool.

"As you can see," he said, "I have a bit of a mess on my hands. I need to get some of these in the deep freezer, but I'm not quite in the mental state to do that right now."

He looked cheerful enough, Gale thought, and even kind of elated, as he smiled. But the glassware in the hall...

"I nearly dumped them all on the side of the road," he confessed, grinning at her.

She could feel the little "11" forming in her forehead as she considered that statement. He laughed.

"I know. Crazy, right?" And he hummed. He sorted through some of the plastic bags, which had been labeled hastily with black marker. "I'm not as interested in the plants, though. I'm interested in something that came back from the desert."

"The desert?" Gale echoed.

"Yes. Atacama."

"Oh yes, the group went down last summer, and they've just gone back, right?" she asked.

"Yes," said Jack. "Only we've not heard from them in a few days. They did send some samples back, which, remarkably, made it through customs."

"Samples of what?" asked Gale, for she knew that the plants before her did not grow in any desert. They were, if she had to guess, from some kind of deciduous tree. Maybe beech.

Jack walked around to the back of the lab and extravagantly waved his arm for her to follow. She did. There were Petri dishes laid out in an orderly fashion, carefully labeled in a different handwriting from Jack's, with what looked like coordinates on them. Inside each dish were what looked like sand, and soil, and some mix thereof. Different dishes held slightly different looking samples.

"Soil's not my purview," Jack told her. "These were supposedly full of seeds, but those have been sifted out. I don't know who these samples are for. I *do* know that I don't quite like them. Watch this."

He retrieved a hulking Geiger counter from the opposite bench and turned it on. He waved it over the dishes, and the machine buzzed and crackled. Gale backed away.

"How dangerous is it?" she asked.

"Not so much now," smirked Jack. "But whenever the meteor hit, I guarantee the animals at the time didn't think so."

"How long ago?" Gale wondered.

"Long," said Jack. He adjusted his high-end glasses. Then he looked over them at her.

"But that's not the most interesting thing about these. And I think, Gale, I might be losing my mind."

With that extraordinary proclamation, Jack waved his arm and said, "Look what happens when I approach them up close."

She watched as he walked up to the dishes and held a hand close to them. The grains inside rose toward his hand.

"What?" said Gale, breathless. "Why are they doing that?"

"No idea," answered Jack. "I wouldn't ask you to do the same, but—"

She surged forward and held her hand over the dishes and the grains leaped up, and the dishes burst open and spilled their contents all over the lab floor. She and Jack jumped back and then found themselves creeping backward toward the lab door. For the dirt began arranging itself in ornate patterns on the floor and making little bridges from the floor into the air, like so much scaffolding, made of sand and dirt from a moment of impact by a large object into the earth eons ago. The connections bridged and stretched and bridged again until something resembling a possible creature emerged. The scaffolding stepped forward, purposefully, toward Gale and Jack.

"My God," whispered Jack. "What did they bring back from that desert? And what happened to everyone who's there now?"

Gale swallowed. "I don't know. But I think we should *run*!"

**(from "The Scaffold" in *THE SHADOW GALAXY*,
by Jendia Gammon, writing as J. Dianne Dotson)**

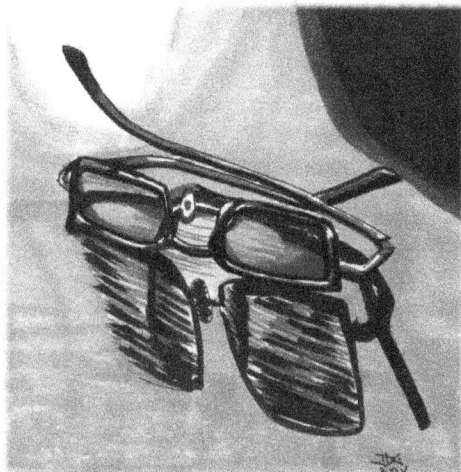

CHAPTER 1
COLD NEWS FROM A HOT LAND

One thing Fiona learned: good news is rarely told in cold silence. She sat uncertainly at her seat, with its mini desktop swiveled in front of her, and she twisted her fingers upon it. Then she pushed back, fluffed her shirt a bit from where it stuck to her sweaty skin, and leaned back appreciatively under the vent of the air-conditioned auditorium. Fiona watched the door to the great room open, and two graduate students fumbled forward to help the professor. He gave them a pinched look through his wire-rimmed glasses. The students adjusted the microphone at the podium. Dr. Bingham's face looked strained, and she could faintly hear his voice drift over to where she sat, midway up the stadium seating.

"Leave it," he said tersely to the students, a young woman and a younger man. They twitched in servile concern. He stared over his glasses at them, and each finally realized he meant for them to leave him be. They scurried to seats in the front row, centered before him. He adjusted the lights at the podium; someone in the back of the great room dimmed the overhead lights, illuminating only him. He fussed with a pen in his shirt pocket, scribbled something on the papers he had set at the podium, and glanced up at everyone. He cleared his throat.

Dr. Bingham said, "I am deeply saddened to bring you terrible news this morning."

The din of the auditorium extinguished, and the only thing Fiona could hear was Dr. Bingham shuffling the papers before him. He cleared his throat again, coughing a bit. He looked up at everyone again and then cast his eyes downward.

"As some of you may know, the Gilden expedition arrived in the Atacama Desert twelve days ago. At that time, Dr. Bridget Gilden alerted us of their arrival and had met with a guide to help them. Five days ago, the signals of everyone's phones suddenly dropped at the same time."

A ripple of whispers undulated through the hall. Fiona bit her lip.

Dr. Bingham went on, his voice barely tremulous, "Now, I knew Bridget well, as most of you know. At first, I wasn't concerned and just assumed the signal was poor. It was a remote location. We all knew that. But I remembered she had a sat phone and could have dialed for assistance if she needed to. I heard from her on Thursday of last week. And last night—last night—"

He paused, and he looked first up, and then down, and then up again. He caught Fiona's eyes, which had widened in interest and concern. He bent his head down.

"Last night," he said, and his voice began to shake, "I received word from the consulate of Chile that eight bodies had been recovered in the desert. I am devastated to tell you that the entire Gilden expedition is dead."

Loud gasps, broken cries, and looks of devastation threaded through the hall.

Fiona's heart pounded, and tears sprang into her eyes. She didn't know Dr. Gilden well, but she did know someone on that team. She did not want to believe the words from Dr. Bingham's mouth.

No.

A smile in her mind, a laughing voice.

No.

Someone stood up quickly, phone in hand, texting, their face blanched, and hastened out of the room. Fiona's fingers twitched, as she was tempted to text Marian herself. But she resisted.

Marian Haglund had planned to go on the expedition and had backed out at the last minute, owing to her mother's illness. Fiona's eyes stung as she remembered Marian saying, "They say she'll be okay, but Mom wants me there. She would never tell me that, not before something like this. But I know. So, I'm staying."

Fiona shivered then. Marian survived only because she had not gone on that trip. Marian knew everyone on the doomed team, of course, but Fiona only knew Alva. She had been—and she hated thinking of her in the past tense—a remarkable researcher for her age, as she was twenty-two, brilliant, kind, a great teaching assistant in botany. An awful, hollowed-out sensation sank into Fiona's spirit and settled there, a sudden and unwelcome guest. She could not believe that someone so positive and young and vibrant had died. Alva. Her friend—it couldn't be true.

She watched Dr. Bingham. He cleared his throat and held out his hands, placating, beseeching. He looked so pale and exhausted that she would not have been surprised if he had dropped dead on the spot, adding to the death count of the dark day. But he did speak.

"There's a lot of questions we're trying to get answered. We've informed the next of kin." He glanced down at Fiona. "Other...members of the lab may not all be aware, and I'm asking all of you: give them the chance to find out from us."

Dr. Bingham scooted his papers around with gnarled fingers and pushed his glasses back up his nose, where they had slid down. He sighed. The hairs in his ears shone in the odd lighting at the podium. It made him resemble an owl, Fiona thought wildly. Her thoughts bounded through many things at once, and she wondered why he would look at her right as she'd thought of messaging Marian. She had resisted, but the person who had left hadn't, nor did several other students.

Piff-piff.

Dr. Bingham tapped his shirt mic, clipped onto the collar of a button-up shirt that was white with thinly lined blue checks, and said, clearing his throat again, "I don't have much else to go on, but if anyone has questions..." His voice dropped off into another sigh.

Voices rose again, and he nodded to one person with their hand up, illuminated in the light from the podium.

"Was it a gang?" the young man asked.

Dr. Bingham's eyes flashed. "Really?" he barked, and his face flushed. "I'll not have that kind of talk. You're dismissed. Get your bag and get out."

The room went deadly quiet, though Fiona heard someone whisper, "Dayum!"

The professor trembled.

"I apologize," he stammered. "This is all a bit much. I'll send out an email as soon as I know anything." He brushed his hand over his eyeglasses and then waved outward. "You can go."

Fiona clutched her backpack on one shoulder, and it pulled uncomfortably as she stood. She pushed past the rumbling throng of students swarming Dr. Bingham, who raised his hands up as if to try to quell them. She hesitated, thinking she would simply go and text Marian, and he shot her a look. She held back, and finally, Dr. Bingham shouldered a messenger bag and approached her, back hunched over.

"You'll tell Marian?" he asked her.

She was surprised. "I...I can," she answered, not wanting to admit how close she had come to doing so already.

He closed his eyes and nodded.

"You know, she—" he began.

"I know," said Fiona.

Dr. Bingham's forehead pushed together in a tectonic mess of wrinkles.

"Come with me," he said quietly. "There's more to discuss."

CHAPTER 2
THERE WERE VICUÑAS

Puzzled, Fiona followed the professor out the side door, where a sudden blast of sun and humidity struck her. Dr. Bingham shuffled along the sidewalk in between the sleek science and engineering building to the quite aged Hansen Biology Building and said nothing. He looked more stooped to Fiona than usual, and she did not like the way his left leg dragged a bit as he walked. She had never noticed that before.

"I'll get the door," she said quickly, and he nodded vaguely, squinting in the bright sunlight, but he only seemed to react to stimuli rather than fully notice them. Mentally, the professor seemed not to be present at all. He even stood absently while she held the heavy old door open, and then with a start, he remembered where he was and walked through, thanking her offhandedly as he did so.

She felt a little spark of indignation; even someone as nice as Dr. Bingham remained stuck in the old science guard's ways. Still, she had experienced far worse in the biology building alone, and in her undergraduate experience generally. She breathed in the rich, fertilizer scent of the first floor of the biology building, where many of the botany laboratories and the greenhouse sat in relative peace at the moment, between classes in the afternoon.

And many of those classes she had attended alongside...

No.

Walking in the main foyer of the building, Fiona's shoes crunched on something, and she looked down. Not seeing anything, she checked their soles. She found a piece of broken glass embedded in her right sole, and she pulled it out carefully and stared at it. It was curved, like lab glassware. She looked around and did not see any other pieces on the floor, so she wrapped it in a piece of tissue from her bag and carried it until they passed a trash can, and she dropped it in.

It must have been tracked from somewhere else, she reasoned.

She sped forth to catch up with Dr. Bingham, who had turned down another hallway to his office.

A stack of dirty seedling trays sat pushed up against the wall of that hallway. The other hallways were far more pristine, and the upper-story labs were primarily used for more sensitive work, like plant genetics experiments and PCR. Dr. Bingham's office, however, did not reside on one of those more hallowed floors. He led Fiona down the shabby, earth-scented hallway to his office at the end of it and fumbled with his keys for the old brass lock.

The upper folks get the good stuff, she reflected bitterly, not for the first time. Dr. Bingham was a renowned biologist and tenured, yet the university shunted his office down the most unremarkable corridor in the entirety of Hansen Biology. He deserved better. It made no sense to Fiona, but then, nothing about academia's politics made sense to her anyway. She followed him into his dimly lit office, with one rather pathetic window whose view looked out on a slot alley between buildings. *Good thing he's got plants in here*, she thought. Otherwise, it might have looked like a sterile, lifeless basement.

Shuffling papers on his desk, Dr. Bingham muttered something indecipherable and then, as though he had forgotten Fiona stood there, frowned, and said, "Oh." She blinked at him. "Did you hear anything from anyone? You were friends with…I'm sorry."

No. No. No.

She stared at him, almost wishing time might stop, that he might not say anything more. That she could pretend, even for a moment, that her friend might still be alive.

Alva.

She closed her eyes, opened them, and blinked.

No.

Dr. Bingham took his glasses off and rubbed his eyes, pushing his crepey skin into ripples. Then, looking up at her from his seat, he said, "I don't know what's going to happen next. But as this is now an… international incident, it might help…that is, if you have anything. Letters, texts, emails…anything that might indicate something went awry. I'm asking everyone who knows the team members. Not singling you out or anything."

Her mouth hung open for a moment.

"No, I know," Fiona said numbly. She felt dizzy.

She had texts from Alva at first, and after delay and poor signal, a few emails. In those, she could see the desert through Alva's words.

"There are vicuñas here who try to befriend you or head-butt you or steal your food."

Fiona grinned at that, thinking of the slender, shorter-haired alpaca-like creatures.

"We drink tea in the morning, and it tastes like minerals."

"These fucking influencers. You should see them. We had to walk through a big stretch of desert, absolutely parched, my lips cracked, skin burnt, and we walk up and see a fully-set, long-ass table with candles and flowers (from where?) and shit. In the goddamn desert. Ain't money a drug?"

"I've been to the Hand. It reaches up not to seek heaven, I think, but to warn anything that might be looking that this is hell. It's a stop sign."

"The volcanoes look unreasonable to me. I dread them every time I see them, and it's hard not to. They thrust upward like knives, and at any moment in history they could cut the sky and make it bleed. I keep thinking that the 'any moment' is imminent."

But Alva always did have a way with words. Fiona did not want to think that those might be crystallized forever. That there would be no new words from her friend with whom she had roomed her freshman year, who had vomited in their shared sink after a frat party, and then after entering major courses, who had gone on to grab every A and scholarship she could.

How much does it matter now if she's dead?

Fiona focused on the "if" because with a lack of data in front of her, that vibrant young woman could not be dead. It simply wasn't possible.

"Just," Fiona found her voice at last, "a few emails. I knew she had spotty service."

She did not tell him about the letters, the real ones. The ones Alva had mailed. She did not know why she did not tell him. Some instinct stopped her.

"Hmm," said the professor, "well, one would. Bridget had a sat phone for emergencies. I don't understand…"

He sighed. The air floated with dust motes, it reeked of old flowerpots, and he looked quite as if he had regretted not taking the offer of emeritus status he had been offered the past summer.

"There were vicuñas," Fiona said absently, pulling on a piece of dead skin on her chapped lips.

He looked at her over his glasses.

"Go home. Make copies of all that stuff. And get some rest. If you can come back tomorrow, we'll go through old files."

She walked the half-mile trek across campus to her parking spot.

What does a vicuña do when it sees a dead body? she wondered.

CHAPTER 3
TOMATO SOUP

S he turned the door key with a click, grimacing at the sound of the neighbors arguing *again*. The apartment complex sat tucked back inside a leafy pocket right off the main highway to the university, and she liked that aspect of it. She could hear wood thrushes and sometimes, at night, a great horned owl. Cicadas ricocheted their caustic sounds through the trees on hot summer days, and katydids eased the night sounds into a soft cacophony of rasping and scraping music all their own. The in-between hours, not quite dusk, were sultry and soporific. Mosquitos drifted up as if they had waited all day for her to come home from work. She smacked one on her neck and drew her hand back to see the small smear of blood and smashed legs, and she wiped her hand absently on her backpack. Turning the door handle, she entered to hear the TV and smell a freshly microwaved Hot Pocket, and she became tempted to close the door and pretend she had not come home at all. Then she could go to her ancient, maroon Honda Civic, turn the key, drive off up into the mountains, and wend her way down the other side into North Carolina…then keep going until she ran out of road, presumably at Wrightsville Beach. And from there, where?

Anywhere but here.

"Hey babe," a voice called, and she felt her shoulders fall in disappointment.

Graham muted the TV, which showed late-season baseball, and approached her, arms wide. He was a sweet young man, and she knew he was trying to be accommodating to her, but many times he overdid it, or crowded her. She felt suffocated at every turn, and guilty that she did. She hugged him. He smelled like pine-scented stick deodorant and Head and Shoulders shampoo. As ever. But he was solid, and his arms were strong, and for a moment she forgot her troubles and just leaned against him.

"Tough day?" he asked into her hair.

"Yeah," said Fiona, and she backed away from him, for his deodorant was so strong and faux-woodsy that it made her nauseous. So did the lingering scent of the Hot Pocket. In fact, everything made her nauseous.

"You look super pale," Graham noted. "Can I fix you something to eat?"

She held up her hand, warding off the urge to vomit, and said thickly, "No, no thank you. I'm. I'm going to lie down for a bit."

He crinkled his brow at her, and she gave him a weak half-smile and walked past him back to their bedroom. She was glad it was quiet at the moment. The neighbors had stopped yelling. The green screen of the woods behind their apartment shone through the tall, skinny bedroom window and cast a green glow across the floral comforter, cream-colored cotton covered in embroidered vines. She sat down on the bed. It sank, its cheap mattress soft, and then she let herself fall back, still with her legs dangling over the side of the bed. She stared up at the white ceiling fan, its globe shade dingy ivory.

The blades need dusting, she thought absently.

She rubbed her temples. Her head hurt. Her stomach churned. She felt cold inside. Not ice cold. But underwater cold. Like the time she had fallen off her dad's boat in the lake in spring, when it was too cold to swim. The dark green liquid pressing in on her as she stared up at the shafts of feeble sun in starburst form above the water. She had heaved herself up, not being a good swimmer, and when her dad pulled her out and she sputtered, she shivered for a good two hours after that. The instant cocoa he had handed her tasted more like instant coffee, likely from residue in the mug, and she had held the enamel mug gingerly. Cocoa tasted different outside. Metallic. Burnt. She remembered that now.

There would be no lake in the desert.

But then, she wasn't sure.

She heard Graham turn on the stove fan and set a pan on a burner. She wanted to sit up, but she felt pressed down.

Was there a lake? It's a desert. But.

She turned her head and looked at the antique cherry dresser, which had been her grandmother's. Its deep auburn finish was coated in a fine layer of dust. When had she last dusted? On the surface of the dresser, a couple of old doilies lay like fossilized spiderwebs. An ornately painted batik jewelry box sat with its lid partially ajar, hastily dropped back after she had seized a necklace out of it at some point. It wasn't that morning. She wasn't wearing any jewelry, except for her engagement ring. It kept catching on her shirt, and she longed to take it off. She did whenever Graham was not around and felt relieved by doing so. And then she felt bad for feeling relieved.

She remembered Alva's face when she had entered their Biochem 260 class. Fiona hated that class, but having Alva there had softened the blow of its egomaniac professor, flush with gaining full tenure and refusing to call anyone by their first name unless they had an A. Alva was an A student, Fiona was not. That never changed. But Alva's face did, that day. She saw the ring immediately. And her mouth twisted just a fraction off center as she smiled.

"Oh my God!" she'd whispered as class began. Fiona had grinned, and felt a strange mix of embarrassment, pride, and dread. It seemed more real then; she really was engaged. She was in public. Alva knew.

The two had whispered back and forth during class until Dr. Bacheldor stopped talking and glared at them, and then their faces glowed from suppressed laughter. Fiona had felt better then, about the engagement. Bustling out of the class among fellow students like so many salmon up a stream, the two girls had giggled and chatted. But Alva's expression haunted Fiona.

"What is it?" she had pressed.

"What?" asked Alva.

"Your face," said Fiona.

"*Your* face!" laughed Alva.

Fiona grinned and rolled her eyes. "I mean, when I showed you the ring. I'm sorry I didn't tell you sooner."

Alva gave her the funny look again.

"That's it, that's the face!" Fiona pointed.

Alva shook her head and briefly closed their eyes.

"I'm happy for you," she said, and she gently nudged Fiona with her elbow. "I know. Let's celebrate! Tomato Head! On me."

"Whaaat," Fiona laughed. "Copper Cellar, if you're buying!"

"Ow!" said Alva. "Okay, fine. Since it's you. And anyway, the tomato bisque is good."

"The rolls, though," sighed Fiona, dreaming of splitting a steaming roll open and slathering it with butter. Then they both sighed and marched off chatting, walking down the hill and toward the restaurant.

That had been a fun day after all.

Fiona blinked, stared at her dresser, and sighed, not from pleasure, but from not knowing what else to do.

What do I do?

"Hey babe," called Graham. "I made you a grilled cheese and tomato soup!"

Fiona jerked, and her breath caught, and she coughed. Then she lifted her legs to the bed, and seized them about the knees, and turned in fetal position to stare at herself in the dresser mirror.

She said to her reflection, "I don't know what to do."

"What, babe?" called Graham, and he opened the door and stared at her. "Fi," he said softly, and he sat next to her and put his hand on her back. She flinched. "What's wrong, are you sick?"

She didn't answer. She stared again at her own face and ignored his reflection next to hers.

"Did something happen?" said Graham softly. "Tell me."

Fiona kept staring until finally her eyes began to sting. She blinked.

"Alva's dead."

CHAPTER 4
NO SHOW

When you tell someone that something has happened, that a life-altering event has occurred, it usually makes it more real. It had for Fiona when she told Alva she was engaged. And she assumed, fleetingly, that telling Graham about Alva would make it seem more real. In truth, the experience made her feel like she was watching from a doorway, watching herself, watching Graham flail for the moment before gathering his composure and slipping back into pleaser mode. He had learned this tactic from his turbulent childhood, always aiming to please, but never seeking out what would truly help him. He preferred helping others first. Fiona had loved and admired that about him, until she had realized the origin of his response. Then she felt ashamed. Like now.

"Oh my God, Fi, what?" he cried. "Why didn't you call me, I'd have come to get you! What! What happened?"

Shut the fuck up! she thought forcefully, and she gasped at the power behind the thought. It was what she wanted to say just then. And she wanted him to leave. But he was in pleaser mode, and desperate to help. Again, she felt the sensation of watching the two of them from a distance rather than actually being in the moment.

"Fi, I'm so sorry. Fuck." Graham hugged her, while her arms hung limply at her sides.

She didn't want him touching her, and for a moment she felt revulsed by his presence. She twitched her arms, and he misunderstood and picked up a throw blanket—also her grandmother's—and placed it around her, clucking like a mother hen. Then he dashed off, and for a moment Fiona felt intense relief.

Maybe he'll never come back.

He did, though, bearing a tray with the soup and sandwich. He set it on the dresser.

She felt pure rage.

Do I look like I want to fucking eat right now?

"Your color's coming back," noted Graham. "Good. I was worried you were going to faint when you came in. Now I know why! Here, babe. Eat something. Even just a bite. Please."

She did not want to eat anything. She did not *want* anything except for him to go away. Or to get into her car and drive off forever.

He poked the corner of the sandwich at her mouth, and it took all her willpower not to knock the thing away. She stood then, seized the sandwich from the tray, took a bite, and then dropped it back on the plate. She chewed and swallowed while Graham stroked her arm.

She looked at him, and in that moment, she knew she would never spend the rest of her life with him. She wasn't even sure she could bear the next five minutes with him.

It wasn't his fault, she knew. But she was not the same person she had been when she had left their apartment that morning, and she never would be again. But he would not change. It was over, and she thought that fact calmly. It didn't really matter when she said it to him, it only mattered that she knew. Now wasn't the time to say it, though, and so she kept her mouth shut while he hugged her. And while he did, her eyes drifted to her old filing cabinet, dented from various moves, and she knew then that she had to wait until he was gone in order to open the cabinet. That's where Alva's mail was. Suddenly the few real, paper letters from her friend had become the most valuable things she owned. Far more valuable than the department store engagement ring which she loathed.

She sifted through Graham's placating attempts to comfort her and heard "What happened?" and "Does her family know?" until finally, just to get him to stop talking, she answered.

"We don't know," she said dully. To get him to stop touching her, she walked out of their bedroom and back to the living room, and to the kitchen, where she poured a glass of water for herself. Sipping it absently, she noticed the skillet covered in grease from the grilled cheese sitting on a cold eye, off to one side from where he'd cooked. She rinsed the skillet.

"I have to go to Dr. Bingham's in the morning," she said absently, as Graham looked at her with eyes full of sympathy. She could not look him in the eyes.

"I'll take you—"

"No. Thank you. I'm going to leave super early," she said, her voice level.

"Oh," said Graham. "Okay. I just want to help."

"I know," she said to him. "I know. I just—this is a lot, and I—I need to think, you know?"

By his expression, Fiona knew Graham pouted, but was putting considerable effort—for him—in trying to hide it. She felt the coil of rage well in her again. Then the interlocking spiral of guilt to go with it. A double helix, but not of the plant DNA she studied. One of pure dysfunction instead. She knew it, and she hated it.

Graham, looking forlorn, retrieved the food tray and set it on the kitchen bar.

Sighing, Fiona took the soup spoon and sipped at the reconstituted tomato soup. It was no Copper Cellar bisque, but it was food. She slowly began to eat, and she felt a little warmer.

Her phone vibrated in her pocket, and she jumped. She pulled it out and saw that she had a text from Dr. Bingham.

"Please bring any communication with you tomorrow. Also, have you seen Gale Thompson? We had an appointment, and she didn't show. You know each other, yes?"

"Why are you texting me, old man?" she said in a low voice.

Graham perked up.

"Who was it?"

"Bingham," she answered.

She texted back, "Ok. Yes, I know who she is, and no, haven't seen her. See you tomorrow."

She felt irritated, outraged, and more fatigued than she ever had in her life just then.

Graham held his arms out. "What can I do to help?" he asked.

Fiona pressed her lips tightly together.

"You've done plenty, babe," she answered. "Thank you for the food. I'm going to shower. And maybe just...I don't know. Watch Jeopardy or something stupid like that."

"Whatever you want to do is fine with me," Graham assured her.

I don't care, she thought. She nodded and went to her room, gathered her pajamas and clean underwear, and then shut the bathroom door, thankful for the privacy. She locked it, just to be sure she had those moments to herself. She let the hot water spill over her face, but still, she did not cry.

CHAPTER 5
THE LAKE

She woke with a flinch, as Graham had touched her back. It was morning, and she'd slept uncomfortably. She pretended to go back to sleep as he made his way to the bathroom to shower. As soon as the water gushed, she padded out of the bedroom and to the kitchen bar, where she had left her purse. She retrieved her keys as quietly as she could, holding them tight in her balled fist so they would not jingle. The living room was dark save for the orange border of light around the vertical blinds from the sickly streetlamp outside, which she loathed. She quickly walked back into her room. She listened: the shower was still on.

She faced her filing cabinet and stuck the tiniest key in her keychain into its lock and turned it. She pulled the bottom drawer out very slowly, so that it would not make its telltale scraping noises.

Inside, she found a file labeled CORRESPONDENCE in her messy scrawl. She yanked it out, closed the cabinet, locked it, and came close to running with the file back to the dining room. She thrust the folder under a pile of sales papers and junk mail on the edge of the table and then hurried back to her room.

She climbed back under the covers and slowed her breath. The shower turned off. She shut her eyes. Graham exited the bathroom, towel around his waist, she knew. She heard the flop of that towel on the bed, which made her seethe.

Why can't he just hang it up? Why does he put the wet towel on the bed every time?

He opened the dresser drawer and pulled things out: socks, underwear, T-shirt, jeans. She knew it was all these things without looking, because Graham was a creature of habit.

"Babe," he called softly.

She shifted slightly but didn't turn to look at him.

"It's time to get up, babe. You said you were going in early."

She stretched and mumbled, "Changed my mind."

He sighed. "Okay. I'll make you lunch. Don't forget to text that you're going in late."

"Mmph," she responded, and she shut her eyes and drew her blankets close around her.

He left the room, but also left the wet towel on the bed. She felt a flare of frustration ripple through her and gritted her teeth. She reached over to the nightstand and pulled her phone off it, and then propped herself up in bed to look at it. There was a missed call, and she would have checked to see from where, but a series of texts began pouring in.

Three in a row were confirmation texts for an appointment. She squinted at them, and assumed they were junk. She had no upcoming appointments, not anytime soon, anyway. She sifted through the texts and found a message from Dr. Bingham.

"Can you come in soon," was all that it said.

She puffed out a sigh.

"Ok," she texted back. "Am running a bit late."

No word back. She put the phone back and sank down under the covers.

Graham opened the bedroom door and peered in, but she was turned onto her side like before.

"Hey," he whispered. She said nothing. "I set out your bowl and spoon. I'm headed out. Your lunch is in the fridge."

"Mmmmm," she murmured, as if half asleep. "Thank you," she whispered.

"I love you."

"Love you."

Graham shut the door and she waited. She listened closely. She heard him leave the apartment, shut the door, and lock it behind him. She waited a few more minutes. She heard his pickup truck start, and the sound of it backing up, going into forward gear, and then leaving. Then she sprang out of bed.

She pelted to the dining room and opened the coat closet on the wall opposite. She pulled out her backpack, and then she turned to the table with the sales papers. They had been moved.

Oh fuck.

She felt her whole body sting with adrenaline as she seized the pile of papers.

The folder was there.

She gasped in relief.

But then she felt a crawling unease. She opened the folder and flipped through it.

Had he looked through the folder? If he had, did he take anything?

She felt sick. It wasn't just from wanting to help Dr. Bingham. The contents of the folder now seemed priceless to her—not to mention private.

There were old letters and cards, and among them, letters and postcards from Alva. With shaking hands, she leafed through them.

"I think everything's here," she whispered to herself, but she felt on edge. She checked among the sales papers and junk mail to make sure none of the folder's contents had fallen out. It looked like it was intact. She then stuffed the folder into her backpack. Then she dressed for work and class.

She glanced at the cereal bowl and spoon Graham had left out. She opened the fridge and found a sandwich. Glancing at the bowl and the sandwich, she shut the fridge, shouldered her backpack, threw her crossbody purse over her shoulder, and held her keys, jangling this time. And she left the apartment and locked the door.

She saw a shape move past and turned her head quickly. Someone had walked in front of the apartment, but there was a walkway there between the housing and the parking lot. So that was not unusual. Still, the hairs on her neck sprang up. She peered around the corner and found no one. Possibly a neighbor, then, who had gone inside. She looked at her car and thought wistfully of careening out of that parking lot and heading toward the mountains. But she sat in it placidly.

Why am I so nervous?

She texted Dr. Bingham: "On my way."

While she was driving out of the parking lot, he texted back, "We've got company. Don't text back. Just come."

She blinked and took a breath, and slowly exhaled it.

What was going on?

She drove down Chapman Highway and remembered she needed to eat, so she pulled into a McDonald's drive-thru. The line was long, so she sat still for a moment in the car. She opened the backpack, sagging in the passenger seat, and withdrew the folder. She pulled out a postcard. It showed a lake on the front. On the back, she touched the stamped postage from Chile. She traced Alva's familiar, clean, looping handwriting.

Fiona had remembered correctly. There was a lake in the Atacama.

CHAPTER 6
CURBED

She parked along a leafy side street north of Cumberland Avenue and turned her wheel to the curb on the incline. Her visit to San Francisco had taught her to do so, after receiving an ominous warning about parking tickets. She was still traumatized from parking outside her old dorm building on the southwestern side of the Tennessee campus, having received an eyebrow-singeing ticket for her five-minute dash inside and back out a few years back. She made her way southeast and crossed the major street. From there she eyed the hill, green with lush grasses and full-foliage maples, oaks, and tulip poplars, and sedate and covered in brick and concrete buildings. The moisture from the nearby Tennessee River seeped through the air, rendering it with a syrupy, soporific scent. She had never felt farther from a desert.

Where's Alva's body? she wondered suddenly.

As she pumped her legs up the hill toward the biology building, she felt queasy remembering a zooarchaeology class she'd taken the prior summer, and the use of flesh-eating beetles to strip the bones of skeletons. She leaned against a magnolia and dry-heaved.

Her phone chimed.

It was Bingham.

"ETA?" the text read.

"5 min," she texted back.

There was no way around it; she'd have to swallow, perhaps literally, her nausea and quaking disbelief, still, about Alva's death to be able to face anyone, even the even-keeled Dr. Bingham. She walked along the sidewalk toward the science building, and she saw a little woman come running out, puffing, glasses steamed. It was Mrs. Laird, the main secretary of the front office for life sciences. She barreled straight for Fiona.

"Fiona," gasped the lady, stopping for a moment and leaning to one side, holding herself. "Oh! Side stitch. Sorry." She shook it off and her round-lensed glasses bobbed on her button nose. Her hair was dyed dark brown, and her eyebrows were drawn on with a sort of reddish pencil.

"Dr. Bingham's waiting for you," she announced, her forehead beading with sweat.

"Yes, thank you," said Fiona, managing a grin. "He just texted me."

Mrs. Laird held up her hand and shook her head.

"Don't go in yet."

"Why not?" Fiona tilted her head.

"Someone's in there with him. He told me to come tell you," Mrs. Laird added. She smoothed her dark violet blazer and skirt. Fiona looked down at the low, black leather pumps the woman wore. They were clearly too small; Mrs. Laird never really wore anything that fit just right. Her toes bulged a bit, as if protesting the insult of the shoes.

"Who?" asked Fiona.

Mrs. Laird looked over her shoulder, and Fiona noticed a man leaning against the side of the building, apparently looking at his phone.

That man had something about him…an indefinable aspect of tidiness that seemed to clash with everyone else who worked or studied on the science hill of campus. There was an effort to look casual, as if to try to fit in. Blue jeans. Nondescript white shirt, rolled up at the elbows, white tank top barely showing through. He was tall, with a lot of black hair on his arms, and a slicked-back, curly hairdo cut short. He wore dark, thick glasses, and the first thought that went through Fiona's mind was…

"Who's Clark Kent over there?" she blurted out, but quietly.

Mrs. Laird looked up at her and pressed her lips together and shook her head very slightly.

Fiona glanced up at the man, still several feet away. She only responded by biting her lower lip for a second. With a thin nod, she said, more loudly, "Thank you so much for reminding me! I'll put the order in soon. I don't want anyone to be without their bagels at group meeting. The grad students get kinda savage with me, the lowly lab tech!"

Mrs. Laird gave an indulgent chuckle. She then hurried ahead of Fiona and entered the stone double doors, one of which was open. Fiona approached the door and then found herself facing the preoccupied stranger. He looked up then.

The glare coating in his shaded glasses gave him a strange look, a green-hued one. He smiled in a way that salespeople smile: plastic and well-practiced.

"Hello!" he said pleasantly enough.

"Hi," she answered, and she passed him and entered the room.

He followed her in and pulled the door shut behind him. Its clang echoed in the hallway. Fiona bent her head to look back at the admin office, and she could see Mrs. Laird at her desk, glancing up quickly and then back down again. Fiona saw two more strangers, a man and a woman, again both dressed nicely without being formal…but too refined to be staff in an old, rickety, grant-starved set of labs and offices.

Fiona swallowed. She pretended not to pay attention to them. They stood so strangely, as if waiting for something, or someone. The man behind her joined them, and she could feel their eyes on her, but she did not look back. She stopped briefly to use the restroom along that hallway. After washing her hands, she felt the unease that she'd forgotten something. Drying her hands, she blinked at her tired expression in the bathroom mirror. The fluorescent lights above cast haggard shadows under her eyes.

She proceeded down the hall to Dr. Bingham's office. Her ears were ringing. She stepped forward and was about to open the door to his office when she drew in her breath.

She'd left the backpack in the car.

Fuckshit.

She opened the door.

Dr. Bingham sat at his desk, and in the chair before him, *another* man sat, and still another stood. The one standing was younger, possibly about twenty-eight, and crispy dressed. His freckled, pale skin and his slate-grey eyes and reddish hair made her think he might be of Scottish descent; not unusual in the Tennessee highlands, but he did not look like a local.

What the hell is going on?

"Ah, Fiona, good," said Dr. Bingham, with a closed-mouth slight grin; nothing unusual there either. He did look paler than usual. "I was just talking to Jack, here…er, Dr. Jack Cordeiro," and the man in the chair turned to look up at her.

It was the Clark Kent fellow; he'd gone ahead of her, and there he sat.

Wow, she thought.

He was extremely handsome, with dark brown, wavy hair and hazel eyes with long, dark eyelashes behind those thick glasses. They looked expensive. He stood, and he towered over her. She was not a short woman, either. But this man, this Dr. Cordeiro, was impressively tall. She gave him a rapid glance up and down, saw the points of very fine boots under his dark blue jeans, and then she composed her face to look as placid as possible.

"Dr. Cordeiro, this is Fiona Hawthorne," Dr. Bingham introduced them.

He smiled at her with striking white teeth and outstretched his hand.

"So nice to meet you!" he exclaimed, taking her small hand in his two large ones and shaking it three times, firmly but gently. His smile then vanished and, as he held onto her hand a bit longer, he shifted his face to one of concern and said, "But I am so sorry for the loss of your friend."

He glanced at Dr. Bingham, who nodded.

"We, ah," Bingham said, his eyes darting to the other stranger, "we have some visitors today, here investigating the…incident in the Atacama."

Fiona raised an eyebrow. She pulled her hand away from Dr. Cordeiro.

"Shouldn't they be doing that down there?" she asked, looking at the redheaded stranger to whom she had not yet been introduced. "You know, in the desert where they died?"

Dr. Bingham's look at Fiona only made sense in the context that she had known the man for a few years, so she could translate very quickly the flicker from exasperation, irritation, mild shock, and still, admiration. She could tell he wanted to smile but, for various and sundry reasons that she was *not* privy to, chose not to.

"That's exactly what I was wondering!" said Dr. Cordeiro.

She stared at him. Despite his charm, something about him seemed...off to her. "I don't know you," she said bluntly.

Bingham cleared his throat. "Dr. Cordeiro has been out in the field collecting."

"Please," said the man, pressing his fingertips together under his chin, "call me Jack."

At that moment a tremendous crash of broken glass startled them all, including the blank-looking redheaded fellow. Then a large series of mechanical thumps echoed through the lab.

It was the garbage pickup, backing into the brick dead-end made by the Hansen biology building just behind Dr. Bingham's office and lab...hence robbing him of any view.

Jack made a wincing face and said, "Ah, that's all the glass—my fault," and he glanced at Fiona congenially—too much so, she thought, for having just met her. "I—had a little accident in the lab the other day."

A clipped sigh escaped from Bingham, and the redheaded man finally asserted himself.

"We're here to ask a few questions," he declared. "Nothing more."

"We?" said Fiona. "Who, you and Jack?"

Jack shook his head vigorously. "What? No, I don't know this man. I'm assuming," he said to the redhead, "you're referring to the others out in the hallway? I've not seen any of them before."

"You hadn't seen me either," Fiona pointed out.

"No, and a pity, that!" declared Jack, cocking his head to one side.

Fiona drew her brows together in a stern line and said, "What sort of questions? Who are you? Who are you with?"

Dr. Bingham nodded his head to the redheaded man and said, "I'll let you explain. I'm going to get a cup of coffee from the front office. Anyone want something? Tea?"

Jack held up a hand, and said, "I'll take coffee, please and thank you!"

Fiona frowned up at him, and snapped, "That coffee tastes like day-old shit."

Jack burst out laughing and looked over at the redheaded man, who looked as though he didn't approve of the joke.

Doc Bingham closed the door behind him with a bit more force than Fiona had ever heard from him, and he walked out of sight.

The redheaded man said, with no obvious accent (therefore taking away much chance he was a local, as she'd suspected), "We're representatives of the agency who provided the grant for the Gilden expedition."

"Again," Fiona interrupted, "who's *we?*"

At that moment she felt the vibration of her phone and pulled it out of her pocket absently.

"Don't show them anything you have," a text read. "They're coming in. I'm right behind them. Delete this."

All from Bingham.

She felt little prickles of alarm bounce up and down her back. She swiped on her phone to delete their text history.

Good thing I left the backpack in the car after all. And I didn't park in the lot.

CHAPTER 7
500 PANCAKES

She exited Bingham's lab office, but the two stiff individuals stopped her.

"Sorry, Miss," said the lady. "We're conducting a confidential investigation, and you'll have to come back later. If you like, I can escort you—"

"No." The word came emphatically. "I—have to get to a class."

"Don't you work here?" simpered the woman, eyes cold and unflinching on Fiona's face.

Fiona kept her breathing level.

"I'm a working student," she replied, gritting her teeth.

The life of the lowly lab tech strikes again.

"Let me get your number and I can call you when—"

But Fiona did not wait. She turned on her heel and charged forward, intending to leave the hall and race back to her car. She collided with a wiry obstacle at the end of the hallway, however, in the form of one Lafe Lambert. Lafe was a former fellow student, erstwhile smartass, now a post-graduate working researcher like her, but in these days in engineering, not biology. In many ways, though, the subject that most hung in the air between Fiona and Lafe was chemistry, and not the kind taught in any university.

"Whooaaa." The lean young man gawked with his protuberant grey eyes and rascal's grin. "Where's the fire?"

Fiona swallowed, glanced up at him for a moment, and planned to flee the hall and race back to her car. She could think only of rushing to check on the backpack. Lafe cantered after her and caught up with her just before she left the building.

"Fi! What's going on?"

"I—" she began, twisting her fingers together, her engagement ring catching on her right palm. That frustrated her. It kept spinning, too loose against her finger, but her large knuckle prevented its coming off.

"Something's happened."

"Why are you whispering?" Lafe whispered back.

"It's Alva. And…her team."

He considered her face, and his mouth drew into a tight line.

She darted her eyes behind them, down the hallway. Just then she saw Jack saunter out, oozing charisma and sweeping his gaze to his left and right. He struck up a conversation with two lab assistants who looked to be just under twenty years old. While Fiona could not hear his exact words, she could hear his laughter, and that of the girls as well.

Lafe narrowed his eyes.

"Look at this fucking guy!" he hissed, his eyes gleaming, bordering on predatorial, the crease between his wild eyebrows deepening. "Fake as fuck."

Fiona snorted.

"You say that about everyone who dresses well."

She grinned down at Lafe's faded red Chucks, their laces frayed at the ends.

Lafe frowned.

"Steer clear of him, Fiona."

"Didn't you say that about Graham?"

"He's a goddamn *bore*. Different reason here. This dude's dangerous."

"That's a bit extreme to say about someone you've never met."

Lafe sniffed. "I know the type. Trust me."

She followed Lafe's gaze and watched Jack laughing with his too-perfect teeth, and the casual shrug of his muscular shoulders in his white shirt, sleeves rolled up to the elbow. The young women around him, now joined by one young man, gazed at him with dizzy awe. She recognized their expression, for she had borne it herself upon her first glance at Jack.

He holds us in his sway.

Lafe's sharp elbow nudged her in the arm. She blinked, stirred from her reverie.

"Pancakes?" he whispered.

Turning her head, she caught the words, "...seen Gale?" from a passerby. "She was supposed to set up those plates."

"I'm sorry, I don't know anyone by the name Gale," Jack answered, hands outstretched.

The other lab tech shook his head in irritation. "There's a whole day's experiment dead, along with my cells." He stormed off, leaving Jack Cordeiro and his new little cadre.

Jack threw his hands up in the air and laughed, and so did his admirers.

It set Fiona on edge.

Where was *Gale, after all?*

"You know what, I am a bit hungry."

Lafe slapped his hands together, grin manic and wry. "Only took you four years. I'm buying."

"Damn right you are."

She threw her crossbody bag over her shoulder.

"Besides," muttered Lafe, stepping between Fiona and Jack's line of sight, "dude makes my skin crawl, and I wanna talk about him *way* out of sight or earshot."

She hooked her right forefinger into the circular mug handle, and despite the warm temps outside, she liked the heat of the thick coffee mug against her hands. She slipped her thumb around the rest of it and took a sip. Acrid coffee, it would win no barista awards, but the gum-chewing waitress with the teased, bottle-blonde hair swiveled by often enough with refills to justify tolerating the swill.

"Run it by me again."

Lafe had a mesmerizing habit of staring intently with his bulging, aggie marble grey eyes. Typically Fiona remained resistant, but today wasn't typical.

"He comes in like he owns the place." She sipped again from her mug and scowled. "There are two others—"

"Two goons, got it," Lafe nodded. He shoved an entire stick of ramrod straight bacon into his mouth and crunched. He followed that with a chaser of syrup-lacquered pancake wedge stabbed ferociously with a fork. "Who you never saw before."

"Never." She sighed. "I'm really tired."

"That's what the coffee and pancakes are for." Lafe pointed his fork at her plate.

Again Fiona sighed, but she took the hint and ate a few bites. The syrup was not real maple, her favorite, but some ersatz drizzle, likely corn syrup based, she guessed. The butter oozing into a pool on the top of her pancake stack glowed in a suspiciously bright yellow.

Don't knock a free meal, her father's adage tickled her thoughts.

Besides, she knew Lafe was broke. It didn't matter how many times he'd asked her to get pancakes with him over the years. He grew up poor, he was there on a scholarship and a couple of small grants, and his funds were strained to the max. She need only look at his feral expression to know he remained hungry in more ways than one. And *one* of those ways she refused to relent to. He had never outright asked her for anything but pancakes, but she remembered vividly his reaction to the diamond on her hand. He hadn't needed to say a word. His eyes shouted what he felt. Then as now.

"Fi," he began, and a plate crashed in the kitchen of the diner, startling them both. He shrugged nervously. "I don't want you near that dude."

"He works on campus, Lafe," she drawled, attempting another sip of coffee, struggling not to sneer at its taste out of politeness.

"Stop pretending. It's basically boiled piss."

She blushed. "I'm sorry."

"It wasn't the point of all this. Anyway. Why do you need to go back?"

"You're kidding, right? I *work* there. And Doc Bingham needs me."

"Does he? Does he need you accosted by a couple of likely techbro-funded goons who masquerade as government officials?"

"You don't know—"

"Goddammit, Fi, I don't *need* to know."

She shivered. "Anyway, Graham's going to worry—"

Lafe scowled. "Like he's not tracking your location right now."

"I could turn off the find feature."

"Oh good, so if you disappear none of us can find you."

"Fuck you, Lafe."

He smirked and ate his last wedge of pancake, and a clatter of applause rang out.

The waitress whooped. "By our count, that's your 500th pancake, Lafe!"

His eyes popped. Fiona glared at him and mouthed, "Five *hundred?*"

He bared his teeth awkwardly, and the staff descended on him.

"You get the bronze fork!" said the waitress, Wendy, and loud claps ricocheted through the diner.

Lafe bowed and took the object, a slightly oversized, bronze-coated fork, with the words "C'mon In Diner" etched on its handle. He promptly handed it to Fiona.

"What am I supposed to do with this?" she demanded.

Lafe leaned back. "I don't know. Keep it for a salad or some shit, in your purse. You're welcome, by the way."

She stood and shouldered that very same purse. Her cheeks burned.

"I'm going."

He stood too.

"Fucking fine," he said, a little too loudly.

"People are staring at us."

Lafe swept his arms out and bowed to the entire diner. Then he nodded to the waitress, threw down a twenty, and followed Fiona, her cheeks burnished from embarrassment, out to the parking lot.

"Where'd you park?" he asked.

"Over by Sylvie's again," she said.

"I'll drive you back. But not by the main road. Scenic route."

She halted her steps and gave him a sidelong glance.

"What are you up to?"

"Indulge me for once, would you?" His words cut the air like lightning. She could practically smell the ozone.

She buckled into the faded, cracked passenger seat and scooted several stained papers around beneath her feet. Lafe turned the car over and she noted that this time, the check engine light flickered on as if in annoyance for having been awakened at this hour.

"You should get that taken care of," she said.

"Okay, Mom." He shook his head. He checked the rearview and side mirrors, eyes half-lidded. He swept the shock of dark brown hair out of his eyes.

They pulled out of the parking lot and then Lafe gunned it. Fiona gasped. Lafe turned the car quickly down a side street and sped ahead, slowing only briefly at a four-way stop. He jerked the car down side roads and snaked in and out of neighborhoods.

"Where are you taking me?" she gasped, unnerved by his focused expression.

At first, he didn't answer, but after flicking his eyes back to the rearview mirror a few more times, he pulled down another street in an older neighborhood. Run down yet not completely abandoned, it had been planted with dogwoods many decades prior, and in spring they would sway with foamy pink blossoms. In summer they sat languid, drooping over old chain link fences and cracked sidewalks, the houses peeling and careworn, when once they thrummed with happy smiles and the pounding of busy feet. Some were abandoned. One old yellow Queen Anne sat forlorn back from the road. It must have been extraordinary in the early 20th century, but now it made her think of a broken dollhouse.

Lafe pulled forward into its gravel driveway and drove all the way to the back, toward a decrepit garage.

"Lafe," Fiona said, not liking the situation.

"Just a minute," he muttered. He left the car running and jumped out. He edged over to a bent screen door, fumbled with something in his pockets, and brought forth keys.

"This your place?" she called out.

He didn't answer. He disappeared for a moment and then reemerged with a backpack and a baseball bat.

She crinkled up her eyebrows at him as he opened his car door and threw the items into the back seat.

"What are those for?"

"Insurance," he said.

She felt cold all over.

CHAPTER 8
FLOORING IT

Lafe's car protested, climbing the hill near campus. His slate-hued eyes darted to and fro as he urged the car up.

"Which one is it?"

"Maroon, up on the right." Fiona pointed.

He backed his car into the only empty slot on the sloping street, turned the wheels to the curb, and yanked his emergency brake with manic zeal.

"Get the backpack," he urged.

"You seem pretty unnerved by all this," she pointed out.

"Because I am. Go get it, and we'll keep driving."

"That's your plan? We just…drive around? I've got to get home at some point."

"Let's get out of the car. Keep your purse in here."

She got out and scraped her car door on the buckled sidewalk. He saw and winced at first, then shrugged.

"It's ancient. Fuck it. Leave the purse. Shut the door."

"Why are you being like this?" She pushed her purse underneath the passenger seat and shut the door. She noticed he'd left his phone inside the car too.

"If you're being traced—"

"Oh, for fuck's sake, Lafe!"

She laughed, but it was a shallow laugh. Then she shuddered.

He walked over to her and looked down into her green eyes.

"Fi," he said quietly, "something's really wrong about all this. I want to talk away from our phones, away from anything. You said you had cards, letters and stuff in your backpack. From Alva. Don't take it home, don't give it to anyone else. Let me take it. I'll hide it."

"I don't understand," she protested. "Why would those be valuable at all?"

"Everything you've told me just screams it. There's info in there. Something that could implicate guilt. Let's go through it. But not here, back at the house. I'm going to hang back. You go get the backpack casually and just walk back here to me."

Fiona felt cold in the sultry sun.

"Lafe."

"I know. I *know*. I'm always flapping my wings over something. I get it. But this is…it's not right."

"If it's just one of your vibes…"

Lafe grinned, his eyelids half closed, and he said, "Then I'm a goddamned idiot, and I still got to have pancakes with you."

Fiona snickered and shook her head. She walked to the old maroon Honda, with its Darwin fish sticker on the back, and inserted her key into the car and popped her trunk. Walking around the car, she glanced over her shoulder up and down the road. She saw nothing untoward. A cat yawned on a porch. A dog barked, maybe on the next block, out of sight. She looked into the trunk to see her faded beach towel, covering a lump. She pulled the beach towel back, exhaled. There sat her backpack, unremarkable, in the same position she'd left it. She pulled it out, threw it over one shoulder, and shifted the beach towel back into place.

Something flickered across the street, diagonal to where she stood at the end of her car. A faded, blue pickup truck sat there, and she caught movement in its cab. A trail of smoke drifted out its open window. Someone sat there.

She bristled yet pretended she hadn't seen. She walked back to where Lafe stood concealed under an archway of ivy at the front of a 1950s duplex. She opened her eyes wide, and he slowly eased out of his spot. One glance and she could see him discreetly turn his eyes back up the street. He nodded to her, just barely.

They walked to his car and got in. He rolled the windows down partway. He started the car. They sat there for interminably long seconds, and then he glanced at her and mouthed, "Hold on." She gave him a terse nod back.

He shifted the car into reverse, released the parking brake, and then jerked the car into the street and quickly turned it around. An oncoming car honked, but he didn't let that deter him. Fiona could see his eyes gleam in satisfaction. He'd waited just until someone was coming, so he could put a car between them and the blue pickup.

He whipped the car forward down the hill, and only then did Fiona look back. The blue pickup pulled out behind the car between them.

"Fuck," she whispered.

He put his finger to his lips and patted the seatbelt across his shoulder. She tugged to make sure hers was secure. Then he floored the car, and they sped down the hill. He careened down streets, up and around and down again. Fiona dared to look back.

He cleared his throat and slowly winked at her.

She recognized some of the streets from earlier, and realized she'd been tensing her shoulders. Now she let them sag a bit. He pulled into the driveway of the old Queen Anne house and back far enough from the street that nobody could see. But as they walked to the side door, Fiona saw a sleek, black vehicle slowly roll past the house. She pressed herself back and into Lafe, who watched.

"Probably fine," he said, but she heard the tension in his voice.

"What are we even doing?" she hissed.

He pointed at the door, then unlocked it.

It was dim inside, with all the curtains drawn. It smelled of old coffee, fabric softener, and the moisture-rich scent of earth and fertilizer from Lafe's many potted house plants. She walked through the little mudroom and found the kitchen to the right, a galley kitchen, but with decent light from a south-facing window and trailing with plant tendrils from little shelves along the window frame. A speckled white countertop, likely made in the 1950s or early 60s, was stained from an old burn mark. A half-filled coffeepot sat partially off its base. A frayed, olive green dish towel languished over the sink faucet.

She followed Lafe forward to the living room, which was sparse except for plants and some old bookshelves. A blonde acoustic guitar and an African drum sat in one corner, above which hung a tapestry. She could not discern what image was woven into it for a moment. But then she tilted her head and found it was made of letters, and they spelled "FUCK OFF."

Smirking, she said softly, "So this is where the great Lafe Lambert resides."

"Sometimes."

He picked up a small dish from a worn, likely 1970s coffee table, and shook its contents, old piles of incense ash, into the kitchen trash.

"I thought you said you had a cat?"

She spied an empty, silver two-bowl set in the kitchen. It looked recently cleaned.

"My ex-girlfriend had the cat." His voice was flat, but she heard the faintest acid tone.

It didn't end well, then.

She thought of Graham. Then she remembered she'd turned her phone on "do not disturb."

When she pulled it out of her purse, Lafe held his hands up and shook his head.

He mouthed, "Turn it off."

She felt cold then. She'd said Lafe's name aloud earlier. Should she be worried about that, too? But he had not responded to it in anger.

She held up a finger and mouthed back, "One sec."

She looked, and indeed there were messages. The topmost held four from Graham.

"What do you want for dinner? Should we get Mandarin?" Then, "Someone called the landline asking for you." Then, "Someone came by. Is something going on?" Then, "Where are you? I see you're over in Doyle Heights."

Her whole body went cold.

Goddammit!

She turned off her "find phone" feature then.

Then she read the next text. It was from Dr. Bingham.

"Could you bring those files by that we talked about?"

And then the worst one of all, sent later from him.

"The bodies disappeared. I'm sorry. I'll contact the families."

The time on that one read 12:26 PM.

She turned her phone off with fingers sweaty from shock. She watched Lafe turn his off as well, eyeing her the whole time.

"You're shaking," he noted. He motioned to the couch. "I'll make some coffee."

"No. I'm—I'm jittery enough."

"Okay, herbal tea then. Chamomile?"

"Okay."

She held her quiet phone in her hands and stared at the backpack, perched on the floor in front of her. In a few minutes, Lafe brought a steaming mug of tea that smelled like moldy flowers. He set it on an old, black rubber coaster on the coffee table.

"Dump the thing out," he said, pointing at the backpack. "Let's see what in the entire fuck is really going on here."

So she unzipped the backpack and turned it upside down, letting the letters and cards of a dead woman cascade onto the faded hardwood floor.

CHAPTER 9
THE ASTRONAUT AND THE DESERT

Staring at the postcards, letters, and a few printed photos from Alva, Fiona's mouth went dry. *Dry as the desert?* But Alva had told her stories.

"You *feel* the moisture being drawn out of your body," Alva had written once in an email. "There's nothing drier than this place. You can't even imagine it!"

Yet somehow, Fiona could. She imagined every drop of water in her body evaporating, leaving her cadaverous, mummified, hollowed of her flesh. She'd been told she was too empathic, that she put herself into others' situations to her detriment. Now she stared at the writing of someone not merely dead but *disappeared*. Why? How? Her mind stumbled.

Then she felt empathy for Dr. Bingham. Having to tell the families. How to explain such a thing? What impossible wording could anyone come up with?

"What is it?"

Lafe reached out and put his hand on her shoulder and squeezed.

"Fiona!"

She looked from the letters on the floor to the mug in her hand. It was a bit too hot, but the mild discomfort kept her, for some reason, grounded, when nothing else did.

"They're…they're gone."

"Who's gone?"

She whispered almost out of Lafe's hearing range.

"The bodies."

Lafe released her shoulder, stood, and ran his hands through his wild hair.

"Oh holy *fuck*. What happened?"

Fiona simply shook her head, eyes on the letters, especially one whose envelope Alva had sketched the famous hand onto, underneath Fiona's address, on its side; rather than reaching up, it reached out. *Accepting alms.* The errant thought flickered through her, and she shook herself.

With a shuddering sigh, she pointed down at the disgorged contents of her backpack and said softly, "That's all that's left of her, then."

And now they were even more priceless. Whatever the investigators wanted, Fiona could not give these to them. They belonged to Alva's family. Fiona did not dare to contact them. She only vaguely knew they lived in the Newport News area. Her father had been in the Navy, Fiona remembered.

That intrigued her, because some of the grant money funneled into the department was military; but largely the grants came from the Army. Endangered species on military grounds, etc. allowed for some smaller funding. Then the eco-evo groups provided some as well. It was the private sector grants that had always given Fiona pause and with the presence of the strange investigators at the college, she now wondered even more.

And what had Alva's father done in the Navy? She thought back to snatches of conversations. Fiona had some difficulty making temporal sense of them now that Alva was gone. She longed for a linear time stream of their interactions and communication, but her brain simply would not comply.

Pilot. He was a pilot.

"…had flown over it once…" Fiona remembered Alva telling her that her father had flown over the Atacama years ago on a return mission from somewhere. And that, prior to that, he had pursued becoming an astronaut. He had made it fairly far in the training, too, before fracturing his femur on a climbing expedition. And not long after withdrawing from the program, he'd had Alva. She continued calling him an astronaut, even nicknaming him "Astro-Daddy."

An astronaut's daughter disappeared in the same desert where, off to the east, NASA scientists worked on astrobiology projects unrelated to Alva's work.

Life is strange. Fiona slid to the floor and shuffled her hands through the letters. *Death is strange too. Alva's, anyway.*

Gone! Disappeared! Missing! The words burst in her mind, little blasts of disbelief.

"Fi." Lafe sat down next to her and peered at the letters. "What if she's not dead? What if…something else happened, they were kidnapped, I don't know."

"No." The finality of it startled her. "Bingham would never have announced that publicly if there were any doubt."

"No bodies though." He rubbed his eyes. "Smells like a coverup."

"You think *everything* is a coverup, Lafe."

"Maybe everything is. But this? Come on. Tell me this doesn't seem suspicious."

"I know Bingham. He'd have had reassurance. This is already an international incident."

"Which is why those goons of yours want to cover it all up and grab every bit of evidence related to those folks they can. Maybe you're not the only one being followed."

"That could have been anyone in that truck."

Lafe leaned back on his heels and crossed his arms. "That's some bullshit, and you know it."

"But why? Why pursue me? I wasn't down there. I'm just her friend."

"Maybe it's her parents," Lafe suggested suddenly. "Maybe they hired some PI team to go find out what really happened."

Fiona grimaced. "They'd be justified, but...I doubt anyone would move this quickly, and definitely not like these people. It's not impossible. But...that guy. He seems...invested."

"The well-dressed creeper I told you was dangerous? He's definitely involved somehow. And no professor has money enough to dress like him anyway."

The contempt oozed from Lafe. That made Fiona smirk.

"He's a scientist who's known at the lab. Jack Cordeiro. *Kind* of famous, loads of publications, up for tenure."

"Does fame give people tenure?"

"Not necessarily, but probably it doesn't hurt."

"Anyway, he gives off douche vibes."

Fiona took a deep breath and slowly exhaled it.

"Let's look through these." She handed some of the letters to Lafe. "Now," and she bit her lip, "there might be some…private stuff in some of them."

"Oooh," Lafe crowed, and he held the letters above his head and bowed to her. "To what do I owe the honor?"

Fiona rolled her eyes. "Just help me out."

"Count on it."

Lafe carefully removed a letter from one of the envelopes and stared at the top of it.

"What the hell is that supposed to be?" he asked, pointing at a sketch of something roughly ball shaped.

Fiona tutted. "Maybe read the letter first?"

"Mmkay."

He skimmed down through and then said, "Oh. Salt geodes, basically. Cyanobacteria…they must have looked really cool. I mean, aside from her sketch."

"She said it was their version of snow," murmured Fiona, tapping her chin with her finger. "I remember one time she told me that they still talk about snowfall like it's some kind of myth, but it wasn't that long ago. Even rain seemed holy to residents there."

"Then snow must have felt apocalyptic to them."

"The end of the world at the end of the world." Fiona shuddered. Now that she'd said it, she wished she hadn't. She sipped at the tea, which at best tasted like mold smelled. Still, somehow, it had a calming effect. *Maybe not so much from the tea, but from its intention.*

Lafe picked up a printed photo, slightly crumpled in one corner. Alva and three of her research team, sunglasses on, hats, and yet Alva's smile glowed more brightly than the others'.

"She was stunning," sighed Lafe.

"Yes, she was."

He looked at her, and she avoided his gaze.

"You two were quite the dynamic duo in class," he said, and she felt her cheeks sting. She shook her head.

"Alva was far more glamorous. She'd even modeled for a little while. Good summer cash flow in college, that sort of thing. Outdoor wear."

Lafe nodded. "Pretty much what you wear, then."

Fiona looked down at her khaki pants, starting to fray at the hem, and trail shoes, scuffed and stained from trampling through the Smoky Mountains and up the little tributaries of the Little Pigeon River on fishing excursions. She was a terrible angler in the mountains, but that wasn't the point of her sojourns. The elusive brook trout, with its vibrant spots, proved a worthy opponent, wily and wary, and if one of her hand-tied caddis flies happened to fool the little things, it only worked once. There was no room to cast in the highlands. She could only cast with a sort of flick of the wrist while sprawled ungracefully over a boulder to hide herself from the watchful brookie. It didn't often work but felt so vindicating when it did.

Can't fish in the Atacama.

Abundant moisture defined East Tennessee as much as its dearth defined the Atacama.

Lafe read aloud, "'Remember to take a deep breath for me in a rainstorm. I miss petrichor. My nose is bloody and full of dried snot. Lol, sorry…just one of the things we have to deal with down here.'"

He continued reading silently, and Fiona watched his expression ripple from interest to surprise to concern.

"Listen to this part. 'We had a visit from someone who claimed to be funding the mine.'"

"Oh, I remember that," Fiona said. "There was some kind of kerfuffle."

"But do you remember this part?" Lafe made eye contact with her. "'There were two people, and they were really well dressed. Not for the desert unless you were, like, cosplaying. Safari couture, practically. No labels or anything. But they knew the land. They knew the old mine, and said they'd bought it off the former owner. So Bridget shrugged and said we'd had an arrangement and grants to work there. I started getting kind of freaked out, because what if they stopped the study? But then later she told us that they'd allowed us to continue, that'"—Lafe clenched the letter, and Fiona sat up straight. She remembered now, and yet here came the words— "'Jack had cleared it and would smooth things over. I knew he'd been here on another expedition but didn't know he was still working down here. I didn't like the sound of that, because of that time at the brewery social, do you remember?'"

"Jack...Cordeiro!" breathed Fiona.

"Damn," said Lafe. "So what happened at the social?"

"I'd forgotten all about it." She abandoned the tea now entirely and took the letter from Lafe. "I didn't really interact with Jack, but Alva knew him, and I'd sort of forgotten. I think he'd hit on her. I wasn't with her when that happened, though, I was off with Graham, probably in a corner."

"Of course you were. Exactly where he'd want you to be."

"What's that supposed to mean?" she demanded.

Lafe shrugged. "Keep asking yourself that until you figure it out."

Fiona wanted to bite out a comeback to that, but nothing good came to mind. And she cringed, because she knew why; what Lafe had said was irrefutable.

"Speaking of," she muttered finally, "I'm going to have to go home at some point. I'll say my phone battery died or something."

"Totally plausible," Lafe replied absently, skimming through more letters. "Check this out. 'We got some new equipment today, thanks to you-know-who.' Well, I don't know who. Jack? Anyway: 'There's a new dig on the property. Bridget cleared it, and we start tomorrow. Preliminary. If we don't find anything, we're packing up and moving on. I don't think she likes the new owners, but she's not outright said it. I guess you don't bite the grant hand that feeds you. Anyway, here's hoping I have something to work with. Everyone seems excited, like it's a sure thing. One more shot at wrapping things up, then it's *Nature*, baby!'"

He sighed.

"This is really sad, actually. Look at the date. Not that long ago. She had high hopes."

Fiona nodded.

"They all did."

"But look…the new owners, Cordeiro being there, it's all looking pretty fucking fishy right about now, don't you think?" Lafe tucked the letter back in the envelope. "Like, there's nothing super incriminating here, except the sexual harassment maybe. That's vague though. But…I don't know. I'll keep reading."

Fiona stood.

"Just please keep this quiet," she said. Lafe stood as well.

"I will, you know I will," he answered.

They stood in a frozen moment of awkward eye contact. Fiona heard a car go by.

"I'd better get back. Should I call a ride?"

Lafe shook his head. "I'll call it." He turned his phone on.

"Thanks. Not just for the ride. The tea, the hiding. The pancakes."

He grinned. "Anytime."

She sighed and gave him a quick, friendly hug. He smelled like clean laundry and potting soil. Breaking their eye contact, Fiona waved her hand at the letters and pictures on the floor.

"Let me know what you find."

"Tell me what happens next."

"If we're tracked?"

"Keep it light. Maybe we use a code."

Fiona giggled. "Pancake code."

"Perfect!" Lafe's eyes crinkled up. "Short stack for news. Whipped cream for 'be on the alert.' Strawberries for when some really big shit's going down."

"Love it," agreed Fiona.

"Your ride's here. I'm gonna follow it on the phone until you get to your car. Let's meet up tomorrow outside the greenhouse, down by the dumpster."

Fiona laughed. "Sounds like a smelly place to be secretive."

"The nose knows."

She laughed again, shook her head, and tossed her purse strap over her shoulder. She glanced back at the backpack, and then reached down to retrieve it.

"You've got everything you need from it, so I'm going to take it back."

"I'll stow it all someplace safe when I'm done. Okay?"

"Okay. Bye."

Then she was off, hurtled by her driver up and down the streets lined with summer green, the horizon muddled with building cumulus clouds. There would be rain that night, possible thunderstorms, and more moisture in any one of those clouds than the desert would ever allow to waft over its salted expanse.

She exited the ride and waved off the driver, who barely looked at her. She glanced up and down the street to see if anyone sat in a car. She eyed her own car, walked around it twice. Nothing unusual. She opened the door, sat inside, bristled from the heat assailing her skin and lungs. She rolled the windows down to let it escape, sweat collecting in every crevice. She turned the ignition and the car started as usual. Her emptied backpack sagged in the passenger's seat. She plugged her phone up but did not turn it on. She could have run the air conditioner, but she wanted to feel the sticky air. She wanted to breathe it in. Just as Alva had asked. She wondered if Alva's father had ever asked her to appreciate breathing as well. He would have known, practicing to become an astronaut, helmeted for long periods. A man with lofty ambitions who fell broken to the Earth, and now, Fiona guessed, he must feel broken in other ways.

CHAPTER 10
INDENTATION

She dreaded going home. She was tired, her mouth tasted funky from her tea, and she was suspicious of every car behind her and around her. A fog of fatigue and grief and unease settled over her, and she slammed her brakes before running a red light next to the Dunkin Donuts off Chapman Highway. A screech of tires and a stream of profanities rang through her open window from someone in a pickup. Not *the* pickup. But still, she trembled in her seat, tugged at her seatbelt absently, and drove more slowly from then on, traversing the light traffic of early afternoon.

Her hands sweated as she gripped her steering wheel and turned into her apartment complex. She had not bothered turning on her phone yet. It sat cold, attached to its charger, in the passenger seat next to her backpack: a useless slip of glass, dormant.

What happened to Alva's phone?

And for that matter, what happened to *Alva?*

She turned off her car and sat still for a moment, the hazy cloud-filtered sunlight rapidly seeping through the windshield. *If I stayed in here, the temperature would rise to the point that my brain began to cook.* She shuddered and opened the car door. Shouldering her purse, she walked in the syrupy air toward her apartment.

She halted in the little causeway between it and her neighbors and looked out at the entanglement of summer leaves and vines and breathed in the tangy-sweet air of loamy undergrowth and decaying leaves. The raspy cacophony of cicadas sawed its way into her thoughts. Somewhere, down in that fecund ravine, there were likely sleek white-tailed deer, resting, just out of sight in the sun-dappled depths of the woods, still as small boulders, and watching her to make sure she stayed beyond them. She had seen the deer sometimes; a flick of the white tail as they bolted, the soft shiver of leaves as they advanced and foraged upon tender shoots. She sent a silent plea to them: *Save me from this. I don't want to go in. I don't want to face him.*

No deer came to her rescue.

No vicuña had come to Alva's. Yet still Fiona hoped.

If the bodies are gone, what if they weren't really dead?

The thought tickled her mind again and again, and it hurt, the way touching a canker sore with your tongue repeatedly might. She wallowed in that repeated anguish.

The door opened before she could unlock it, and she faced Graham.

His expression puzzled her. He put on his great, beaming smile and threw his arms wide to hug her.

"I'm so glad you're home," he said. He smelled of garlic toast, and an orange tinge to his lips betrayed a snack of Cheetos. She pulled away from his attempt at a kiss. "I was so worried."

He followed her into the kitchen, where she dumped her purse and keys upon the bar.

"Sorry," she said distractedly, pulling her phone out of her purse. "My phone died."

"Someone came by." Graham encroached, arms out again. She stepped away from him again and took a tall glass from the maple-stained cabinet next to the sink.

"Oh?"

"Fi, is something going on? Are you in some kind of trouble?"

"Who came by?"

She turned to face him then, and stared fully into his face, until his light brown eyes darted away from her. She clenched her teeth.

"I don't know. They left a card." He gestured to the bar, but then his eyes dropped to the floor. Her purse had swept a card there when she had put it down. He retrieved it and handed it to her.

He was being cagey, his eyes shifting. She did not look at the card, only him. Something was different.

"I need a shower. It's really goddamn hot out there."

"Fi."

She walked ahead to move past him, and he stopped her, standing rigid, his feet shoulder-length apart, not letting her pass.

"What is it, Fi? Who are these people?"

She glanced down at the card and rolled her eyes. In metallic orange embossed letters, CUPRUM ASTRA blazed out of the high-quality, thick cardstock. She closed her eyes while running her fingers over those letters.

A front if there ever was one. And now I'm thinking like Lafe.

"Are you going to let me by?"

Her voice rang like a hammer on stone.

Graham's eyebrows pinched together, and he licked his lips.

"If you're in trouble, you need to tell me."

Blood surged to her face, and she hissed, "What sort of trouble do you think I'm in, Graham? Because I was out for a few hours? And some solicitor comes by?"

She moved past him only by pushing on his arms, for he blocked the kitchen. She shook her head and walked toward their bedroom, Graham tailing her. She tugged clean underwear, leggings, and shorts from her drawers, and then something caught her eye.

Graham was saying something like, "You weren't at school, and then your signal was gone. Then these people show up—"

Her file cabinet. She approached it and stared. It was dented, and not only that, but it was partly pulled open. Someone had pulled on her locked filing cabinet, and it was stuck about an inch and a half open. Enough for someone to pull something out of it...

She wheeled.

"Why is my cabinet open?"

Graham narrowed his eyes.

"Who is he?" he bellowed.

Fiona's eyes flew wide.

"Who is *who*?"

Graham sputtered. "I found the poem. About how much you missed him—"

"Oh my *fucking god*!" she shouted. "You broke into my filing cabinet! You got my old poems out from grade school! What the fuck, Graham!"

His face went magenta, and he flailed his arms. "What was I supposed to think, you're writing about some guy—"

"My old neighbor from childhood! Those poems were written when I was maybe 14, reminiscing! How fucking *dare* you break into my stuff!"

Graham held his arms up, panting, and protested. "They came by. They wanted to see stuff. I said I didn't know what they were talking about. They said—"

"WHO!" she shouted.

"Those people. The CUPRUM people."

"You let them *in* our home?" Fiona's blood drained from her face.

"I mean, they seemed official, like you were in trouble, and—and—"

There stood a man completely unspooling before her, and if she had not been so enraged and outraged simultaneously, she might have found his expression hilarious, flicking to and fro between upset and guilty.

"Did you open my cabinet in front of complete strangers?" Her voice slid like an ice dagger between them.

"N-no," he said. "No, Fi, I swear. I shouldn't have opened—"

"You literally broke the cabinet. You took things out. Why? Why would you do this? These are my private files!"

"You shouldn't keep secrets from me!" Graham roared. "We're getting married!"

Fiona glared at him, and her fingernails dug into her palms.

"Not anymore."

Graham blanched.

"What?"

"It's over. You betrayed my trust, you let strangers into our home, you went through my files. Did you give them anything?"

Graham's eyes welled with tears. "No, I sweartagod, I didn't let them into the cabinet. They just—they asked if you might have one, and I told them I didn't know, I swear, Fi! And I asked them to leave. They never came back here."

"But *you* did." She pointed at the dented cabinet. "You went through my things."

"I was worried about you."

"You were suspicious of me," snapped Fiona.

"I thought, I mean you weren't where you said you were, you were acting weird—"

"Stop, Graham!"

The air between them hung thick with unsaid words, with all her boundaries and trust disrespected, all her moments wishing she'd been able to be with friends, but Graham had insisted she stay with him constantly, all about stroking his ego and making him feel better at the expense of her own well-being. She loathed him in that moment.

And then…

No.

She shook her head.

"My friend is dead. Not just dead but missing."

"I know, I'm sorr—"

"Stop. Just stop. What we have isn't loving, or healthy, or good. You know it. I see it in your face."

Her shoulders shook and she could not stop them.

"Please don't end it, please," he pleaded. He reached out to her, but she held her hands up.

"Don't touch me."

"Okay. I'll—I'll get my stuff, I guess." He sniffed and wiped his eyes.

Fiona sat on the bed and stared at the damaged cabinet.

Thank God. Thank God I got those letters out. He's lying to me about some of it. I don't know what all. But at least he had nothing to give those goons. Just walked into his own goddamn trap.

"You stay here," she said suddenly. "I'm going. I don't feel safe here. I feel violated."

"I'm sorry, Fi—"

"Stop. I've heard enough."

"Where will you go?"

"I'll figure it out. I'll be back in a few days."

She opened a closet and sneezed, pulled out a dusty suitcase. She unzipped it and began to dump clothes into it. By now Graham was sobbing.

"I didn't mean anything. I swear. Can't we fix this? Can we go to therapy?"

She wheeled on him.

"Can't you let me *grieve*? Can't you let me breathe, for that matter? Can't you for *once* give me the benefit of the doubt that I'm a whole person who can take care of myself? Make my own sandwiches? Work my own job? Dress how I want to? Hang out with friends? Let me be *me*?"

It all gushed out of her, a dam broken. She took her engagement ring off, the ring she detested, that caught on all her clothes and ruined them bit by bit. She set it on the dresser, a tiny circlet of defeat.

Graham snuffled and wept and tried to approach her and she held her suitcase before her like a shield.

"I'll call you in a few days. I'm busy at work and helping Bingham with everything during this mess."

She strode past him, rolling the suitcase, seized her phone and purse and keys, and walked out of the relationship, out to her hot car, pummeled by the disorienting thrum of cicadas. She drove toward a future that was uncertain, except for one thing: she would not be owned. She would die before being caged again. That much she knew.

CHAPTER 11
SNAPSHOTS

She made it to Marysville before pulling into a Taco Bell drive-thru, then parking in the lot and choking down a burrito. Then she convulsed, opened her car door, and vomited the thing in the space next to her.

"Gross, fuck!" someone yelled.

The tears streamed after that. She shook in her seat, the salt in her eyes making its way to her mouth, filled with the bitter tang of bile. Aware of stares at her, she shut the door, turned the car back on, and kept the AC running.

Just exactly the same shit I judge other drivers for.

And she wailed in the hermetically sealed safety of the car, emptying herself of all the anguish and anger and horror and disappointment of the past week. Hiccupping with the horrible taste in her mouth, she scrounged her glove compartment for napkins and breath mints. She found the former but not the latter. So she swished her mouth using the lemonade she'd ordered, came close to gagging again, and opened the car door to spit it out onto the hot blacktop. She gasped and gasped and finally composed herself, shut the door again, and buckled herself in. Three deep breaths and she turned her phone on.

She would have turned it back off again immediately—she was prepared to—but there was a message from a local number that said simply, "Cat bowl time!"

Lafe.

She thought back to his empty cat food dishes. She didn't know this number. She had to hope it was him, writing in code.

She responded with a thumbs-up and turned the phone back off.

"Why the fuck am I in Marysville?" she asked herself aloud, staring at her odometer.

The soft blue undulations of the Great Smoky Mountains beckoned. All she wanted now was the cool, secretive depth of a good trout river. To feel the rush and pull of the strong water in the lower elevations of the Smokies surrounding her, pressing on her, welcoming her. She wanted to step into that river, in up to her waist, with no waders, and march along until her legs could move no more and she could sit on a boulder and become one with the thing, gather moss, and disappear.

Tell the trout I'm ready for them.

She jerked herself upright and decided.

No mountains today.

She set her car in reverse, then in drive. She pulled back onto the highway to head back, but then she considered. Lafe's house was in a historic neighborhood just down from Interstate 40, where it curved in sight of Knoxville's old downtown, with the 1982 World's

Fair Sunsphere gleaming gold in the forefront of the skyscrapers. She was not sure she could remember exactly where the house was.

Why the fuck did Knoxville even have *a World's Fair? It's* Knoxville.

She knew why and shook her head; it seemed such an innocent idea, that Knoxville would be at the forefront of some new age. In reality, it had taken extraordinary effort for its shining university to get a library refurbished, when so much more money funneled into the university's football team instead. Much of the ecosystem of the city seemed to subscribe to the sports behemoth, but she wondered what might have been, had more of that cash flowed into research.

For her own department was destitute. With technology leaping forward, rendering so many thinkers obsolete, and pushing life scientists more into technology and corporate opportunities, the halls of Hansen rang hollow. Yet somehow, money did seep in. Not from sports, but from benefactors with vested interests…such as the military, and perhaps, she reasoned, shadowy corporate bigwigs like this CUPRUM.

She wended her way back through the leafy streets, taking a scenic route, but ultimately still crossing the dark green arc of the Tennessee River and proceeding onward. Avoiding the university as best she could, she found herself gazing wistfully at the throng of students walking along, blissfully ignorant of anything she had to deal with.

Onward and through and around the Old Town, past a brewery where she had remembered Alva being hit on (unsuccessfully) and where Fiona had first tried IPA and came close to retching. The lingering taste of bile in her mouth reminded her as much as seeing the brewery itself; no fan of bitter tastes was she. She preferred the porters and stouts, or perhaps a red ale. Her stomach protested at these thoughts, and she continued on.

The shade trees on Lafe's street stretched in tired arches over the cracked road. It must have been a grand neighborhood a hundred years prior, but now it was given over to junky old cars on front lawns and broken fences, badly peeling paint, and a sense of malaise. At night, she mused, this would be the perfect setting for a horror film: the old child's swing swaying, its seat apparently empty; the litter blowing down the street as if pushed by ghostly hands. During the day, it looked bleached and downtrodden and bereft of much spirit, save the occasional windchime or faded yard décor. As she rolled slowly past the lots, one of which was empty and held only an old, concrete foundation partially covered with fallow grasses and dandelions, she saw one pale, plastic flamingo overturned, its vibrant color drained, its painted eye listless. She had never related more to an inanimate object in her life.

She parked her car in front of a house four doors down from Lafe's and stepped out onto the bright sidewalk, reflecting the strongest summer rays on a now-sweltering day. She turned her head left and right, and her shoulder-length, golden brown hair began to frizz in the dense humidity of the day. She saw nothing suspicious. She took a shuddering breath as another wave of nausea coiled through her, and she swung her purse across her body and began to walk.

A dog inside one of the rundown houses began to bark at her, and she glanced up to see a small, white terrier perched on the back of a couch, pawing at a window. Hands reached out to pull the dog down, and beige lace curtains closed up. Still the dog barked, but its sound was muffled, almost in a Doppler effect. She assumed its owner had taken it into a back room against its wishes.

A crumbling set of circular stones peppered the scraggly front yard of Lafe's house. It looked to Fiona as though no one ever used the front yard at all; there was a front porch, with an old, rickety looking wooden porch swing, a dented, metal screen door with a tear through its mesh about a foot long, and a sagging, black mailbox hung next to the door. She considered the walkway, the porch, and the mailbox, and ultimately decided not to draw attention to herself by attempting to knock at the front. She slipped along the side and walked down the driveway, making her way to the side door. A June beetle landed on her hand just as she raised it to tap, and she hissed in irritation, flinging her hand a bit, but the beetle stayed there.

She tilted her hand backward and forward to see the beetle's iridescent wings. It seemed quite content to stay latched onto her, and given her biology roots, she had no wish to harm the creature. She carefully lifted the thing and placed it into her left palm. It extended its wings and pumped up lazily, having satisfied its curiosity with her, and bumped against the faded siding of the house as it flew away.

She stood watching it and then heard the clearing of someone's throat. She jumped and looked up to see Lafe staring at her through the open door.

"You seem mesmerized," he noted, glancing toward the beetle's path; it was now gone.

Fiona blinked up at Lafe, whose dark grey eyes were half-lidded, not wild and bulging.

"June bug," she responded, pointing.

"Okay." He grinned for a second, then his brow went stern. "What happened?"

She blinked again and followed his gaze toward her waist. A splatter of dried vomit betrayed her. She blushed.

"I got sick."

He sighed.

"Come in, I'll get you a clean shirt."

She stood staring up at him and her eyes began to sting.

"I left."

"I know. Come in."

She stepped in, breathed in the smell of the houseplants, and her shoulders relaxed. He shut and locked the door behind her. She walked into the living room and the old wooden floors creaked. The room was dim, the curtains all drawn, and the scent of ancient smoke wafted from the fireplace, no doubt heated by the baking sun outdoors.

"Did you find anything?" she called out.

Lafe had walked up the stairs, which groaned and popped, and she could hear his steps on the floor above. She wondered what could be up there, and why he lived alone in the old house. And what might it have been like in its younger days? There was a lot about Lafe she didn't know.

"Shirt first," he called back down the stairs.

Finally he clambered down and emerged into the living room, a T-shirt flung over his left shoulder.

"Not your size," he said, holding it out to her, "but it's clean."

It was a soft, cotton tee, and on its front "Thistle Holler Hoedown" was written in swooping, rainbow letters, with the silhouette of mountains and a banjo placed in front of them. The date was three years prior. She could tell it had been worn many times. It was a woman's shirt, too.

"One of the reminders."

"Thanks."

She went into the bathroom and turned her eyes from the stains in the sink and in the tub, exposed from an open and quite worn blue shower curtain. A framed print of a Far Side cartoon with a dachshund hiding from an alien hung over the toilet.

She removed her stained shirt and scowled at the smell of it, and then groaned in embarrassment. A curled-up tube of toothpaste proved to be too great a temptation, so she squirted a small blob on her fingertip and scrubbed her teeth with it and swished with water. She pulled on the clean tee and stared at herself in the mirror. Dark circles under her eyes stared back; flecks of ruined mascara dotted her eyelids. Her hair couldn't decide between lank and floofy, and settled somewhere in a bad combination of the two, reminiscent of 1980s hairdos.

"Fuck," she whispered.

She peed, flushed, washed her hands, and emerged feeling, if not better, at least more respectable.

"Not my best day," she said, but Lafe was not within sight. "Hey, where'd you go?"

"Tea," he called from the kitchen.

"I don't think—" she began, dreading the funk of the tea from her prior visit.

"Don't worry, it's ginger tea."

She sighed in relief.

"Good for the stomach."

He brought it out to her, and she smirked at him. He didn't return the smile, and so hers faded.

"What is it?" She didn't like his expression.

He set the mug of tea down on the coffee table and gestured at an array of pictures on the floor.

"Take a look at these photos. I put them in what I think is chronological order. Notice anything?"

He pointed to three of them.

In one, Alva and Ken Hatch, another grad student, stood smiling, sunglasses reflecting bright sun, and they both gave peace signs under a fuchsia awning with a table behind them. In a second one, a picture of a table spread with an assortment of fruits and platters of food, with various people lined up and smiling. In a third, a group photo of several people, including Alva, piled onto a yellow pickup truck.

"I don't see—" Fiona began.

So Lafe picked up the three photos and brought them to her.

"Look closely."

She held the first one with the awning, and at first could not see anything unusual. But then, on the table behind Alva and Ken, in large, white letters: CUPRUM. She felt cold prickles go up and down her back.

"Not exactly a university logo," he muttered.

Lafe gave her the second photo. She didn't see anything unusual at first, but then, a bright smile shone out, distinctive, at the foot of the table; someone waved at the person taking the camera, and Fiona assumed the photographer was Alva. As for the person...

"Jack. Fucking. Cordeiro," she gasped.

Lafe handed her the third photo.

And there stood Jack, suave and fashionable, among the group.

Everyone in that group was now dead.

Except for Jack.

CHAPTER 12
STATE CHAMP

She sipped the ginger tea with trepidation, but found it neutral enough to tolerate. She nodded to Lafe in thanks. He tilted his head in reply. He took the three photos and fanned them out like playing cards.

"So…how well did Alva know that Jack douche?"

Fiona shook her head. "I didn't think that well. He'd hit on her. I'd have to go back through my emails to see."

Lafe frowned. "How many emails do you have from her?"

"I don't know. A few dozen?"

"Show me."

"What, on my phone?"

Lafe pointed to his desk. "Log in there. Everything's encrypted."

Fiona licked her lips and set the tea down. She stood, sighed, and plucked her phone from her purse.

"I really need to check my messages."

Lafe sighed. "Well, good luck. I can maybe block the location a bit with my equipment."

"What do you mean?"

"I have this place tricked out," he answered with a lopsided grin, his hair falling forward into his eyes. He swept it back.

"Jesus fuck, you *are* paranoid," she murmured. "I don't know whether to admire you or back slowly out of here!"

Lafe shrugged, his eyes glinting. "It's kept me going this long."

"Yeah." She reached out and squeezed his hand. "Well, I'm glad."

He squeezed her hand in return, pulled out the desk chair, old and wobbly with a loose caster, and flung his arms out in a grandiose bow. "Milady."

She laughed, sat in the chair, and he pushed her in. She caught a whiff of him then, and something smoky-green, like a beach fire from logs, perhaps. It sent a jolt through her, a remembrance of long ago days at beach campgrounds in the Carolinas with her family. Such a feeling of adventure associated with that scent, but also of good memories and, somehow, home. She glanced up at him, and he looked back down at her, and she felt her cheeks tingle. She giggled, and he did too.

"Dork," she said softly.

"You're a dork." He gestured toward the keyboard.

She stared at the screen and entered her password, which required security codes and her thumbprint on her phone. It was then that she saw new messages, and with an irritated sigh, she flicked through those. None were from Graham, fortunately. She did not want to deal with him at the moment. Not after what had happened. Then she paused.

"Doc's sounding on edge," she murmured. She took another sip of the ginger tea. Whether it was the tea or the company, she felt soothed; the nausea faded.

"What's he saying?"

"People are looking for Gale. 'Can't get in touch with Sykes or Franks. Might need you to come in early tomorrow.'" She shook her head. "I don't want to go in."

"Guess you have to, though, right? Maybe you can find out more info. Are the spooks gone?"

Fiona texted back, "Ok. Something personal going on, might be in a bit late, definitely by 10 at the latest. Is anyone still there this afternoon?"

A couple of minutes passed, and then the message reply: "Empty as a tomb. I'm not getting any clear answers from anyone, so anyone asking me isn't getting any either. Take it easy. Get pizza or something. I'll see you at 10."

Lafe nodded. "He's a good boss."

"He is," agreed Fiona.

She found another message, from Marian Haglund: "How are you doing, hon?" Fiona felt a pang of guilt then, for not checking on Marian sooner.

"I'm hanging in there," she texted back. "How's your mom?"

A couple of minutes passed and then Marian wrote back, "Tired. She has another surgery tomorrow, and it's looking like she'll need physical therapy. I'll be here a bit longer than I thought."

"Take all the time you need. Sending every good wish for your mom." Fiona texted back. "Big hug."

"Big hug to you, too, hon. I know you and Alva were so close."

Fiona sent back a heart emoji but then set the phone down. Her eyes stung. She turned her face so Lafe could not see.

Lafe walked back into the kitchen and turned on music: Earth, Wind, and Fire streamed through his speakers. Of everything in the rundown house, at least the speakers were of good quality, she noted. He whistled in the kitchen while Fiona searched her emails from Alva.

"That's weird." She twisted her fingers together above the keyboard.

"What?" he craned his neck around the kitchen door.

She shivered, staring at the screen.

"There's…there's only a few emails in here. This isn't right. We had dozens. We had dozens! I'm telling you!"

Her voice rose and her tears fell. "Where the fuck are these emails?"

"Hold on, hold on," Lafe soothed. "Check the trash folder."

She shook her head and flung tears from her eyes. "Nothing there."

Lafe bit his lower lip. "When was the last time you read these emails?"

"Two days ago."

"Fuck." He ran his hands through his hair. "Is there anything left?"

"There's one."

"Show me."

She brought up the only remaining email between her and Alva. It read: "You'll never guess who showed up!"

Fiona stared up at Lafe from her seat.

"Did you reply?" he asked her.

"No," she admitted.

"Well, I'm guessing we know who she's talking about."

"Jack."

"Probably."

"The emails though." Fiona sat still and stared at the screen, her shoulders shaking. "I didn't print them, I didn't forward them. They're gone."

Lafe put his hands on his hips and threw his head back.

"Someone's been digging through your shit. Was it Graham?"

She glared at him. "You know, I wouldn't put it past him, after what he did. But why delete them? And anyway, I wasn't logged in at the house. So I'm not sure."

"Someone else, then, maybe," reasoned Lafe.

"Who, though?" She tapped her finger on her chin.

"Look, I'm going to do some digging. Go chill for a while. Pick out new music, raid the fridge—on second thought, don't look in there. Fuckin' biohazard. You hungry?"

"Come to think of it, I am craving pizza."

She stood, and he took her place in the chair.

"On it," he said, and he opened a new tab. "Enter your toppings."

She chose mushrooms and green peppers; he chose pepperoni. He placed the order and handed her the mug.

"We might need coffee later," he mused.

"Oh?"

"It's going to be a long night, because I'm doing a deep dive here, and reaching out to some old chums for help."

"Nothing illegal, I hope?" she asked uneasily.

She could see the curve of his lips reflecting the pale glow of the computer screen.

"Nothing you need to worry about."

Well, now I'm going to worry about it.

But she chose to take her tea and peruse the living room.

"What's upstairs?"

"Poltergeists."

She snorted.

"Fuck it, have a look around. It's a goddamn mess."

She carried her tea with her up the creaking, popping stairs, and the air grew mustier and hotter with each step.

"No AC?" she called down.

"Heat pump is shit," he called back, "barely pumps up the cool air. It's actually on, believe it or not. Feeble as fuck."

"Get a window unit!" she remarked.

"There is one; it's gross, don't look at it."

She continued on out of earshot and held onto the top railing and looked back down. Then she studied the pictures on the hallway walls. Old black and white photographs; she assumed they were his family. A huge pennant hung from the hall ceiling, red with yellow lettering, that read "1987 STATE CHAMPS." A framed vinyl album cover of The Doors hung at the end of the hallway, along with a mercury glass mirror, scuffed and smeared and fogged up in the lower right corner. One room's door sat ajar, an upstairs bathroom stood open, and another bedroom, the largest, was open, expansive, hot, and bright despite the aged curtains. It smelled like old wood polish and a bit of mold. A rickety window AC unit wheezed in one of the windows. A queen sized bed sagged under a drab brown blanket, smushed in the middle. Two blue and white striped pillows bulged from just under the blanket. Another guitar sat in the corner, electric, red and white, glittering. Bromeliads hung from the low walls; the ceiling was sharp and angled here, and low on the western side of the room. She knew it must be Lafe's bedroom. It looked to her a bit abandoned. Forgotten. She wondered if he actually slept there at all.

Finding it stifling, she ducked back out into the hall. She pushed a partially closed door open; this room was darker, smaller, and cooler. It was full of boxes shoved up against one wall, an old desk, and a twin-sized bed, crisp and tidy. A small, red bookshelf sat next to the bed. The room smelled a bit of mold and cardboard and old books. Something thumped in one corner, and she jumped.

Poltergeists, she remembered him saying, and she laughed at herself and rolled her eyes.

She heard Lafe and walked back toward the stairwell.

"Pizza's here!"

She held the handrail with one hand and her mug with the other, and walked down the stairs. Her ankles popped with every step. She smelled the cheese and sauce, and her stomach contracted and her mouth watered.

"Well, good thing my appetite is back." She took his offered paper plate and scooped up a hot slice, catching a string of cheese with her finger.

"Maybe not for long though," he said.

"Why is that?"

"My digging has already brought up some…interesting results. But first, pizza."

She sat on the couch, he sat at the computer, and for a few minutes they ate in silence. After they'd finished their slices, he wheeled around and put his hands behind his head.

"So…tell me about the space connection here."

"What?" she asked.

"Our friend Jack, here, tried to get NASA funding and failed. Did you know that?"

"No, and really, I don't know a whole lot about the guy."

"I wonder if anyone really did. He got funding, all right, for some astrobiology projects. But not from NASA. From CUPRUM. And something seems to have soured there."

"What do you mean?"

"Jack here is one shady motherfucker. I don't know what he was doing in the Atacama desert, but it wasn't in the best interests of your department. There's money flooding into his accounts from somewhere—CUPRUM, maybe, but it's not above board. This guy's soul is as dark as space itself."

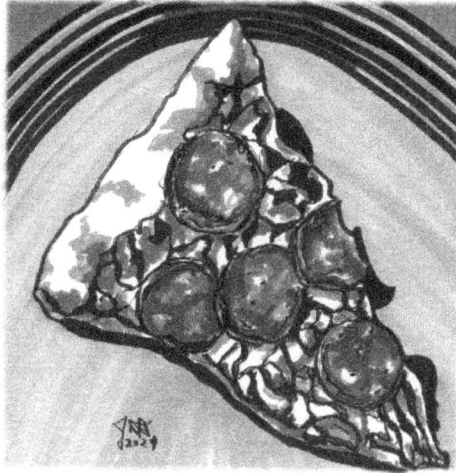

CHAPTER 13
THE PUZZLE

Fiona snorted at Lafe.

"Poetic," she cracked.

He shrugged. "Maybe. Look, how close were Alva and Jack?"

Fiona shifted where she sat. "Well, that part's not so clear to me."

"What do you think CUPRUM really does?"

His brow had gone stern again, and with his sharp features and staring, he resembled a twitching eagle.

With several panels open on his desktop, he brought up forms that, to Fiona's innocent eyes, looked official, some with the seal of the U.S. Army and the Department of Defense.

"Lafe," her voice warned. "Where are you looking for these documents?"

Shrugging again, he tapped the screen with his finger and expanded another set of files.

"Looks like CUPRUM here outcompeted the Army for some grants for the department. Best I can figure, maybe CUPRUM funded Cordeiro to fast-track some new technology. Something they found in the desert. But...a falling out."

"But," Fiona thought back, "he seemed okay with the CUPRUM reps who showed up to interrogate Bingham."

"Hmm," was the only response.

Sighing, she took her used paper plate and dropped it into the kitchen trash. Then she went to the bathroom. Her face looked blurry, as if the sheen of grease from her pizza obstructed her vision. She washed her hands and looked down at the crusty edges of the sink. A very bachelor scene, she surmised, with an old bar of soap and a stick toothbrush. Lafe was a bit retro, she realized then. Except for his computer.

She walked back into the living room and Lafe whistled.

"So...CUPRUM bought the mine from the original landowner, best I can tell, and wanted to take over the dig."

"Hang on," Fiona said, her thoughts sparking. "I seem to remember now that Bridget had put her foot down on that, and Jack took her side, or something. The landowner had an agreement with the research team that wouldn't have interfered with Bridget's team."

"How'd that factor into things?"

"Something Alva said." Fiona felt her thoughts and memories betrayed her, for she could not remember Alva's exact wording. And that had not been very recent. The emails were gone now. But her last in-person conversations...snatches of them flicked through her mind, like flipping pages.

"Sounds to me," Lafe rubbed his forehead and pushed out his lower lip, "Ol' Cordeiro here must've been with Alva's team quite a bit. Even though they didn't have the same site."

He stared at the photos laid out on the floor.

"He was with Alva's team recently."

"How recently, though?"

"Can you think of anything Alva said that might tell us?"

"I don't...I can't remember for sure. And the emails are gone, so I can't go looking."

She loathed her memory lapse right then, and she knew instinctively that part of it stemmed from grief and the surreal shock that someone she knew was dead. That she would never hear from Alva again.

"The emails grew more sporadic," she recalled.

"When?"

"I don't know. Less than a month before...before they disappeared."

"Nothing strange?" Lafe pressed.

She felt a low-moving chill traverse her body.

"Something," she murmured.

"What?"

"Well, the emails were sporadic as I said, but also...weird."

"Weird how?"

She chewed on the inside of her cheek and wracked her brain for any vestige of memory. "She said things like, the mood was bad, morale was poor, there were arguments all the time. A few people had bad dreams. And then...yeah. Someone tried taking over the site. Guessing it was CUPRUM. A land grab."

She stood. "I remember now. Alva said, 'That shifty-ass motherfucker came back around and may have fucked us all.'"

"He was there. Had to have been. Still. And within weeks."

"Maybe."

"And she didn't trust him then," Lafe pointed out.

"No," agreed Fiona.

"So he was in support of Bridget's team, or appeared to be, then he did a 180, and CUPRUM swooped in for the land grab. And then everyone died. Fiona."

She locked eyes with him.

"It seems obvious to me," he said.

"We can't know that," she whispered.

"What the fuck happened down there?" Lafe wondered aloud the thoughts she held. "Why would they move in and do that, too? What was so important about that site?"

CHAPTER 14
CURRENT

Even as the oldest desert on Earth, the Atacama was a thing of newness compared to the Appalachian Mountains. Its age belied its impermanence. Alva had told her many times about the contrast between the Atacama and Appalachia. Fiona could only dream about this; she had never even been to the American Southwest and could not fathom such a thing as a desert. The pulsating, forested, and populated surfaces of the Appalachian Mountains masked their ancient roots, she knew.

"Older than the rings of Saturn," her geology professor had intoned, tugging at his salt and pepper ponytail and setting the young minds before him dreaming.

Older than old. Anything that had grown from those ancient roots had worn down again and again, weathered and eroded and pocked by toothy caverns holding primordial, quiet, colorless creatures in their dripping depths. Upon their surfaces, Fiona climbed again and again, in every season, to experience each in its fullness: the crunch of dead leaves in winter, the flame of them drifting down in autumn; summer, the sweat and the insect bites prolific under a filtered green roof, spring with nascent shoots and buds and little, growing secret notes passed between courting birds.

Her friend had died far from a land of vines and flowers, far from family. And for what?

And for what?

It didn't make sense to her.

Lafe's insinuations wormed deep into her mind, and she wanted them not to be true. For now, they had more questions than answers. And Lafe implicated a company in mass murder, along with Jack Cordeiro.

Alva talking about the friction in the team and the bad dreams…Fiona could not guess what that had to do with anything, but she kept replaying the words in her thoughts over and over. It painted a picture of unease, and maybe everyone had been on edge.

"Could be," she said slowly, "one of the team freaked out. And—and—"

"What, assassinated everybody else?"

She nodded.

"But why?"

"I don't know. But the desert. It…Alva said it does things to people." Fiona then felt silly for verbalizing something she'd been dancing around.

Lafe looked at her as if she'd turned turquoise.

"What the hell does that even mean?"

Fiona's lips twitched. "Well, she'd been there enough, so she knew. The place sounded…strange. And, for lack of a better word, haunted."

Lafe crowed loudly. "I'm the one with the poltergeist! Not a research operation!"

Fiona managed a small laugh.

"She was really affected by the desert, though. Said it changed her and she—she couldn't ever really let it go, even when she did come back. Like she came to dread going back, but loved it when she was there. 'The desert is my new family,' she told me once. 'The hills my mother and the valleys my father. My ancestors buried in some ancient pit somewhere, maybe.'"

"That's a helluva thing to say to you."

"She was always saying things like that, though."

"And *I'm* the poet?"

"There can be more than one poet."

Lafe smirked.

"I guess I see now why CUPRUM came sniffing around. And Jack too."

"We still have no idea if any of what you're suggesting is true."

"Something went down. Alva and her crew talking about bad dreams, bickering over the site, the land grab. Come on, Fi. That was a predatory takeover."

"So, what, the desert made everyone crazy?" Fiona pressed her hands onto her cheeks, which had gone hot. "Maybe. I don't know. It was a weird place, based on everything she told me."

"Nah." Lafe shook his head. "Something happened. Something in that three-week period."

"But what?" Fiona actually stamped her foot, like a toddler might, who had no real way of coping with something she couldn't understand other than to react physically to her own frustration.

Lafe stood and turned off his computer screen.

"I've seen enough of this shit," he said, "and it's low-key freaking me out. I say we go for a walk."

"Where? It's getting kind of late."

"We'll drive. And anyway, what? Do you have plans?"

"Don't be a dick," she sneered.

He threw his hands out. "Just saying. Let's cruise down by the river. I need to get out of here. I feel like I'm stuck in a sticky snow globe and my plants are gonna go nuts and start to strangle me."

It *was* sticky in his house, with the feeble AC straining unsuccessfully against the crush of a Tennessee summer upon a poorly insulated, older home. The daylight slanted gold, and so it would be about an hour until sunset. He was right: of course she didn't have plans. There was nowhere to go back to. She could drive to her parents' home, a couple of hours northeast, but what would she say to them? And besides, she did need to go back to work. No matter how many strange people were around, it didn't solve the issue of her having bills to pay. Working for Dr. Bingham was stable and reliable, and while not glamorous, at least she worked at the forefront of knowledge. Not everything was researched by AI, and she was glad to have the work.

She shook her head, casting her sweaty hair in a swooping arc, and said, "Why not? There must be plenty of mosquitos just *starving* for our blood at the river."

She cast her eyes at the photos and her backpack. He noticed, and then he pointed to the barrel table over near the corner.

"What?"

He rolled his eyes and gathered the backpack and photos carefully and took them to the table. He lifted it up, set the backpack down, and placed the barrel over it, hiding it completely.

She felt idiotic, worrying about that backpack, but she did still, even though she had no real reason to suspect someone would break into Lafe's home and take it.

"Come on," he urged. "I know a good path to walk. It'll do you good."

She sighed. "Okay."

So he pulled his car out of the driveway, and she watched as he darted his eyes up and down the street. She hunched down in her seat.

"I don't know if you need to do all that."

"I'll feel better once we're on a more open road."

He glanced sideways at her.

"You really are jittery right now."

"Well?" she flashed. "My friend is dead and my engagement's off. There's weird fucking people dicking around my only place of work, stirring up shit. Don't I have the right to be jittery? And it's rich coming from you, Mister Conspiracy!"

Lafe's mouth went o-shaped. "God*damn*!"

And for a while, they rode in silence, as Lafe careened through the golden hour light of Knoxville's streets. Rush hour traffic had begun to release its grip on the city, with Interstate 40 breezing along at a good pace above them. As Lafe drove under the underpass toward downtown, Fiona sighed.

"I'm sorry."

"For what?"

"For blowing up at you."

"Don't be. I earned that one."

"Still."

He twitched his shoulders up and turned on the radio. It was an old car, and still had a regular radio, so he flicked through the dials and found an oldies channel.

What's oldies to us was new to someone, she mused, thinking the tunes weren't even from her parents' generation, but the one in between theirs and hers.

They descended toward the river, in a lush neighborhood with bluffs overlooking parts of it. Further along, they wound down a road to a dock, and a waterfront path. Lafe parked the car along the street and Fiona opened her door with a loud, squeaking creak.

"Oof," she said.

"Yeah, she's not getting any younger, but neither are we."

They walked along and felt the humidity of the early evening air envelope them. It reeked of river, of the lake-ish, slightly fishy scent that the Tennessee River held in its dark and rushing column. The river here was wide and powerful while seemingly still on the surface. And such a lot of water. Alva had remarked on that every time she'd come back.

"There's so much water here. You don't understand," she'd say. "It's kind of embarrassing, somehow."

Fiona stared at the current and then jerked her arm, feeling the tiny prick of a mosquito.

"Shit."

"Most useless creatures on Earth," spat Lafe. "Not one good function for them except to make us suffer. A true parasite."

"Maybe we just haven't found how they fit," she reflected.

"They fit to spread disease; that's literally their only function. They're instruments of suffering and nothing more."

He smacked the back of his neck and swore.

"Loathsome fucks."

Now he seemed irritable and restless.

"Look, we don't have to walk here," she told him.

"It's not bad," he replied, "just the damn mosquitos. Anyway, I needed some space to clear my head. If the *stupid. Fucking. Mosquitos* would take long enough to stop."

She tried not to laugh, but a peal of laughter loosed from her, and then another, and then she spasmed, doubled over, laughing.

His lips twitched and his eyes glowed in the fading light.

"Fine, I fold," he said. "I've got a plan."

"Oh? What's your grand plan, Lafe Lambert?"

He swiveled to her and bowed extravagantly. "Lady Hawthorne, we are going to sneak into the lab tonight."

CHAPTER 15
GREENHOUSE BLUES

Taking a quick, sharp breath, Fiona cried, "The hell we are!"

"Oh, we are," nodded Lafe, rising up and down on his toes, his eyes manic with mischief.

She shook her head and held up her right forefinger. "No."

"Yes!"

Rolling her eyes and placing her hands on her hips, she said, "You're not making sense. This is ridiculous."

"What, you've never been to the lab at night before?"

He lowered his face and looked at her with puppy-dog eyes. She shuddered.

She *had* been to the lab late one night, having ruined an experiment and needing to redo the entire thing within a few hours. She'd never told Doc Bingham that she'd done that and definitely didn't divulge that she'd had help. They'd needed data to present the next day, and he'd been out of town. She knew she'd face consequences if she didn't have the data.

She frowned.

"How'd you know?"

He hooted. "Well, if I hadn't known before, you just verified it."

"There's nothing wrong with working at night!" she sniffed. "I prefer it, actually. Not stepping over the grad students or triggering their egos: I count that as a win."

"So you can go in, no problem."

Exasperated, she hissed, "Sure, but what's the point?"

"I want to do some digging."

"And get us arrested? No thanks."

It was his turn to roll his eyes, as he swept his hair back from them.

"We can say you needed help with an experiment."

"Are you going to snitch about that time?"

"No, and besides, Doc would probably have *loved* that shit. Who else is gonna come in late and miss their shows"—Fiona clicked her tongue at him—"and miss out on domestic life with the most humdrum fiancé in the universe, all for the love of science?"

"What are you saying?" she demanded.

"That you're a fucking nerd," he replied easily. She turned away from him to march back to his car.

"Just take me home."

"Which home?" he called.

She paused her steps and placed her hands on her temples and let out a small rage-shriek.

He approached her.

"Lafe." Her voice, low, carried a warning to him.

He held up his hands.

"Look," he offered. "We go in, act like you need to work on something. I take a look around. We get out, we go back to my place, you take my room, I'll take the spare bedroom. Come back tomorrow ready to face the world, but maybe with a bit more info. Come on! It'll be fun."

"You sure have a warped idea of 'fun,'" she pointed out, glaring at him.

"You should go look in a mirror sometime," he snapped back. "Come on. You know I'm right: this is a good chance to check things out without any spooks around. Say…fifteen minutes, and we're out."

She folded her arms and tossed her chin.

"Fifteen. Tops."

"Tops," Lafe agreed.

"I think you're nuts for this, officially," she muttered as they walked back to the car.

She felt a tingling sense of adventure laced with unease.

"That's the nicest thing you've ever said to me." Lafe grinned at her as he opened the car door for her and then whisked to the other side to drive.

She stared at the dark river and the lights of buildings on either side of it as they pulled forward. The river slid behind them as they climbed, its deep presence a constant despite its motion.

The campus was well-lit by night, for the most part. But the parking spot Lafe chose off-campus sat in darkness, under a large silver maple, far enough from streetlamps that they would not draw attention. Or so Fiona hoped. Still, both she and Lafe looked all around to see if anyone watched them. Feeling the prickling of unease upon the base of her neck, Fiona chewed on her lower lip.

For a long while they said nothing, and more or less strolled casually up the hill, past the great hall, and then turned in the courtyard toward the Hansen building. The only sounds were katydids, the *beent-beent* of nighthawks zigzagging their way through the night sky, siphoning up insects, and the high chattering laughter of a small group of young people. More chipper and less grandiose than grad students, and with their very presence after five o'clock not signifying another tech like her, she assumed they were undergrads. The sound of their joviality turned a corner and vanished, and she heard the hum of the large air conditioning units and giant freezers and all other ephemera associated with the science and engineering buildings. Labs glowed yellow into the night, and she could see a few people in the upper floors working away, but by and large, the first floor of the Hansen building was dark. She stepped toward it, but Lafe hissed.

"Not the front door, God!" He pulled gently at her elbow and gestured down the walkway.

"The greenhouse?" she mouthed, her face lit by one of the older halogen lamps. It shone on Lafe's head, casting unsettling shadows onto his angular features, making him the vision of a silent film vampire. He nodded.

They slinked into the shadows alongside the path to the greenhouse. The staccato sound of boots froze her momentarily, and her nerves sang. Lafe darted ahead and out of sight, and she gripped her shoulder bag against her and ran, praying the campus security hadn't seen them.

Skidding a bit, she collided with a stack of small seedling trays just outside the greenhouse and whispered, "*Fuck!*"

The pair of them whipped their heads back and forth. The algal-green gleam of the old greenhouse panels, perhaps a hundred years old, shone in lurid, phosphorescent hues, unnatural in the darkness. Fiona felt that every panel of the thing had eyes, and they were all turned on her.

"I think we're clear," Lafe whispered. "Got your badge?"

She nodded, retrieving it from her wallet. She held it up to the greenhouse door. She took a breath.

What if it didn't work?

What if an alarm went off?

Who has a record of entry for this?

All these questions flitted through her mind like a drunk hummingbird.

But the security panel went green. The door clicked, and she turned the lever and entered.

The crush of moisture and fertilizer gagged her, but Lafe urged her on, and glancing left and right out the door, he pulled it shut.

"No one's here," she said, her pulse hammering.

"Good. We've got the entry into the hall."

"But what's the plan?"

Lafe thrust his hands in his pockets and pulled them out. He tilted forward and backward.

"I'm scouting," he answered, shrugging.

"But for what?"

"Anything. Any clue."

"Okay…"

"Why don't you head to Doc's and see if there's anything amiss?"

She felt a moment of cold panic.

"Where will you be?"

He put his finger to his lips, and she shook her head and groaned.

"Lafe, dammit. This is so risky. Where do we meet? Back here?"

He thought for a moment. "There's a space behind Doc's office, right, by the trash?"

"Yeah," she replied. "He likes to say that's what the department considers him, and that's why he's there."

"Douchebags," muttered Lafe. "But aside from that, let's meet back there. I don't want to go back the way we came in. That rental cop will be on the prowl out front, mostly."

"I hope you're right."

"Mmhmm."

"Okay, off I go."

Lafe opened the greenhouse door and they both took breaths of the cool, drier air of the air-conditioned old building. The tang of chemicals and old wood polish filled Fiona's nose. She used to love that smell; now it put her on edge. He gave her a short nod and loped off toward the main entrance to the building, where he swept around and up the stairs to the second floor. The squeaks of his sneakers told her he'd reached the hallway and after that, she could not hear him.

All that she could hear was the hum of the long, fluorescent lights in the ceiling, the air conditioner, and the drone of lab equipment like chest freezers in the hallway, or refrigerators. She was surprised at how empty the building was, but she knew that likely somewhere, someone leaned over a tray of Eppendorf tubes and pipetted away, or ran analyses on experiments, or otherwise burned their evenings in the manner of so many would-be or actual scientists. She wondered if Doc would be among them, so she stepped quietly along the hallway toward the one with his office.

The fluorescent light in this hallway spasmed, giving everything a lurid, pulsating look, and she grew self-conscious of her own footfalls, staring down at her Keds and wondering why she hadn't replaced them in so long; there was very little arch support left, many scuffs, and the navy blue canvas had faded. She looked over her shoulder multiple times as she padded along, not really sure why; just that she had been watched enough recently, and had come to expect that *someone* might be there. But no one was.

Outside of Doc's office, a tall stack of empty seed trays listed, and she felt a pang of guilt that she hadn't been there. She was tempted to carry the trays back to the greenhouse then and there, but the office beckoned. She peered through the glass window of Doc's office door and found it dark inside, and still. She reached into her bag and felt for her keys, slowly, firmly, so as not to jangle them. A snap sound jolted her and she swiveled around to check the hallway, but nothing was there. She thought for a second.

Was that the greenhouse door?

She stood very still, holding those keys. On the keychain, her car key took up considerable space, and it had an alarm feature. She glanced along the hall walls and also found the fire alarm pull behind acrylic. The light flickered. The hall sat still. No more snapping sounds.

With a shudder, she turned back to the office door and inserted her key. She had only rarely ever been inside the office outside Doc's working hours, during rare vacation days for him or when she had come in on weekends to work. This felt different. It felt like a violation of trust. But she needed to see…what, she did not know yet.

She turned the lever of the door and its sound rang through the empty hall so that she felt even more on edge. Still, she saw no one. She entered the office and locked the door behind her, and turned on Doc's desk lamp.

His chair sat empty, its vinyl seat cracked and lined with duct tape, its polyester-covered arms fraying. Piles of papers and files littered his desk, and a two-thirds-eaten, open pack of Lifesavers sat under the green lamp. A faded picture of a much younger man and a young woman, framed in dull bronze, sat shoved back up against a section of the cream-painted cinder block wall that his desk was pushed against. This was Doc and his wife, many years ago; she had died not long before Doc hired Fiona a couple of years back. Hiking accident out West; she'd fallen down a crevasse. Fiona did not know what Doc was like before his wife's death; she had only heard through others that he seemed never to stop sighing since then.

She had never thought until that moment what it must be like for him to go to his home and not have his wife there, after the accident. How it might feel even to be married that long, and for it suddenly to be over. She thought about Graham and realized, again, that she could not imagine being married to him for decades; and now, for any length of time. But to love someone and lose them in such a strange, sad, random way…she couldn't fathom it.

As she thought this, she forgot for a moment to be careful, and gasped at the squawk of a walkie-talkie. She turned the lamp off and ducked out of sight.

The security guard walked down the hall and tested the door. Her heart hammered.

Will he come in?

She panicked, and her eyes shot to the window that faced the garbage bin outside and little more. For a wild second she thought of leaping into the garbage and she snorted, and then clapped her hand over her mouth. A wedge of flashlight blazed through the door's window, and then the walkie-talkie squawked again. She heard a heavy sigh.

"Yeah? No, I didn't. Okay. I'll check it out."

The light extinguished and the guard turned and clopped away on his boots. She dashed over to the door and could just barely see him retreat, and then he was out of sight. She heard the front door of the building open. She hoped Lafe was nowhere around it.

Then she quickly stepped back to the desk and turned the lamp back on, and began shuffling through the papers. She found a white legal envelope with something sparkling on it and seized it.

"CUPRUM" blazed in a shiny, copper, modern font on the front with an infinity symbol below it. The envelope was open, so she reached in and pulled its contents out.

Her eyes darted across the cotton page: "…pleased to…" and "grant extension" and "ten years, or until completion of the project." She sat down in Doc's chair and it creaked loudly. She winced.

"So," she muttered, "CUPRUM's taking over Doc's grants. Fuck."

Then she read the letter more slowly, and felt her face blanch and then grow scarlet. She read, "…maximum of two part-time research technicians affiliated with CUPRUM, and no university affiliations."

"Me!" she hissed. "They're talking about me and my job! They don't want me here."

She could barely see straight. No way would Doc go for this. Would he? Would he fire her, so he could get all the grant money he would need for the next ten years?

"Of course he would," she groaned.

Something rustled and scraped outside in the hallway. She froze and turned the lamp off. She carefully placed the envelope back where she had found it.

If it's that goddamn guard again…

But she heard no boots, and no walkie-talkie, and no flashlight appeared. She waited. Silence.

She finally crept over to the door and leaned just enough to see out the small glass window. She could see nothing.

Where the fuck is Lafe?

She waited again. Silence.

I'm totally filling the emptiness with my own imagination. Fuck.

She bit her lip and unlocked the door, and turned its handle slowly. She pushed it open an inch and peered through, and saw no one. She opened it further. An empty hall. Exhaling slowly, she closed the door behind her and locked it with her key. Then she tripped and fell onto her knees.

The seed trays.

They had been moved. Not by the guard, she realized; it was the noise she'd heard after he had left. Had Lafe come looking for her?

No. He'd have tapped on the door or something.

Someone else had moved the trays.

Irritated, she restacked them, and then, sighing, she adjusted her shoulder bag and picked up the lot of them. She carried them in her arms toward the greenhouse door, and then the guard entered the building. She froze. He froze. They stared at each other.

"Oh hi!" she said in too high a pitch.

He nodded uncertainly. "You work here?"

"Yes," she said. "Just cleaning up."

"Can I see your ID?"

Her face flamed. She said, "Sure," and set the trays down on the hallway floor. She tried to still her trembling hands and she found her entry ID and showed the man. He sweated, and she could see a shave rash beneath his too-tight collar.

He nodded again.

"You have any trouble tonight?" he asked her.

She disliked his smell: cheap aftershave, and too much of it, yet she could smell his body odor beneath that.

"No, no trouble," she answered. "Is everything all right?"

"So long as I'm here," he said, and he grinned then.

She felt a little spike of warning in her mind.

She smiled and said, "Well, thanks so much for taking care of things. I'd better be going."

"You need a hand with those?"

"Oh, no thank you. Good night!"

And she seized the trays and hefted them up against her chest like a shield, and marched toward the greenhouse door.

"Let me help you with that—"

But she raced to open it before he could, and then his walkie-talkie squawked again.

He swore and then answered it, and she found herself inside the greenhouse door, its moisture soaking her, but at least it provided a barrier between her and the guard. She set the seed trays down on the floor in the dim room and then straightened and then…

She saw it standing in the far corner, behind some hanging ferns and extinguished glow lights. Something. Something standing in the corner.

A man?

Her heart hammered.

She could not make out any features but then she could see it move. Not toward her, though. It moved in place. It shivered. It shook, it trembled, it wriggled all while standing, and it was a pale shape. Sucking and slurping noises emanated from the shape. It was as tall as a man, but it was nothing she had ever seen before.

She backed into the greenhouse door, and, still facing the expanse of plants between her and that…shape…she reached behind her and fumbled for the door handle and turned it. She pulled the door open slowly, just far enough to squeeze herself through, and then she shut it. And then she ran.

She ran wildly toward the front door, and charged out of it, expecting to see the guard, but he was gone. As big a creep as he seemed to her, she preferred finding him to dealing with...whatever it was she had seen.

Where is Lafe?

She could see no one outside. She only heard the nighthawks and distant sounds of cars and the constant, constant thrumming of machinery in the science buildings on the hill.

Oh god. Lafe.

She put her hands on the front door again and pulled, and found it locked.

"Shit," she whispered, and she dug again for her ID card. She swiped it in front of the door, and it unlocked. She entered the building hesitantly, eyes on the hallway of the greenhouse. Then, movement above her.

She let out a small cry. It was Lafe, staring at her from the top of the stairwell. She briefly covered her face.

"Jesus," he hissed down at her, his eyes large, "what the hell's wrong with you? Get up here!"

She ran up the stairs, her feet protesting at the sunken concrete of each step, compressed from over a hundred years of footsteps up and down. And she ran at him and threw her arms around him.

"Jesus," he said again, this time into her hair.

She gasped and squeezed him.

"What is it, Fi?" he whispered.

She stepped back from him and darted her eyes down the stairs below.

"There's something. There's...something."

"Something...like what? The guard? What's going on, you're babbling. Fi!"

She shook from head to toe.

"I don't—it's not the guard. I saw the guard. Talked to him, even. There's something in the—" She began to hyperventilate, thinking again of the quivering shape. "Something—"

"Breathe slowly, in through the nose, out through the mouth," Lafe soothed.

"Greenhouse," she wheezed.

He took hold of her shaking hands and looked into her eyes.

"Something in the greenhouse?" he repeated.

She nodded, taking breaths in gulps.

"What?"

"I don't know. I don't know. But we need to get out of here."

"Um...okay, but I need you to see something first."

"Lafe, we *need to get OUT of here.*"

"Just two minutes."

"Lafe."

"Look, there's a back door, remember? Down to the garbage chute near your doc's office. We'll go out that way. But come and look at something."

Fiona shook her head. "I don't know, Lafe, I don't think—"

"Help me out with this, and I'll help you out with...whatever the other thing is. Because something is happening here and we need to know what."

That stilled her and made her curious. She took a deep breath and felt nauseous, and strongly tempted to vomit, but she swallowed her terror and tried relaxing her shoulders. At least she was with Lafe and not by herself alone with...no. She could not focus on that right now.

"Okay," she gasped. "Show me."

He held her hand and pulled her gently along one hallway and down another. Its lights were also flickering, just as the one downstairs had. Directly above the hallway with Doc's office and the greenhouse, she realized.

"What is it?" she asked, staring at the hall full of labs.

"See anything unusual so far?" he asked her.

"I don't—" But something caught her eye. Something shiny.

She walked toward it and knelt. She picked it up gingerly.

"Glass. Broken glass. I found some the other day, down Doc's hall…" Her voice trailed off as she considered the shard. Two pieces of broken glass on two different floors. *Why?*

"Yes, I found another piece here too. But come down here. Did you know about this?"

She followed him and the two of them stopped before one of the laboratory doors.

It was completely sealed all around its edges. A biohazard sign was posted on its little window.

It read, "Decontamination in progress. DO NOT ENTER. Department of Health and Safety."

"What the hell is this?" she murmured.

"Right? I've never seen this sort of thing before. Hey, will your key work?"

"Lafe," she warned. "I'm not breaking into a lab with a biohazard sign on it."

"Okay, but maybe we should."

"Fuck no. I do still have a job, which I'd like to keep for…as long as I can. More on that later. And I don't want us contaminated with…whatever happened in there. Also, we'd break that seal and everyone would know."

Lafe sighed. "Dammit. I really want to see what's in there."

"I really want us to get the hell out of here," she reminded him.

"But wait, what's this stuff?"

Lafe knelt and examined the floor. Its banal, speckled white tiles revealed an unusual tinge: a vibrant blue.

"Powder," murmured Fiona. "Blue powder."

"What could that be? What's blue that would—"

Then they said it in unison: "Copper sulfate."

They stared at each other.

"Why is there copper sulfate on the floor outside a sealed off room that's contaminated?" Lafe asked their shared question aloud.

A snapping sound echoed through the hall from the floor below.

"What's that?" Lafe said.

Fiona's eyes went huge and her heart raced.

"The greenhouse door. Lafe, go!"

They ran for the stairwell.

CHAPTER 16
DIVE BAR WISDOM

S kidding on the slick floor, which thankfully had very little blue powder on it, they ran full-tilt for the stairwell door. Lafe threw himself against it and held it open so Fiona could bolt down the stairs. In the sickly light of sparse fluorescent globe sconces, they ran down and then reached the ground floor. The stairs continued their descent toward a basement level, and the two of them looked at each other.

"Ain't no way I'm going down there," Fiona said, voice firm for long enough to get the point across.

"Hell to the no," Lafe agreed.

They turned to face the door to the garbage area.

"This doesn't take us past the greenhouse, right?"

"No," he reassured her. "There's an alley that goes to the back parking lot behind the building."

She nodded and shoved the door open.

The reek of garbage hit them both, and they gagged.

"Good God," Lafe choked. "There's something out here that's not your everyday garbage. What the *fuck*?"

He was right. Something sickly and rotting festered in the dumpsters.

She shuddered, thinking of the thing in the greenhouse.

"You're looking wild, Fi," Lafe noted. "What the hell happened?"

"Can we please just get out of here?" she snapped. "I don't want to talk about it right now."

"Fine," he answered, and they pulled their shirts up over their noses to mask themselves as they swiftly walked out the dark alley into the parking lot. There they froze: the security guard's car sat there, door open, light on inside the car, but he was nowhere to be seen.

Glancing at Lafe, Fiona tilted her head back to the north, away from the car, and the two of them slinked in the shadows among the pipes and tubes of the back side of the biology building. The squawk of a walkie-talkie made them both jump.

Shit. We're busted.

But Fiona saw no evidence of the guard. The walkie-talkie, however, repeated its chatter.

Lafe looked back from their shadowed hiding place toward the guard's car.

"Did he take a piss or something?" he whispered.

"It's coming from over there." Fiona pointed.

Lafe bent down.

"It's sitting on the ground. This is weird."

"Let's *go*," she urged, pulling at his elbow desperately.

And so, he turned toward her, for the first time reflecting her own expression: fear. And they ran. They pelted behind the engineering building and ran along the small lane that sloped down the back side of the Hill and then out to the main street. Reaching that street, they both doubled over and gasped and choked.

Fiona felt some relief, though, somehow, just seeing cars pass by. They stood under a large oak tree and caught their breath. She held herself, feeling the stab of a side stitch.

"Come on," she said, and without another word, she sprinted across the street, not bothering with any crosswalks, and hearing him shout, "Fiona! Jesus!" She wasted no time and kept going.

Her feet pounded pavement, then concrete sidewalk, then stairs and finally she found the car and sank down beside it. Lafe caught up with her.

"That was crazy, you could've been hit by a car!" he sputtered.

"I wasn't," she pointed out. "Get us out of here."

He opened the car door for her. She threw herself in and seized the door, slammed it shut, and locked it from within. She held her purse against her chest and squeezed it, staring straight ahead with wide eyes. Lafe sat down beside her, glanced at her with a stern expression, shut his door, and turned the ignition.

"Jesus Christ, Fi," he muttered. "Now where to?"

She shook her head. "I don't care. Away. Anywhere. Go, please."

"Can we talk about—"

"Not here. Go."

"Fuck's sake!"

But he did go, and they drove a long time in silence. He turned on back roads and they traveled away from the heart of the campus and away from downtown. She glanced at him occasionally, and he at her, and both their expressions remained grim, their brows creased.

She managed to relax just enough to start feeling sick.

"Not doing so great," she said thickly.

"Are you gonna barf?" He began to pull over.

"No, I…I think we need to eat."

"Not much open this late, other than a gas station," he muttered. "I don't even know where the fuck we are."

Fiona spied a flickering neon sign, flashing red and blue, in the distance.

"There," she pointed. "Stop there."

"A *biker bar?*" he asked incredulously.

She could see, then, a row of glistening, menacing-looking gigantic motorcycles.

"Oh," she said.

"Well?"

"Yeah, do it."

"Oooooohkaaaaay," he said, and then he whistled.

He pulled into a crumbled asphalt parking spot, the only one not occupied by assorted Harleys and other bikes. Fiona noted in her drained state that some were painted with skulls, others with flames, and some with both skulls *and* flames. She exited the car and stood staring at them, and then felt Lafe's hand brush her arm.

"Hey, you're looking pale."

"It's the…neon," she muttered, blinking.

"Hmm, no, don't think so, come on." He clasped his hand in hers and pulled her along with him. She noted the asphalt looked far smoother under the bikes, as the colors of red and blue flashed across her, dazzling her, and she began to tremble.

Shivering in place.

Like the thing in the greenhouse.

She let out a small, hiccupping sound and covered her nose with her free hand. Clouds of cigarette smoke wafted from the other side of the bar, where a group of bikers stood and laughed and spoke loudly. For a fleeting second, she imagined them as pirates on the bow of a ship, the masts hidden in blue and red fog. Lafe urged her gently toward the door, an old, wooden contraption, smooth and worn. It even had a porthole window.

Well, maybe I'm really at sea after all, she thought wanly. *I'm bobbing like I am.*

Disoriented, she blinked as she entered the bar, which somehow was darker than the night outside, devoid as it was of outdated, orange streetlights and neon. Steely Dan music met her ears and she blinked again, and the bar shone from what at first looked like glowing, bloody teeth. She stared at one of them a long time and realized, finally, that they were plastic chili pepper lights. An enormous man turned to face her and Lafe, tall, with a barrel chest and large belly wrapped in a snug, white T-shirt and an open, sleeveless, black leather vest. His great arms were covered in white hair like that of his head and bushy beard.

A rock god Santa.

And for a moment she half-smiled, but then she focused her eyes on the rest of the room, and she felt the gaze of everyone there. She heard the *clack* and roll of a billiards ball, the guitar filtering through the loose groups of bikers, and an occasional raucous laugh.

She had never felt more out of place in her life.

"Is, uh, the kitchen still open?" Lafe asked, his voice an octave higher than usual.

The bartender smirked, or at least, Fiona hoped that he did; his beard and mustache twitched. "Fryer's not empty yet. Grill's closed. Want some fries?"

He and Lafe turned to Fiona, eyes questioning.

She did not feel like eating just then, but she did feel that sort of slightly nauseous fatigue of low blood sugar overtaking her prior adrenaline surge.

"Okay."

Lafe blinked, and she realized then he must be relieved. She felt anything but.

The bartender set two tall glasses before them: a yellow beer for Lafe, and a Coke with ice for Fiona, a straw bobbing among the fizz. She drew the straw between her lips and took a sip. She nodded to the bartender in gratitude. He nodded back, poured a glass of whiskey for another customer, and then walked through the swing door to the left of the bar; she assumed that was the kitchen.

"Tell me," Lafe pleaded, as they faced each other on stools, their knees close but not touching each other.

"I don't know what to say," she admitted. "I saw something."

Lafe tilted his head. "Something?"

She sucked in a sharp breath. "In the greenhouse."

He squinted.

"Like what? Some plants?"

"Oh, fuck you, Lafe," she sighed, but her lips curled just a bit.

"Sorry." He grinned wryly at her while taking a sip of the beer and scowling as soon as he did.

"On the house," called the bartender.

Lafe lifted the glass. "Thanks!" Then he whispered to Fiona, "It's shit."

"Free though."

"Thank fuck. Okay, so. Something in the greenhouse. What?"

She shook her head. She felt so very tired. She wanted to rest her head on the bar—which felt sticky to her hands, its gnarled edges weathered from many drinkers over decades, some of whom had probably also seen some odd things in their lives, she pondered. But maybe not quite what she had seen. And what *had* she seen? She could not quite decipher how to describe it to him.

"I thought it was a person at first," she said slowly. She took another sip of the Coke, its zippy-sweet flavor sizzling on her tongue, and she swallowed. The fries arrived just then, with an accompanying bottle of ketchup. "Thank you," she told the bartender with a weak grin.

"You okay?" he asked, gruffly but not unkindly. "You've got that look. Like something went down."

She blinked at him. "I'm okay, I'm just—"

"Spooked," the man finished.

She stared at him.

"Yeah."

He nodded and flung a bar towel over his shoulder. "Well, nobody's fucking with you in here," he told her. And some of the other patrons heard and whooped.

"Whose ass do we need to kick, Hoss?" one of them shouted in a voice like shaken gravel.

Some of the people inside the bar had turned to look at Fiona, and her face spiked with heat. She turned away from them and held the Coke glass in both hands for a moment. She snatched a fry off the plate and blew on it, then took a bite. She crunched on the salty-starchy thing and chased it with Coke to keep it from burning her tongue. She did not want to be there, but at the same time, the bartender's statement grounded her.

Maybe he's even right, but I can't be sure of anything right now.

"So," Lafe pressed, "you think you saw a person in the greenhouse. Maybe it *was* a person?"

Fiona shuddered. "No, I...I don't think so. What would a person be doing hanging out in the corner of a dark greenhouse at night?" And then she rolled her eyes. "Besides *us*, before you say anything."

Lafe shook his head. "Maybe it was just a big plant."

"No," she said. "It was person sized. They don't have plants like that in there. It was tall. Like a man."

She trembled. She ate two more fries and took another sip of Coke. She could feel a bit of energy returning, but more anxiety.

"It quivered."

She stared at a beer mirror sign on the other side of the bar, and her reflection shone back, broken by gold letters. Her eyes looked dark and sunken. She did not recognize the expression because she had never quite felt it before.

"So," Lafe began, and he grimaced after drinking more beer. "You saw something tall and quivering in the greenhouse. Like...I don't know what that means. Could an animal have got in there?"

"Oh, a really tall animal?" She wheeled around and bit the words at him. "Just casually, a really tall animal in the greenhouse. Which was locked, by the way. Remember?"

He threw his hands up and closed his eyes for a second.

"I don't know! I'm trying to figure out what you're saying."

"I'm trying to figure out what I *saw*. And what I saw was no animal."

"Then what was it?"

"Goddammit, Lafe! I don't know! I've never seen anything like it before."

He rubbed his eyes and sighed. He said, "Okay. Fine. Something weird in the greenhouse."

"The Meth Man," bellowed the bartender, making them both jump.

"What?" Fiona shot him a stern look.

"Sorry," he said, this time grinning genuinely, "that's what we called it. Anytime someone I know had a bad trip, they saw a figure, and so we called it the Meth Man. Everyone sees the Meth Man sooner or later."

"I don't do meth!" Fiona hissed.

The bartender chuckled. "I believe that! But if you've ever had anything...the wrong cold medicine, a funky joint—"

"I didn't have anything at all," she said vehemently. She secured her purse on her hip and stood. "We're going."

Lafe stayed seated. "Fi, finish the fries at least. You're coming down from a scare and you needed to eat, remember?"

"Not worth being insulted," she growled.

The bartender rested his chin on his hands and looked imploringly at her. She felt unmoored by the Santa-like biker in such a position. Which, she realized quickly, he likely intended. And she was angry with herself that it *worked*.

"Hang out a bit longer. I'm sorry. I just know that when folks are stressed or—not in your case!—on something, they can see things that aren't real."

"This thing was real," she said, her voice sharp and short. "I don't know what it was but it was *there*. And then the guard went missing, too."

She looked down at Lafe, whose eyes grew larger.

"Well, we don't know that."

"His walkie-talkie was on the ground, Lafe," she reminded him.

"Still. Maybe let's just...go with what we know."

Fiona sighed and sat back down.

"We don't know anything."

"Exactly."

"But I did see *something*, and it scared the shit out of me."

"Fair," agreed Lafe.

"I'm tired. Can we go?"

"Go where?"

Fiona yawned. "I just...I need to sleep."

Lafe sipped more beer and twisted his mouth. "Where? Not back to your place, I take it."

She shook her head.

They sat, staring straight ahead, and not at each other, for a long moment.

"Mine then? Upper bedroom. I'll take the couch."

"I don't want to impose," she answered quickly. "I can get a motel."

"You wouldn't be! And no, I don't think it's good for you to be alone. At least I have decent tea, after all."

He grinned, looking roguish in the dim light, his sharp features etched by neon above the bar, blue and red.

She felt on edge about it, on one hand, because she was not stupid: she knew he'd had a crush on her, but hadn't allowed herself to think much about it. And he'd never made her feel uneasy. She felt that of everyone she knew—still alive, that is, a falling sensation washing over her as she thought of Alva—she could probably trust him the most. She caught the eye of the grizzled bartender and he glanced back and forth between her and Lafe, his beard subtly twitching. She barely turned her head, almost imperceptibly shaking "no," and the man dipped his head, just as imperceptibly, as if to say, "Understood."

"Okay," she said aloud.

"Okay, what?" Lafe asked.

"If you really don't mind."

Lafe spread his hands on the bar, "Oh, nah. I mean, you're *so* high maintenance and all that, and you'll class up the joint a bit, but, really, it's fine."

She laughed, and so did he. He watched her blinking and yawning.

"Tab us out, please," he told the bartender.

To her surprise, the bartender leaned on the bar and brought his hands together under his bearded chin.

"I believe you," he announced. "Just so you know. It wasn't a 'meth man' at all. I get it."

Fiona could see out of the corner of her eye that Lafe was looking at her, but she simply shrugged.

"I'm glad someone does," she said. "Thank you."

She felt her body relax then. And now, truly, she needed sleep soon.

They drove in near silence on the way back, and she nodded off a couple of times. She heard the rumble of Lafe's driveway as they pulled in, and she jerked fully awake, wiping drool from the corner of her mouth, embarrassed. In the dim light of the car, she could see he scowled.

"What is it?"

"I don't know. I'm…on edge I guess."

"I can stay somewhere else, it's really okay. I can get a cab."

He swiftly looked at her and said, "Hell no. That's not what I meant. It's just. Ah, fuck it. Let's get some sleep. We can chat in the morning."

They entered the dark kitchen, and the sight of Lafe's plants momentarily startled her. She stood still in the kitchen, barely lit by the porchlight outside. The plants in the windowsill looked harmless enough, though. There was no quivering mass in the corner.

"Right," he said, "upstairs you go. See you in the morning."

"Will you be okay down here?"

"Of course. I mostly sleep on the couch anyway. Good night."

He turned abruptly, and she followed him to the stairwell. He looked over his shoulder.

"Good night," she said.

She felt self-conscious, walking on the old wooden floors, hearing them creak and pop with every step. She found the bedroom and upon stepping inside, immediately sneezed. But it felt nonetheless welcoming, a place she knew, even if only briefly, and in the strangeness of the past few days it was the first moment of feeling something resembling *home*.

It was stuffy, hot from the heat rising during the day, so she fussed with the window air conditioner, which looked older than she was. It clattered and whirred on, but the air felt good and cool. And then she sagged onto the bed, not even removing her clothes, and burrowed her head into a musty-smelling pillow, and slid off to sleep, her dreams full of photos of Alva falling like large snowflakes in piles all around her. Only the piles were not photos, and they were not made of snow: they were dunes, dunes in a desert thousands of miles away.

CHAPTER 17
PETRICHOR

H ands on her neck, suffocation. She awoke gasping, gurgling, and then wailing. Footsteps thundering, the door flung open with a bang. Lafe stared at her, eyes wild.

"Fiona!"

She pulled at her shirt, soaked with sweat, glanced at him, and sobbed.

"Sorry," she choked. "Nightmare."

Lafe put his hands on his face, his large eyes glowing through, his brows harsh.

"Jesus *fuck*. You scared the shit out of me, Fi."

She put her own face in her hands, against her knees, and shook in silence. He dared to reach out his hand and touch her shoulder.

"Do you want to talk about it?"

His hand trembled and then he pulled it away.

She shook her head, more aware then that her hair had become matted and tangled from a night of thrashing, and she glimpsed her bra chucked onto the hardwood floor. Her cheeks grew hot and she crossed her arms over her breasts. If he noticed, she could not tell. He didn't take his eyes away from her face, though.

"No." Emphatic. Sure. More so than she *felt*.

"Okay. Coffee or tea after that?"

"It's pretty hot but...yeah. One of them." She sighed. "Coffee..." and her voice trailed off.

"Okay, if you want to get a shower, I'll get the coffee and some breakfast going."

She turned her face up to him then and gave him a lopsided, sheepish grin.

"Breakfast is becoming a thing with us, isn't it?"

It was Lafe's turn to blush, and his eyes softened. He gave her a salute, then a bow, and then she laughed while he loped noisily back down the stairs.

She picked her phone up from where it had lain powered off on the makeshift nightstand (really an overturned wooden crate, painted dark red) next to the bed. She could have pretended, at least until breakfast was over, that this was a perfectly normal morning, that she was safe, that she could imagine some version of her life in which this *was* an everyday ritual. That made her feel warm all over. But she knew, without question, that she would not, and perhaps *could* not enjoy this kind of life. The thing in the greenhouse gave her enough assurance of that.

She felt sick even thinking about it. The fragments of her nightmare came back then, and she tasted bile in her throat. The hands that had clenched her, their intentions murderous, of that she was sure…they were not of flesh and bone. They were gelatinous, yet powerful. She shuddered.

"No," she said aloud to the empty room. "I'm not thinking about that right now." She did not turn the phone on yet.

She showered first, trying not to look at the mold stains on the shower walls or the ancient rust marks. It was a shower, the water was hot, and she would at least be cleaner when she finished than when she had started. The towel scratched her skin and then she realized Lafe probably didn't own a clothes dryer, for it was obviously air-dried and she caught a whiff of mildew.

Her thoughts wandered back to Alva, who on one occasion had talked about the staggering aridity of the Atacama.

"We took a dip in a slot pool in San Pedro. Fi, you wouldn't believe. I got out and in seconds every part of me was dry. Every. Part. And I felt cold all over, even though it was scorching hot. You just can't even fathom how dry it is there."

Again Fiona could only imagine, in this humid, soporific subtropical summer heat, where moisture ruled the day and where cumulus clouds already towered outside. There would be a thunderstorm that afternoon, she guessed. Perhaps a severe one. The air hung thick and oppressive and ominous. It wrecked her hair into frizz as soon as she'd combed it out. She stared in the mirror and witnessed the toll of the past few days: the dark circles under her eyes (she'd forgotten her allergy meds back at her apartment, so allergic shiners had decided to make themselves cozy), the splotchy skin, the haunted look.

There was no face to go with those hands.

She realized this as she stepped slowly down toward the kitchen, her phone tucked in her jeans pocket. She would need more clean clothes soon. That meant seeing Graham. She did not want to turn the phone on, did not want to deal with that part of her life, to say nothing of whatever was going on with the lab. She felt again the tug to leave, to flee, to put distance between herself and the maelstrom of chaos and grief and terror that swept itself around her, pulling her down. She was put in mind of one of those great spillway drains in the TVA lakes system. How she had stared at it in deep horror as a child: the deep funnel of rushing water, sucking down into unseen depths, pulling everything into it. Inescapable. That was how she felt now. Everything pulling her into something powerful and incomprehensible. She longed for a safe shore.

For the moment, Lafe offered the only shore.

He looked askance at her, and the air sort of fizzed between them. She took his offered plate of two fried eggs, toast with a smear of butter, and then they sat at the couch again, where her mug of coffee wafted steam into the already murky air.

The pile of Alva's photos lay on that coffee table, and Fiona found herself staring at them. Lafe noticed and set his plate down, shuffled the photos together into a neater stack, and turned them over so that she could only see the backs. They ate in silence, and only after she had stood and seized his empty plate did he speak again.

"Don't worry about those. I'll take care of them. But, like…for now, what? What's the plan today?"

Fiona ignored his first remark and took the dishes to the sink, running cold water over them to pre-rinse them. She turned to him and pulled the phone from her pocket. She sighed.

"Time to face things."

In that fleeting second before she turned her phone on, she could see in Lafe's face a moment of pure recognition. She knew from the way he looked at her that he also wished they could make whatever this was happening between them last, and they could go on living something resembling a normal life. His glance at the phone told her more than he could have said aloud, and she sighed again, more softly, and nodded as if to say, "I know." He nodded back.

She turned the phone on and the messages pinged rapidly and with alarming quantity. Emails, phone calls, texts.

"Do you want me to field them for you?" Lafe offered.

She was tempted. It was almost too much. She wanted more just to turn the thing off and crush it into oblivion. Again, the urge to *run*. But she could not. Where would she run to?

"No," she answered, but her voice betrayed some doubt.

"Should we drive?" He reached for his keys.

"Yes."

He opened the passenger door of his car for her, and again that flicker of what-if passed between them. She dipped her head in gratitude. The morning shade of the house had left the interior of the car mercifully reasonable in temperature, and the gathering clouds assured that maybe it wouldn't be quite so hot today. But she sweated, and the sweat did not evaporate. The air thrummed with cicadas, but the birds were muted. She shut the door and he started the engine.

"AC or…?" he asked.

"Windows down for now." She stretched her fingers into the rush of air as he drove up the street. He took a different path. She settled in to deal with the messages.

One at a time. Nobody's making me read any *of these but me.* She felt a lancet of mutiny over it all. Why *should* anyone feel obligation to respond? And yet that pressure in her built up: to answer, reply, fix, ameliorate, acquiesce, and bend. Why? Why was she like this, she wondered? She didn't have to be.

The memory of the cold, slimy hands around her neck sent shudders through her.

Reading texts would not be that unpleasant in comparison. So she did.

She made Doc Bingham's texts her priority:

"Fiona, could you stop by this morning? Not sure where you're at. Your fiancé dropped by and left some things. Are you all right? Call me."

Thirty minutes later: "Fiona, give me a call, please. Something's happened."

She glanced at Lafe, who bopped his head to blues music from the car speakers, and he glanced back.

She then read Graham's message, but did not listen to his voicemail. "I don't know where you're at. I took a box to the lab. Thought you might want some clothes. Hope you're okay. G."

She closed her eyes for a second over that message. Neutral enough. Maybe he was accepting things. Still, his intrusive behavior sent a spike of rage through her. She would have to retrieve all of her things, and put them…where? Where would she live?

A voicemail from her parents. That startled her. They never, ever called…much less left a voice message.

She held the phone to her ear, not wanting it on speaker.

"Hi, honey." Her mother's rich, lilting East Tennessee accent coursed through Fiona's ear: "We just wanted to make sure you're okay. Graham called. He sounded upset. I hope you two can work things out. Call us. Love you!"

She resented Graham calling her parents. Would her mother have said the same thing had she known about Graham's behavior? Fiona fumed.

"You seem tense," Lafe noted. "I mean, more than usual."

She winced at that.

"I guess I've been pretty tightly wound."

"Well, *yeah*."

"I'm driving to campus, unless I hear otherwise."

She tensed further.

"Why?"

At a stoplight, Lafe turned to Fiona.

"I'm guessing, though you haven't told me, that the boss messaged. If he's there, then…then whatever the living *fuck* was in that greenhouse probably isn't. I'll check my goddamn self. So you don't have to. You've got to get back on the horse, Fiona. As your friend, and as someone who believes in you with every single fucking fiber of my being, I know it's what you need to do. Whatever's going on, you're strong enough to face it."

She bit her lip, blushing.

"Thank you."

A car horn blared behind them, and Lafe twitched his eyes to the rearview mirror and rolled forward. They drove along the riverfront, which looked listless and flat on the cloudy day, the river sluggish, but ripples at the shore belying the bass and other fish splashing beneath. A great blue heron soared like a small pterodactyl along the river's edge as they swept by. Willows bowed and the wind picked up. The air bore a sickly scent, portentous, heady, and filled with rot.

Lafe chose to park on one of the leafy side streets again, close enough to the campus but jumbled enough with students' cars among the rental houses that it offered a form of human camouflage. Summer school sessions were in; it was Thursday morning, and while it compared not at all to the bustle of fall classes, it still bore the air of that sort of frenetic, college atmosphere, even in the doldrums of summer. That was one of the things Fiona loved about working in academia, and one of the things she had missed about being an undergrad. She had wanted to hang onto that a bit longer, and working there gave her the chance. Graham had been more interested in moving on, rushing forth, getting a master's degree or working, whichever one he could get more easily. So Fiona had lingered, feeling proud and excited to be working with great researchers.

There had been flaws in her logic, though, because her work lived and died by research grants. And that was before what had happened. Now she wondered if she would even have a job, if by one avenue or another—being fired, or Bingham's funding being yanked, there would be anything left. Another sense of unmooring. And what was left? What could she do? She didn't have a master's degree. She was stuck. She would forever be relegated to being a lab tech, taking classes on the side, lucky if she ever got her name on any papers, which were reserved for grad students and postdocs.

She hated the whole business. Why did academic research have to be so gated?

She let these thoughts, common for her and more so lately, flit through her mind, like dragonflies over a dark surface of water, beneath which something lurked that she did not want to face at all. Whatever had been in that greenhouse, if it truly wasn't there now, was out in the world. That felt like the cold reality of deep water, shifting yet somehow immutable.

They approached the biology building and she heard distant thunder. Something stood out to her at the front door: a police officer. Not campus police, city. Two grad students talking with the woman, who looked to be in her late forties, broad shouldered, short, hair tightly bound in a greying auburn bun at the nape of her neck, no hat. She took notes on her tablet and nodded. As Fiona and Lafe drew nearer, Fiona felt her face go pale. She could see, then, down the slope, an ambulance parked. She heard walkie-talkie chatter.

She checked her phone, and there were no new updates from Bingham. Wouldn't he have told her what had happened? And if not, why not?

"Fi," whispered Lafe.

"Yeah," she whispered back.

"Let's go around the back. I don't want to be stopped by the cop."

"Agreed."

So they slipped down and around, and behind the parked ambulance. A police car sat beyond the greenhouse, behind the building. The same one as the night before. The greenhouse itself was cordoned off with yellow police tape.

She jerked her head to Lafe and he stared back down at her.

"Oh shit," she said.

"Guess I'm not checking out the greenhouse then."

"But, but if there wasn't anything there—"

"We don't know a thing, Fi. What do we do? Want to text Bingham?"

"And say what?"

"Hell if I know. Ask him what's the deal with the thing in the greenhouse, is it okay to go inside, something like that."

Her fingers trembled as they ambled away from the scene and she typed in the text, with several typos that she then had to fix. "I'm here, what's going on?"

Doc Bingham texted back, "Coffee at the Loop, ten minutes."

Fiona showed Lafe.

"Something's up for sure," he said.

"Agreed."

They turned away altogether and began walking down the ramp toward the bridge to the Loop, which was a round campus center just down from the biochemistry building. Fiona heard footsteps and a call out.

"Hi there!" A man's voice.

Lafe froze and his chin worked.

It was Jack Cordeiro, running up to them.

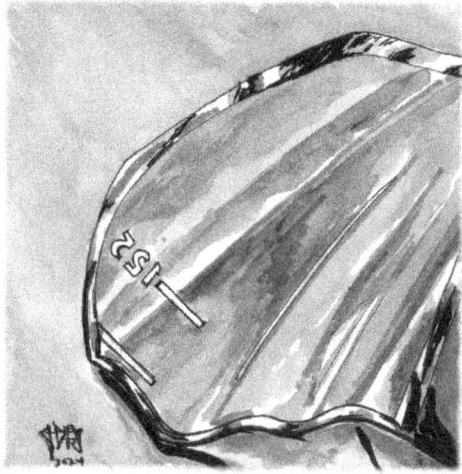

CHAPTER 18
UNDERNEATH IT ALL

Fiona stared at the man, and despite the oppressive heat she went cold as he approached. Suave, immaculately dressed, yet he sweated, she could see. She wondered what this man could possibly want to talk to them about, and she, like Lafe, had decided she didn't trust him at all. It wasn't just because of what Alva had experienced (and now Fiona wondered how much Alva *had* experienced and never told her about).

Today, Jack wore designer glasses, dark bronze in color, glinting at the horned rims, his long, black eyelashes appearing longer than before. His teeth shone too-white and his dark hair looked more slicked back than usual. He wore a linen shirt, rolled up at the sleeves, buttoned most of the way up, but opened two buttons at the collar, so that his chest hair appeared. Even that looked…groomed somehow. His pants were loose yet well-tailored, the hems perfect, the shoes an amber, fine Italian brand, so Fiona guessed. He looked delighted to see them. She wondered why.

"Fiona, good to see you!"

I can't say the same, she thought as she stared up at him with only a half-smile.

"Hello, Dr. Cordeiro."

Lafe said nothing, and Jack glanced at him and spread his arms wide.

"I wondered if you could help me," he said.

Lafe scowled openly, crossing his arms and cocking his head to one side.

A distant rumble of thunder echoed over the campus. Probably the storms funneled along the Interstate, loosed from the plateau and now marching east toward them. It would storm soon, and Fiona realized she had no umbrella. She wanted to put space between herself and Jack more than she wanted to get away from a potential downpour, though.

"How so?" she returned, nudging her crossbody bag over to her hip and clasping her hands in front of her.

"I'm looking for Dr. Bingham," Jack explained, his voice mellifluous, smooth...his smile an attempt at charm, but Fiona found it lacking in that feature.

Maybe it works on most people. Just not on me.

She glanced sidewise at Lafe, and stifled a laugh, for never had she seen such an obvious "Fuck-you" face as the one he gave Jack at that moment. She felt a surge of warmth toward Lafe, and he caught her eye and winked.

"I haven't seen him," she answered, shrugging.

"Try the greenhouse," offered Lafe in a flat tone.

Fiona fought the shiver that ran up and down her spine.

"I did, thanks," Jack replied, dipping his head at Lafe, but quickly turning his gaze back to Fiona. "Well, it's a bit urgent, so if you see him, tell him he's needed back at his office."

"Oh?" Fiona acted slightly but not too curious.

Jack ran his hand through his pomade-laden curls, an affectation, Fiona decided, one he likely used on girls, she would place money on that. Again, she remained nonchalant. She fought the urge to present herself as outright hostile, but Lafe certainly acted on her behalf in that regard, in spades.

"If we see him," Lafe said quietly but evenly, "we'll pass along the message."

A flicker of something passed over Jack's face then. Dislike? Anger? It was so fast that Fiona barely caught it, but she hadn't seen it in him before. So it stood out.

He focused only on her while saying, "Please, I'd greatly appreciate it. I'm in…I'm in his debt, and I would like to return the favor. They're—that is"—and he batted the long lashes, to her disbelief—"there's a meeting and he's needed. It appears there's been an…incident at the building and as I say, it's a bit urgent."

Fiona gritted her teeth but smiled as pleasantly as she could.

"You're so kind to think of him. I'll certainly tell him if we see him."

Jack placed his palms together as if in prayer and lowered his head.

"Thank you so much, Fiona."

She nodded.

She noticed the sweat beading on his face, and how when he'd bent his head, his nose had dripped. She struggled not to curl her lips. He was indeed unusually sweaty. And smooth; perfectly shaven. But his face glistened. He extended his hand toward Lafe in offer of a handshake, but Lafe kept his arms crossed and his dark grey eyes half-lidded. With a buoyant half-bow to Fiona, Jack said, "See you at the lab."

I fucking hope not, she thought. She simply said, "Mm," and smiled without showing her teeth.

Mercifully, he turned on his expensive heels and walked back toward the Hill.

Without waiting, Fiona darted ahead, and Lafe sprinted to keep up. She turned a corner out of sight of Cordeiro and Lafe joined her. They watched him go and Fiona gave over at last to full shuddering.

"Imagine if you'd shaken hands with him," she whispered. "The sweat!"

"Why are you whispering?" he asked, with his mouth twisted a bit.

"I don't know. I don't know! I feel fucking on edge around him."

"Because your creep-dar's working now."

"Lafe, *did* you see how sweaty he was?"

"I don't like looking closely at that man."

Fiona huffed out a frustrated sigh. "He was absolutely covered in sweat. It dripped off his face."

"I mean, I'm not defending that chud," Lafe replied, "but it's hot as fuck out here and humid as a cow's ass."

Fiona giggled.

"What's your plan? Taking the scenic route to the Center?" he wanted to know.

In fact, she did know a better way to the Student Center, out of sight of Jack, should he return. There was a small tunnel beneath the red brick biochemistry building that led there, more of a connecting hallway between the basement levels of the two structures.

She wasn't sure why she feared the man would follow them. It was something…a vibe, not any logical reason. But the tunnel also served a practical purpose, for enormous splotches of rain began bombing down, and then the thunderstorm deluged them. They sprinted inside the biochemistry building, where its air conditioning chilled them in their wet hair and clothes. She imagined hearing her mother say something about "pneumonia weather," although that tended to occur, in Tennessee vernacular, in May and not August.

Fiona liked this building. She'd had an undergraduate research project with Dr. Colman, whom she greatly admired, on the lower floor. Dr. Colman's lab studied reproductive genetics, so it didn't really align with Fiona's growing interest in ecology. Still, it had been a grand experience, and she'd been an enthusiastic learner. She had fond memories of some of the classes there, and that included some with Alva. She sighed. There was no place on that campus that *didn't* remind her of Alva.

"Do you remember Dunham's class?" Lafe asked suddenly, as they walked across the echoing granite floors toward the stairs down to the basement level. They stopped next to a classroom door. Lafe opened it and peered in.

"Right there," he pointed, "fourth row up. That's where we met."

Fiona grinned, her cheeks burning a bit.

"You used to crack me up so bad," she said. "I had to pinch my nose to keep from losing my shit in front of three hundred people!"

"Dunham wouldn't have cared. He was pretty cool. Bought us all those pitchers of beer the last day of class."

"He *was* cool," she agreed. She sat in that memory for a moment: a leafy patio at a sports bar down the road a bit from campus, raucous laughter, no caring about what the next move for the graduates might be. Just a cool ecology professor who was moving to Montana to spend his retirement fly-fishing and phoning it in for guest lectures while he wrote his memoirs.

"I miss that time," she admitted.

Lafe let the door shut.

"Yeah? What do you miss the most?"

She took a big breath and let it out.

"It was simpler. I didn't care as much about my future. I was just starting out, right? Wanted to take a break. Things weren't…weird."

She was not being entirely truthful. For even as she and Graham had been dating, and it had been a decent experience, she'd been less than happy. She'd felt resigned. She had wondered if she had missed out on the entire experience of being a college student, all the fun, all the parties, the dating. Her old roommates never invited her to do anything with them, assuming she would just be spending time with Graham. That was partly her fault, she realized now. She should have made an effort to make friends that actually would have done things with her. Instead she'd felt isolated, even as a couple.

Alva had tried, bless her. Invited her often on group outings. Fiona had mostly refused. She regretted that now, so much.

I could have gone to one party at least. Anything. Bless Alva!

Her eyes stung. She resisted the tears. They'd made it to the tunnel.

The fluorescent lights were quite old in that hallway, and they cast a sickening greenish tinge onto her and Lafe. It reminded her of the upper lab floor of the biology building. Then she paused. An old memory returned to her: one time, while working in Dr. Colman's lab, Fiona had dropped a large graduated cylinder. It had hit the concrete lab floor like a bomb, sending glass everywhere.

"Do you…do you know *where* the copper sulfate might have come from?" she asked suddenly.

Lafe stopped and stared at her.

"Good question. Here, maybe? Or the chemistry building?" He shrugged.

Fiona chewed on her lower lip.

"I hadn't really thought about it much but…you can't just go get copper sulfate from anywhere. I don't think I've ever seen it in the botany labs."

Lafe said, "I really don't know. I've not used it since undergrad days."

"Yeah, exactly," she said slowly. "There's no reason it should have been in that hallway. And then the glass."

"The glass?"

"Remember the glass I found in the hallway? And I'd had a piece in my shoe on the lower floor."

"Oh, yeah. I'd forgotten. What's that got to do with anything?"

Fiona went stiff and stared into Lafe's eyes.

"Glass," she murmured.

"Oooookaaaay, Fi, what's up? You've got that haunted look in your eyes again."

"He—he'd said he had an accident," she began slowly, testing the thoughts in her mind as they swirled.

"Who?" Lafe asked.

"Jack."

"Wait, what kind of accident?"

Fiona saw a grad student heading their way and turned aside, pulling Lafe's arm.

"Glass," she said softly, so that only he could hear. "There was a big dumping of glass by the garbage truck. We all heard it in Bingham's office…scared the shit out of us. And Jack said something about having had an accident. In the lab."

"Which…lab?" Lafe asked her.

Her heart raced.

"He didn't say."

"What kind of accident?"

"No idea, but whatever it was, there was broken glass. In *that* hallway. The one with the closed off lab. And on the lower floor. Not far from...not far from the greenhouse."

Lafe stared at her and swung his head left and right.

"Well, I mean, that's interesting, but not sure how that relates to anything..."

"Lafe," Fiona said quickly. "Who else worked on that hall? Do we know? Think, think!"

"Um...I don't know. Doc's out of town, there's Gale—"

"Wait, what?" she asked suddenly. "Gale? As in, Gale who's not shown up at work and can't be reached? That Gale?"

Lafe's mouth fell open.

"Fiona," he whispered. "Where is she?"

"What's in the lab?"

They seized each other's hands, not knowing what else to do.

"We need to get to Doc Bingham," Fiona whispered. "Fast!"

They walked briskly then, through the tunnel, then out into the basement level of the Student Center.

Fiona felt as though she might throw up. Something was deeply, horribly wrong. The urge to see Doc Bingham, to make sure he was all right, propelled her. She might have run, but she did not want to attract undue attention. They made it to the Loop, a cafeteria, where she'd spent many moments between classes as an undergrad refilling mugs of coffee while cramming for tests, or racing through homework, or chatting with friends over a cherry Danish. She swept her gaze around and found a booth with a man turned away from the rest of the place. She knew that arm, with its gnarled hand. Bingham.

She tried to walk as casually toward him as she could, her heart hammering, with Lafe beside her. She sat at the booth and Bingham jumped.

"Fiona!" he exclaimed, startled, but relieved, she could see. "Thank God. Did you have to deal with any of that mess up at the Hill?"

"We saw it and bolted," she said. "You remember Lafe?"

"Yes, hi," answered Bingham with a short nod, not rudely, but distractedly.

"Hey, Doc," Lafe replied.

"What's going on? Are you okay?" Fiona asked, concerned by the twitch in Doc's left eyelid and his exhausted expression.

"I feel like I should be asking you that!" he said crisply, but warmly. He glanced from Lafe to her. "I'm glad you're not alone. Are you all right?"

Fiona took a breath and gracefully let it out as she said, "I'm okay, yes. Tired. It's been…this week's been a lot."

Bingham nodded. "I gathered. Look, I don't know what all's going on with you personally. I know it's been too much. It's fine if you take off for a while. Take the week. I've got coverage from some undergrads; they're thirsty for their letters of rec, we'll be fine. Seriously. And besides, it might be good just to…get away. To be honest, I wish I could, but there's a new situation."

"What is it?" Fiona and Lafe leaned in.

Bingham glanced out at the crowd of summer school students coming and going for snacks, turned back to them, and said slowly, "There are now two missing persons."

"Wait, what?" Fiona gasped.

"Last night, apparently one of the campus security guards checked on something at the building."

Fiona went ice cold.

Oh fuck. Oh fuck.

She did not dare to look at Lafe.

"He didn't make it back to his car. It was parked, empty, walkie-talkie on the ground." Bingham watched Fiona's face, and while she tried to be stoic, she wondered if she'd betrayed anything. And again, hoped against hope that Lafe had his own poker face, should the professor look his way.

"Yikes, that's weird," she managed to say.

Bingham nodded. "Concerning for sure." He sighed. "But at this point, too, a missing person report was filed for Gale."

Fiona's eyes went wide at that.

"Gale, really?"

"Yes. Which…honestly, Fiona, you had me stressed out, not answering your phone, messages, and so forth. Getting a call from Graham—"

"Wait, Graham called you?" She went hot then. "Never mind, never mind. Back to Gale. When was the last time anyone's seen her?"

Bingham shook his head. "Can't get a straight answer. We did go through lab calibration logs, and she had entered in calibration info for a chest freezer on the third. That's the last day anyone had seen her for sure. And the last time she had any phone contact with anyone, or so her parents say. They got the records, apparently, and there's nothing. It must have gone dead the same night."

Fiona shuddered.

"There's…" She didn't know how to say what she needed to say. Would she sound insane, stupid, paranoid, or all of the above?

Lafe nudged her, and gave a nod of encouragement.

"There's a lab," she blurted out, "on the second floor, closed off. It's Dr. Sykes'."

"He's been out of town. I heard there was a gas leak or something?"

Fiona glanced at Lafe.

"I—we don't think so. There was...something on the floor outside of it."

"Like what?" Bingham pressed, his wild eyebrows doing a lot of work, and his glances between her and Lafe giving Fiona great unease.

"Copper sulfate," Lafe answered. "Not much. But some."

"Copper *sulfate?*" echoed Doc Bingham. "Maybe someone's using it for algae experiments. Well, that's odd, but go on."

"And glass," added Fiona.

"Glass?"

"Broken glass. Lab glass. A piece of that not far from the copper sulfate, outside the closed lab. And I—" Fiona came close to hyperventilating then, thinking of the greenhouse. "I found a piece of glass in my shoe the other day, down near the-the-the...greenhouse."

Bingham squinted at her.

"I'm not really following what any of this has to do with anything."

"Gale." Fiona swallowed and continued, "worked in that hall. She's missing. There's a lab sealed off. Weird stuff outside of it. And glass. And...and Jack Cordeiro said—you were there—he'd had an accident. It was related to glass."

"What are you saying, Fiona?"

She swallowed.

"He's looking for you right now," she said quietly. "There's something not right with him, Doc. And Gale's gone. And now there's a cop gone."

Bingham leaned back in the booth and stared at her; his rumpled fingers interlaced on the table between them. His eye twitched again.

Lafe glanced between him and Fiona and fidgeted.

"Say it," he urged his friend.

She looked at him and shook her head.

"I don't know what to say."

Bingham nodded slowly. "Say it anyway."

"I think it's him. I think it's Jack Cordeiro."

Bingham puffed out a sigh. "That's one hell of an accusation, if you're saying what I think you're saying. That Cordeiro's somehow responsible for two missing people."

Fiona nodded but did not break eye contact with Doc Bingham.

"Well, also," Lafe said suddenly, and she whipped her head around to him and glared at him.

No, don't say that, don't say that, goddammit…

"Yes?" Bingham asked him, eyes stern.

"There was that thing in the greenhouse."

CHAPTER 19
TOUCHDOWN

Fiona closed her eyes, but did not move any other muscles in her face. Lafe had blown their cover, and she knew that if something had indeed happened to the missing security officers, someone, somewhere would be looking at any surveillance footage…and she and Lafe could be investigated if not outright implicated.

Bingham was shrewd, though.

"Greenhouse?" he echoed. "What thing?"

"Nothing," Fiona blurted out. "I saw a shadow…or something. Spooked me."

"When?" Bingham stared at her over his glasses. She felt rooted to her chair by his sharp eyes over his aquiline nose.

"Am I…going to be in trouble?" she asked, eyes wide, locked with his.

Bingham placed his palms calmly on the table.

"Forget I asked. I'll handle it."

She didn't like the sound of that at all. She darted her eyes to Lafe, who sat implacably still, and back to Doc Bingham.

"Handle what?"

Bingham folded, unfolded, and refolded his napkin. He looked quite tired, she realized—and aged as well. It dawned on her that he must have had his own sleepless nights. And likely his own grief over his colleagues.

"I'm sorry." She pulled her humidity-limp hair over to one side and rubbed her temples. "What was it you wanted to meet us here for?"

The professor sighed.

"I think you've told me everything I wanted to know. And some things I didn't. The fact is that a lot of things are happening at once. Missing lab tech. Missing guard. Missing bodies in the goddamn Atacama. CUPRUM breathing down my neck. And Jack Cordeiro hounding my ass."

Fiona blinked at Bingham's raw, chopping words.

Lafe snorted.

"Can't he just…fuck off back to wherever he came from?"

"And where is that, by the way?" Fiona asked suddenly. "Why did he even show up when he did? He was *in* the Atacama. Alva saw him."

"We knew all that," Bingham said with a dismissive roll of his eyes, which irritated Fiona. "But as for why he's been sniffing around here and intermingling with those CUPRUM reps, I have no idea."

His rising tone of voice surprised her. She glared at Lafe, who sat back in their booth with his hands behind his head looking…smug? She creased her brows at him.

Bingham looked at his watch.

"I'm heading back. I suggest you don't."

"What will you do?" she asked.

"Handle. It."

Bingham then rose, nodded to Lafe, and dipped his head at Fiona.

Quietly, he whispered, "You trust him?"

"Completely," she whispered back.

"Good," he answered. He looked relieved. "Stay with him, then. And stay away from Cordeiro."

"Definitely," she agreed.

He hurried on, headed back to the Hill, his messenger bag bouncing on his hip until he adjusted it to move it more toward the front of his body, out of sight of her line of vision. He was a quixotic man, she thought, endearing to a point, and when determined, somewhat powerful in an understated way. She was glad he was on *her* side, for she would not have wished to be his enemy. He was a brilliant person with keen insight. Better to respect and abide by someone like that, she knew, than to draw their ire.

"Well," she said slowly. "We can't go back now. Not until Doc's given us the all-clear. But it's only a matter of time until someone finds footage or other evidence of us being there, I'll bet."

She felt dizzy considering that, and abruptly sat back down.

"Fi," Lafe, said, and he pressed her shoulder lightly. "You okay?"

She laid her head on her arms on the table.

"It's a lot. I...I'm wiped out. Not sure what to do."

Lafe lightly, tentatively put his arm around her shoulders.

"Then do nothing. For now. No one's making you. You heard Doc. Take the time off."

"If I'm not busy," she said through her hair where she cradled her head, "I'll lose it."

Lafe cleared his throat.

"That's kind of the thing with you. You're constantly stressed, constantly worried."

She lifted her head enough to look at him with a frown.

"Shouldn't I be? Look what I've been through."

"I'm not—" Lafe groaned. "I'm not saying it's not valid, that you'd feel that way. But it's not helping you. You need a break."

She made a raspberry sound and leaned into his light side hug. He leaned back.

"Thank you," she said.

"For what?" He looked genuinely confused.

She managed a weak smile. It took work; such was the state of her. Her feeling of overwhelm pervaded every part of her, and she knew Lafe was right. She wondered how far she could go without rest, thinking she abided by physics: that objects in motion tended to stay in motion. She needed to come to rest. But she did not know how. Yet she craved to, with every part of her, no matter how exhausted and distraught and confused she might be.

"For being there," she answered.

They sat in silence for several minutes, and Fiona only half-listened to the bustle and comings and goings of students, the sounds of people eating, the hypnotic din of light clinking of forks and spoons and some muffled music piped into the cafeteria. Some students laughed at their own soaked bodies. Dripping umbrellas stood propped up against tables. An occasional clap of thunder vibrated through the Loop. Eventually the storm moved on. So did everyone there. Everyone but her and Lafe.

"We're closing up until dinner," called one of the staff, a damp towel over her shoulder, her bottle blonde hair tied back. She looked like an undergrad, working part time to make ends meet.

"How long have we been here?" Fiona wondered aloud.

"As long as it takes," Lafe said, and he squeezed her shoulders. She laid her head against his neck. "But it's closing time. Let's walk."

"I don't have my umbrella," she noted.

"I don't have mine either. Fuck it."

She laughed, and they rose, and ascended the ramp to the upper floor which led to the courtyard outside. The rain had indeed stopped, the sky to the east dark, slate blue, with occasional forks of lightning splintering that darkness. The sun attempted a feeble return, and the concrete steamed in that sunlight. The ominous storm had passed, but the oppressive humidity and heat remained. Still, everything looked freshly rinsed, in bright relief, like Dorothy witnessed entering the Technicolor phase of *The Wizard of Oz*. And as soon as Fiona thought this, a partial rainbow appeared opposite the storm. It was not complete, but it shone vibrantly, and its partial arc ended over the football stadium.

Lafe pointed at it.

"Touchdown."

Fiona cackled. "Shut *up!*" she cried, giggling. Lafe laughed also.

"Where to?" he asked her, and his eyes lingered on hers for a moment; he smiled as she did. Fiona felt giddy.

"Away from the Hill. I need to think, and I don't want to see it."

Lafe nodded. He dramatically waved his arm like a showman at a circus. "And here we have…Monument Way, full of ancient, wizened, bygone teachers, in perpetual mourning of all the money they could have received that went to the football team instead."

Fiona laughed and shook her head. "Priorities, right?"

"Always." Lafe's voice rang with bitterness. "Only here could there be a choice not to build a library, but a new stadium instead. Did you know about that?"

She scowled. "I did. I'm glad they sued the university and had the library made."

"Oh God," said Lafe with a laugh. "Remember that time you lost Frankie's notes in the library? After our study group?"

"Jesus," she shuddered. "I was so horrified. *Horrified.* And Frankie was so nice. He also took the best notes."

"Hey!" Lafe clutched his heart, feigning heartbreak. "You've wounded me."

"Well, at least your handwriting is better than mine."

"Fiona," Lafe paused. He looked at her, twisting his face up, his brows curled in feigned tragedy, "you have many talents. Many, many positive attributes." And he studied her face, and his eyes softened and lingered on hers. Then his mouth went impish. "Your handwriting is not one of them."

She howled and elbowed him. "You fucker!"

They laughed and cajoled and walked along pointing and jeering at all the former mace bearers, captured in bronze for all time, past the eternal flame statue, under the colonnades of trees near the Classics building.

"Do you remember Dr. Aldridge?" she asked suddenly, eyeing the sigil of the Classics building.

"Of course. I remember how he smelled like brandy *every fucking time* he strolled into class."

"Lafe!" She screwed up her mouth at him. "He was my favorite."

"Yeah, because you read your Latin with an Italian accent. That's the only reason."

"I was a great student in his class!"

"You're a great student in everything."

"Not organic chemistry," she said darkly.

"Let's not get into that again," Lafe advised.

"That was traumatic."

"I know. I'm sorry. That professor was a dick."

"He sure liked you."

"One of his many flaws."

Fiona shook her head, tossing her hair back.

"I like you."

"Okay, your only flaw."

"But also my handwriting."

"Okay, *two* flaws."

It started raining again, lightly this time, enough to cause her hair to frizz again. They dashed under the awning of the Classics building. It was now late afternoon, and not many students were about. They stood close together, and Fiona could smell Lafe's wet hair.

"You have none," she said softly.

"None…what?"

She blinked up at him.

"You have no flaws."

He shook his head, grinning.

"I have too many to coun—"

She kissed him.

He blinked at her.

She blushed.

Then he took hold of her face carefully, gently, and leaned forward, and they kissed. They embraced, dripped on by the awning, but oblivious to it. Then something caught Fiona's eye, and she stepped back in shock.

A woman stood staring at them, standing in the rain, holding a cream-colored umbrella. Her ivory outfit and perfect shoes suggested corporate wealth. Her affect seemed familiar.

"Fiona Hawthorne?" she asked.

Fiona squeezed Lafe's hand, then let it go.

"Yes?" she responded, voice shaking.

Her eyes fell on the umbrella, and she could see a small, embroidered patch that said "CUPRUM."

"We need to speak with you."

CHAPTER 20
AGAROSE

The woman could have been anyone. Her face was superficially attractive yet bland, the sort of face that was overly sleek, as if airbrushed, digitized, or manufactured, even. Bland and blonde. And strangely cold, like an advertisement for lab products. Fiona found her familiar not just because of that, but because of the woman's affiliates who had met Doc Bingham in his office.

So they're really all the same, Fiona thought.

She stilled her shaking. It wasn't the police, after all. And she didn't understand the extent of the jurisdiction CUPRUM had beyond its vested interest in funding research grants.

"Who's *we?*" she said then, voice hard, and she saw Lafe straighten up and lift his chin proudly.

"You're needed at Dr. Bingham's lab," said the woman.

"Oh? Then why didn't he just text or call?" Fiona countered.

The rain ceased and the woman collapsed her corporate umbrella and tapped its ferrule briskly four times on the paved courtyard. She smoothed back her dull blonde hair. She reached into a small purse on her shoulder, beige in color, and retrieved a pair of sunglasses, which she then donned over her dark blue eyes.

"Professor Bingham," she announced, "is meeting with campus security, our associates, and other members of the department. I've been sent to retrieve you quietly. I would assume you would prefer this, rather than having the police involved."

"Police?" echoed Lafe. "What do the police have to do with anything? What's going on?"

The woman tilted her head just barely and Fiona caught an almost-smirk, but again the expression on her face remained chillingly neutral.

"This is on a need-to-know basis," she replied, her voice as flat as everything else around her. "Now, Miss Hawthorne, if you would. I brought my car around."

"I don't even know who you *are*," Fiona pointed out.

"Berkeley," came the crisp response. "Now, if you please."

Berkeley gestured with her umbrella toward a soft grey little car parked just down from the colonnade of trees.

Illegally parked, Fiona noted. *So she must not know campus that well at all.*

"How did you find us…Berkeley?" she asked.

The woman did not answer.

Fiona's face burned. She felt her phone in her pocket. It had, of course, been on for some time. Lafe glanced at her, and his eyes traveled to where she pressed her hand against her pocket.

"Fuck," he whispered.

Fiona cleared her throat and called to Berkeley, "So you're just going to take us to Doc Bingham, yes?"

"You," Berkeley responded. "You only."

Lafe shook his head.

"The hell you are," he growled. "If she's going anywhere, I'm going with her."

Fiona met his eyes, and though his expression was hard, he lowered his eyelids just a tic, and his pupils dilated as they stared at each other.

A small chime rang through the sultry air. Berkeley looked down at something and her mouth twisted into a slight frown.

"Very well, both of you, then."

She opened the rear passenger doors of the small vehicle, which revealed tight quarters, but adequate and frighteningly clean. Fiona squeezed Lafe's hand as she walked toward the car. They separated to get in on opposite sides of the car. It smelled new, and oddly metallic. Then Fiona wondered if that were actually Berkeley's perfume, or hair product, or the scent of her immaculately pressed clothing. It lingered in her nose. She fought a sneeze.

It seemed innocuous enough, and Fiona felt a little silly about being worried. Berkeley drove them calmly along, saying nothing, obeying traffic signs and speed limits to the letter, Fiona noticed. She looked sidewise at Lafe, who watched Berkeley intently, his brow furrowed, making him look older than he was. She could see the muscles in his jaw working and realized he must be grinding his teeth.

He's dying to say something. But holding back. That's gotta be hard for him.

It was a far cry from their times snorting and giggling in the middle of an undergrad class lecture. And it was an even farther cry from their shared kiss moments ago. That already seemed like a distant time, something imagined, maybe. But she could still taste Lafe's tongue. She could feel the brush of his hands upon her cheeks.

All the years of knowing him, and never dreaming that they would ever reach that point, unlike him. She wondered if they ever would again.

It took just over ten minutes for Berkeley to drive them down past the Student Center, down toward the river, and back up again, for coming from that side of campus, there was no direct route up the Hill. She parked the car behind the Hansen building, not far from where the security officer's car had parked the night before. Fiona felt sick, anticipating seeing the vehicle, but it was gone.

As they stepped out of the car, Lafe let out a grunt. Fiona followed his gaze and caught sight of Jack walking briskly out to meet them.

"The fuck does he want now," muttered Lafe, echoing her thoughts exactly.

"Berkeley!" he called, clapping his hands together in a prayer pose. "Thanks so much for bringing them over. I owe you."

"No need, Dr. Cordeiro," returned Berkeley stiffly. "We have our work to attend to."

Fiona scowled. *Just what in the hell might that involve?*

"I'll take them in. You go on ahead," Jack told Berkeley.

Lafe's hands curled into fists.

"Lafe," Fiona whispered in warning.

Berkeley walked past Jack, using her umbrella as a cane and giving it another tap on the cracked asphalt of the back parking lot of the Hansen building. She walked rigidly up to the back entrance of the building, where a security officer stood. She showed him her identification and was let through.

"I'm so glad you're here," Jack said, grinning at Fiona and ignoring Lafe for the moment. "Dr. Bingham is...rather put out just now. No doubt he'll appreciate your help."

"I hear there's been trouble," she said, eyeing his face. He still looked sweaty. And he smelled…he smelled…

She felt dizzy and reached out. Lafe caught her arm.

"You okay?"

"Fine, fine," she insisted, but a wave of nausea coursed through her.

What was it he smelled like…it was familiar, and strange.

Agar.

That was it. He smelled like an agarose gel, the kind she'd used in college, which had fallen out of use and need due to biotech advancements. Not that Doc Bingham didn't still favor them; he did.

It was a weird smell, neutral, chemical…and not how anyone *should* smell. She blinked at him. She wondered if Lafe could smell the same thing.

The sweat on the man's face, though, and his neck…and his hairline. He was a handsome man, but at the moment she felt disgusted by his entire look and demeanor. He seemed overeager and placating to her, somehow.

"I know you've been through a great deal, Miss Hawthorne." He attempted a soothing voice. "I've made sure everything is taken care of to help Dr. Bingham, so you can go on up and meet with him. He'll update you about everything."

What?

"Oh," she said. "Okay. Thanks. I'm bringing Lafe." She turned to look at him. He still glared at Jack.

Jack led them up to the security guard at the back door. He spoke quietly to the man and then turned to Fiona and Lafe.

"You're all set," he said. "Head on up."

The man let them in, but Jack did not follow. The door shut behind too quickly for Fiona to see what he was doing. She waited with Lafe for a moment.

"Isn't he coming in?" she asked aloud.

Lafe shrugged.

"Fuck 'im."

"No thank you," Fiona muttered. Lafe grinned at that, and then took her hands in his.

"You don't have to go anywhere, you know. We could run away." She could see in his eyes he meant it. She hoped he could see in hers that she wished that they would. Their foreheads touched.

"Time to face the music," she said softly, and the moment was broken.

They walked through the halls and around toward the entry, and then could see a number of people angling for a view from outside. A couple of guards dealt with them, except for one, who joined the crowd from the left. There was some commotion then: cries of surprise, maybe. Fiona paused and stared.

"What's going on?" she asked aloud, but they both figured it out at the same time.

"It's the guard," Lafe said quietly. "From last night."

"So he's...fine? He just...fucked off the job for a bit?"

Fiona couldn't believe it. Not after...

She shuddered.

The thing in the greenhouse.

The missing guard, his walkie-talkie on the ground. The door of his car open.

This wasn't right.

"Can you get a good look at him, Lafe?"

Her breath caught in her throat. She didn't want to see the guard up close. It was too much.

"I mean, not really, there's a ton of people out there..."

And in some of them burst, raucous and celebratory. The guard was being slapped on the back by his compatriots. A couple of PI's greeted him and shook his hand. The guard then lifted his head up and stared directly at Fiona and Lafe for a moment and smiled. Not a warm smile. Not even a true smile. Then he turned away.

"Lafe," she gasped. "It's not him."

CHAPTER 21
INQUISITOR

Lafe stared at her.

"What do you mean, it's not him?"

Fiona had time only to open her mouth and shut it before a city police officer approached the man who looked like the missing security guard. She strained to see through the throng of people.

"I know it sounds insane," she whispered to Lafe. "But it's too coincidental."

"Too coincidental? Isn't it a *good* thing somebody's not turned up dead or missing after all?" Lafe hissed.

"Did you see how he looked at me?" she asked.

Lafe sighed. "No. Does it matter?"

"He recognized me."

Lafe rolled his eyes. "If he did, so what? We didn't do anything illegal. You work here. You came in after hours. Period, the end."

"That's not…"

How could she describe what she felt? She knew it wasn't the guard. She knew, and she couldn't make clear *how*. Which made her, she realized, seem paranoid.

"Well, he's gone now," Lafe updated.

"You saw him leave?" She lifted up on her toes.

"Yeah, I had a clear view of him."

Fiona tried calming her racing heart down, breathing slowly and easily. The crowd in the lobby of the building began to disperse.

"Well, thank God," one of the researchers, Dr. Reddy, said to a student. "I think you can relax now."

"But what about the girl that's missing?" the student, also a young woman, asked with a troubled expression.

Dr. Reddy raised his palms. "I've heard she was on leave. Don't worry about it."

Fiona grimaced.

"Is that seriously what the rumor is?" she said in a low voice.

"Maybe it's the truth, Fi," Lafe told her. "Look, you're tired, you're grieving, you've barely slept, you're seeing things that aren't there…"

She wheeled on Lafe, her eyes blazing.

"What the *fuck*, Lafe! You don't believe me? About the greenhouse?"

Lafe extended his palms out.

"Fi, stop. I…I didn't see it. I'm just. I'm a literal kind of guy. That's all."

"So you don't believe me. I thought after everything that trusted me. You'll buy into conspiracies, but you still can't grasp this?"

He winced visibly. "I'm sorry. I just…wish I'd seen it myself."

She was hot. Her eyes stung. She felt a pit of coiling anguish spiraling down through her.

But before she could say anything else, she heard the chilly call of a familiar voice.

"Miss Hawthorne?"

It was Berkeley, standing in the hallway that led to Bingham's office. She was backlit by the sickly fluorescent lights, giving her a strange halo effect around her pale outfit. With her face in shadow, though, she looked anything but holy to Fiona. For a moment, she couldn't even see Berkeley's eyes, giving her a blank face, a quality of nothingness. Fiona shuddered.

Am I falling apart?

With no real other alternative that made sense, she let her shoulders slump, and she walked away from Lafe to join Berkeley. Lafe followed her, however.

"Fi, I'm sorry."

She refused to look at him.

She trusted no one now. So what did it matter who she followed, and where she went, if no one would really see the truth of her own experience? She fought tears. She coalesced the pain and turned it into rage.

Enough of this bullshit, she decided.

And so she entered Bingham's office renewed somewhat, her shoulders now back and her spine as straight as she could make it, her chin jutting up, defiance shining in her eyes. She joined a crowd inside Doc's office and blinked in surprise at more CUPRUM workers, the same ones who had been in the office days prior. They looked as bland and listless as Berkeley, but noticeably less commanding.

She did not like the sight of another police officer. This time a campus policewoman, but not a security guard.

So two commanders.

And then she heard a voice she had grown to detest from behind her.

"Sorry I'm late!"

She curled her lips at Jack's voice. She turned her head and looked at him, and caught his eyes. He smiled at her. And he was not sweating now. He had, in fact, changed his entire outfit, and looked just as polished, and even slightly glamorous, as he had the day she'd met him. She chewed on her lower lip for a moment and bit back a nasty remark.

She heard Lafe make a disgusted noise, and for a moment, felt in solidarity with him. But then her anger and hurt returned, and she refused to look at him. Still, he stayed just behind her, and notably he separated her from Jack. For that, at least, she was grateful.

Fiona then faced Doc Bingham, finally, where he sat in his office chair, his hands under his chin, looking up over his glasses at the assembled crowd in his already cramped, messy office.

"Fiona," he greeted her in a neutral voice. "Good, I'm glad you've made it." The look in his eyes set her on alert. She knew him well enough to know that something was very, very wrong, and that she dared not speculate aloud just then what it might be.

Her eyes then fell on what lay around his elbows on the desk, and she fought a gasp.

Pictures of Alva. Pictures of Alva in the Atacama, with her cohorts. A folder beneath them with CUPRUM's logo.

Fiona felt as if she were falling, slipping beneath dark water, trying to look up and see light rippling above her.

My friend. My dead friend. My lost *and dead friend.*

She fought the tears.

Jack spoke then.

"Is everything ready?"

And she turned to see who he spoke to; he looked at Berkeley. Fiona wondered what he meant, for Berkeley only nodded and said, "You'll have everything that you need."

Well, that's ominous as hell.

The police officer, whose last name shone on her badge as Goin, spoke then.

"Is everyone here that needs to be?" she asked. She put her hands on her hips and kept her broad shoulders back. Her hair was cropped short and dyed magenta at the ends. She wore a tiny black rose pendant earring on one ear, and on the other, a black skull. In her hand, she held a small tablet that glowed pale orange, ready for dictation or notes.

Doc Bingham said, "Seems to be."

Officer Goin then said, "Begin recording."

The tablet shifted into a paler hue of orange and she said, "Patricia Goin, Campus Police. Investigation of Gale Thompson, August 24. Present staff include Professor Milton Bingham, Fiona Hawthorne, Dr. Jack Cordeiro. And CUPRUM representatives: Nephele Berkeley, John Shuck, Marta Gearhart. And," she turned to Lafe, holding out the tablet toward him.

"Lafe Lambert," he told her.

"Lafe Lambert," she repeated into her device.

Fiona dared to speak. "Officer Goin," she said, and she could feel every eye on her then. She blushed and asked, "May I ask the purpose of the investigation?"

Goin blinked at her, and looked at Bingham, and then at Berkeley.

"Sure. Miss…Hawthorne? I'm asking for information leading to the disappearance of Gale Thompson and also to connect to the overarching investigation of the incident in the Atacama Desert. We want to see if there's any connection. If there is, researchers need to stay stateside while we continue."

Berkeley responded with more force than her typical mannequin visage, staring down Bingham as she did so: "CUPRUM needs to protect our investment contracts in the Atacama. We cannot allow an interruption in operations."

What kind of operations? Fiona wondered.

She blurted out, "We don't need to lose anyone else down there…or up here!"

She pointed at Alva's photos.

Bingham raised his hand.

"One step at a time, please. Thank you, Fiona. I know emotions are running high. The campus police are investigating, but we're in communication with the TBI and the FBI, who likely will take over the case."

A chill settled over them all.

"Then who's going to the Atacama?" Fiona asked suddenly. "Who's looking for Alva? For the team?"

Berkeley said, "We're working with the Chilean government to continue our efforts."

"To do what?" Fiona flashed. "Continue research without finding my friend's dead body? That her parents would like to put in the ground?"

She was shaking now, and Lafe touched her elbow. She tossed his hand off.

"Fiona," said Bingham, and his voice was firm and measured. "Thank you."

Officer Goin had stood very still during all this, positioning her recording tablet so that it caught every word and, presumably, video as well, Fiona realized. She met Goin's eyes and lifted her chin, determined. *She* had nothing to hide, no matter what happened next.

So she said, her eyes still locked on Goin's, "Maybe look in the lab cordoned off upstairs."

Goin tilted her head and raised her eyebrows.

The CUPRUM workers all shifted, just barely. Jack's smile fell from his face.

Doc Bingham spoke: "I was told it was sealed by Health and Safety due to a chemical spill in the lab. Meaning nobody should open it until after it's been properly cleaned. That could take a few days."

Still looking at Goin, and realizing she openly defied Bingham now, she said, "I think you should open it now. It might be the last place that Gale was."

Bingham blinked at her. She did not budge. But Officer Goin did. She looked from Bingham to Berkeley to Jack, where her eyes lingered for just a moment.

"You know," she said slowly, "it's been an interesting week. We just had one of our campus security guys go missing last night for a while."

Fiona stood very still and hoped Lafe did as well. She didn't dare look at him now.

"He's been found, yes?" asked Jack suddenly.

Goin blinked at him.

"Yes, he showed up just a little while ago. Seemed fine. Odd. Anyway." She turned to look at Bingham. "I'm going to contact Health and Safety."

"Sure," Bingham agreed.

"They've already looked at the lab, yes?" Jack asked then. "Didn't they cordon it off?"

Goin tilted her spiky head again.

She placed the call, and asked to speak to the manager of the department. She rattled off the address for the building, checked with

Bingham on the lab's room number, and nodded while listening. No one in the office could hear the person on the other line.

Fiona realized she was clenching her fists, and that she was sweating as well. She felt a tingly sensation of something: the air felt charged, like just before the storm earlier that day. Only the storm was inside now, she felt. In that room.

"Okay, thank you. Yeah, I know. Have a good night!" And Officer Goin ended the call.

She glanced at Fiona, then to Doc Bingham, then to Berkeley, and then to Jack.

"Well, now, that's really interesting," she declared.

"What's that?" Bingham asked.

"I spoke to the head of Health and Safety. She checked the logs. There's no record of any report on any accident involving that lab. She has no knowledge of it either."

"What do you mean?" Bingham demanded.

"I mean," said Officer Goin, "whoever roped that lab off wasn't part of Health and Safety. We don't know *who* did it, and we don't know *what* is in that lab."

Silence held the room in a bubble. Bingham broke it.

"So what do you propose we do?" he asked.

Fiona felt a thrill of fear and intrigue shoot through her.

Officer Goin replied, "We're going to go open the lab."

CHAPTER 22
ALARM

"We're not going anywhere." Bingham's voice was low, close to a whisper, yet commanding, and they all turned to stare at him. "That's Sykes' lab. He's on sabbatical because of the Gilden expedition. I don't need to explain to any of you why."

But Fiona had heard that Sykes and Gilden were a couple. That was a rumor only, because Alva had doubted it, and Fiona had tended to believe what Alva said, given her gregarious nature and connection among the research teams.

Then again, there was always discretion, or perhaps there should have been, among researchers at the university. Fiona had heard of some incidents, now ghostly whispers, of clandestine relationships, inappropriate trysts, and the like from office staff, mostly incidentally as gossip. All of those parties were long gone from the department, but some of their tales lingered.

Dr. Sykes didn't need to be in a relationship with Dr. Gilden for him to be devastated. Fiona knew that as well as anyone. Alva was her best friend.

She wondered who Gale Thompson's friends were. What were they thinking right now?

"We contact two people first," Bingham continued. "Dr. Sykes, and Dr. Franks, Gale Thompson's PI. I know they're offsite right now. If you can't reach them, you need at least to give them a heads-up. No doubt they'll be on board. But do them the courtesy, would you, Officer Goin?"

It wasn't a question. They all knew it. All eyes were upon Dr. Bingham, and Fiona felt a swell of pride toward him.

"Here are the numbers. That's Sykes' first." He held the hand-scribbled note up to Officer Goin.

She nodded to him. "I'll call them."

She stepped out into the hallway then, and the tension seemed to drop. In its place, though, Fiona picked up on something more insidious, as everyone eyed each other. The CUPRUM contingent checked their small tablets and looked to Berkeley occasionally, but she sat stiff and still next to Bingham's desk, her hands in her lap, as if waiting on a dental appointment.

Fiona had no desire to look at Jack full on, but she glanced at Lafe, still angry at his disbelief in her, and beyond him, she could see Jack standing very still against a file cabinet, his hands in his pockets, his face expressionless. Somehow, she found that more disturbing than anything, even beyond the plastic CUPRUM staff's dronelike visages. His only movement was to puff out his pockets with his hands, and move them a bit, as if he were handling keys out of sight.

Officer Goin stepped back in and shut the door; her face pinched.

"So," she announced, "you're correct that Professor Sykes is offsite, and I could barely make out what he said. He told me he heard there's been a spill. So that's interesting. He did give the go-ahead to open the lab. Dr. Franks is aware of the situation and clears my next steps as well. Looks like the only other person we can verify working on that hall that evening was a lab tech, Will Mullins. We've checked in with him and he said he'd left by about 7:30 PM, probably shortly after the last time anyone saw Gale Thompson. Didn't seem like the most observant guy in the world."

Fiona bit her lip at that direct and accurate assessment of Will.

Officer Goins tucked her phone away then and stared Bingham down. "Just so you know, Dr. Bingham, those were courtesy calls. We do not require the clearance of any entity at the University to investigate a potential crime."

"Is that what we have here? A crime?" Bingham demanded. He stood then.

"Sir, we have to—"

"Nah," said Doc. "Let's go. All of us."

He swept his gaze over everyone assembled, bushy eyebrows crowding like thunderclouds, the lightning flash of his angry eyes beneath. He settled upon Fiona.

"Fiona's right. We don't want to lose anyone else. Down there, or up here."

And he walked out of his office into the hallway, waiting for everyone to leave. As the group assembled there, he shut and locked his office door. Then he meandered through the cluster and said at the front, "Hold please." He unlocked a hall closet and pulled out a box. He opened it and revealed unopened N95 masks, and he began to open a packet of them. He distributed a mask to each of them.

Then he pulled forth another box, more rigid, which revealed a set of clear, plastic goggles. He handed one to Officer Goin and took one himself. He did not give anyone else a pair.

"If there's something in that lab that shouldn't be, we may at least have some protection. We're going to open that door, and Officer Goin and I will enter, take any photos, and keep the place clean. Does that work for you?" He turned to Goin, and she nodded.

Without another word, he walked down the hall, with everyone trailing behind him, Fiona trying not to trip to keep up. Bingham was in rare form, energetic, walking jerkily but confident. He stopped by the front office, entered with Officer Goin, and after a few moments, they both emerged. Bingham held another key.

A phone rang, startling them all, and Fiona turned to see Jack pull his phone from his pocket, look at it, and hold it up to his ear. "Hello?"

Doc Bingham looked briefly at Fiona, his expression grim, and then up at the stairwell to the next floor. He gave Officer Goin a brief nod, and they began marching upward. Fiona and Lafe followed closely behind. Lafe had kept quiet up to this point. Now he laced the mask straps over his ears and looked sidewise at Fiona. She did the same. She could not quite decipher his expression, and that would have to do for the moment, now that their mouths were covered. Something in Lafe's eyes, though, mirrored what she felt just then: a twinge of fear.

They made it to the lab, and Fiona eyed the people there. The CUPRUM staff held back, Berkeley at the fore, her hands behind her back. Everyone stood there masked and expectant. But not Jack.

Dr. Bingham pulled purple nitrile gloves from his lab coat pocket and donned them. He and Officer Goin placed their goggles on their heads. She pulled on gloves as well, and patted her hip, where Fiona could see a holster for a gun.

How would that be necessary for a sealed lab? she wondered.

Lafe seemed to reflect her thoughts by muttering, "Guess you can't be too careful. A lab spill could jump out and grab you."

She didn't know if he was trying to be funny or not, but the hairs on the back of her neck rose, thinking of that.

Doc held the key to the Sykes lab in a trembling hand. He unlocked it, and the crowd seemed to hold its breath. He peeled back the sealant tape all around the edges of the door. And then he opened it, revealing a rectangle of darkness.

That dark maw disturbed her. It looked as though it might draw them all in, devour them in its darkness and whatever else lay in its depths.

She noticed that Officer Goin's hands trembled too, as she readied a flashlight in her left hand and placed her right hand on her gun.

Even with the mask on, Fiona could smell something metallic coming from the lab. Both she and Berkeley stepped forward to take a better look, but the officer stopped them.

"I'm going to ask you all to stand back while we investigate. This could be an unsafe environment."

She glared at Berkeley in particular, who looked for the first time actually eager, even under the mask. She really wanted in that lab, Fiona realized. But why?

"I'm going to flip the light on," Dr. Bingham announced. From where he stood outside the door's threshold, he fumbled his hand around the edge and felt for a light switch. He turned it on.

The lights of the lab flickered but came on. What they revealed confused Fiona.

The lab looked as though something had spewed all over it, as if someone had projectile vomited in all directions, and it had dried in arcs of bright blue.

"Copper sulfate," she murmured.

Bingham darted his eyes back to her, and then back into the lab.

Strange patterns looked etched into the tiled floor, again in bright blue.

"What the hell am I looking at?" Goin asked, likely echoing everyone's thoughts.

Bingham's voice shook. "I...I'm not sure. But...but there's—" his voice caught in a gasp-sob. "There's a shape. If you look."

He stepped backward, away from the door.

"Seal it off again," he said quietly.

"What shape?" Officer Goin asked, and she stepped forward.

"Don't go in there!" shouted Bingham suddenly. They all jumped.

"What is it, Doc?" Fiona asked, voice shaking.

"The shape. The shape."

"Sir?" Goin asked, and she spread her flashlight across the pattern on the floor again, illuminating the blue, crystalline pattern. "Oh *shit*."

"What?" cried Lafe.

Berkeley advanced. "Let me see."

Bingham whirled around and shut the door and locked it, and stood breathing heavily. He rounded on her.

"No. Everyone out. Get off this floor, and don't come back. Officer Goin, check the other labs. Now. Make sure no one is up here. We need to close off the floor."

"Doc!" cried Fiona. "What is it? What's the shape?"

"Get. Off. This. Floor. Fiona," he bellowed, pointing at the end of the hall toward the stairwell.

Officer Goin moved them all back several feet, her eyes round and startled.

"I'm going to need you all to do as the professor says. I've called for backup."

"Doc," Fiona begged, her voice cracking. "Tell me. What is it?"

He walked toward them all, alongside Officer Goin, and held up his hands as if to try to push them away.

"Go. Now. I'll tell you more as we know. Go!"

Lafe took hold of Fiona's elbow, and she jerked it away in a fury.

She rushed up to Doc and with tears in her eyes, she whispered, "Tell me. Tell me. Is it Gale?"

He didn't need to say anything. His eyes, hollowed, exhausted, but mostly horrified, said enough.

She stepped back, nauseous, and cast her eyes upon the tiled floor around them.

The blue, crystalline material she had thought was copper sulfate was nowhere to be seen out here. Someone had swept it up. Lafe pulled at her again.

"We're going," his voice, taut with anxiety, said in her ear.

She shook all over as they walked quickly to the end of the hallway and down the stairs.

She heard the crackle of officer Goin's walkie and barely caught the words, "We're going to need a forensics team here STAT. Hazmat gear. Yep. Get on it. We need to clear the building."

Bingham stood at the top of the stairwell with her, and she argued with him over something in a quiet voice. Then she stepped over to the wall and opened a plastic case and pulled something. The fire alarm squawked out and everyone jumped. Workers began pouring out of doorways toward the front exit. Fiona and Lafe followed suit, but Fiona looked back up one more time at Bingham's face. He looked defeated. He held a phone in his hands and nodded, and then pocketed it.

He began to descend the stairs, and then rallied, rounding the staff up, ushering them outside.

The suffocating humidity of the day struck them outside. Fiona began to sweat instantly, despite feeling cold within. She looked around at the growing group of evacuating staff and students, out on the sidewalk and gathering across the lawn from the building. She marked all the CUPRUM workers, the office staff, Doc Bingham, Lafe…but one face she did not see: Jack Cordeiro's.

He was nowhere.

CHAPTER 23
GARDEN OF SHADOWS

"Professor Bingham," Berkeley said, "when can we continue? There's the business of the grant and our assets in the desert—"

"Get out of here," Bingham thundered. His eyes were wild, brows skyward, his face tinged puce.

Berkeley gathered herself up, a human vase in statuesque ivory, facing him with her prim mouth and cold eyes.

"Need I remind you that your research relies up—"

"My research is on its last legs, and you threw me—us—" he nodded to Fiona, who felt a jolt of surprise, "—a lifeline. But I can't support this anymore. We'll find the funds somewhere else, or we won't. Whatever it is you're doing down there, up here: I want no part in it. You've got multiple deaths on your hands now."

"Dr. Bingham, mind your implications," said Berkeley acidly. "Our attorneys are far better funded than you *or* your little hillbilly lab."

"Fuck. Off."

Doc said it deadly calm. No inflection. He pointed to the road curving down from the Hill.

Berkeley finally, *finally* stepped back, her face staining most unpleasantly, the most human thing Fiona had witnessed from her yet.

"We will be in touch," came her cold response. She turned her unreadable indigo eyes to Fiona.

Such was the coldness and flatness of that gaze that Fiona shivered in the August heat. Still, she lifted her chin, and glanced down the road where Bingham pointed, and glanced back. She shrugged.

"Bye," she said, unable to resist a smirk.

Berkeley and her cohort left, walking toward the back parking lot to her car.

Fiona exhaled then, relieved to see the retreat of them all.

Soon a police vehicle and a forensics lab van rolled up the Hill as well.

Bingham turned to Fiona and Lafe.

"You had a box in my office," he said, his tone rueful. "I should've grabbed it. Not sure how to get it to you now, but if there's a way, I'll let you know and when you can come pick it up. I'm sorry."

That last sentence he uttered in a tone full of unspoken emotion.

He looked to Lafe momentarily, and back to Fiona.

"Look after each other. I don't know what happens next."

Fiona stepped forward and looked him in the eyes.

"Take care of yourself too, Doc. Let us know if there's anything we can do."

He nodded. "I have some very unpleasant phone calls to make. Again."

"I know."

"Take the time off," he told her. "I'll handle things inside our lab at least. Might be the only thing I can do, for much longer."

Fiona did not like his tone. "This sounds like a goodbye," she admitted, voice breaking.

At that, Bingham snorted. He shook his head.

"We must really be workaholics, if taking a break feels like the end of the world. Makes you wonder why we picked science sometimes."

Fiona laughed at that, feeling some relief in his twinkling eyes and half grin.

He turned away from her and Lafe then, and they looked at each other.

"I say we get out of here before anything else happens," he suggested.

She was reluctant, and pissed off, and the moment crackled with tension and anxiety.

But as she gazed back, shuddering, thinking of what that lab had revealed to them all, she felt one overarching emotion: the desire to leave that place immediately.

She wondered, again, what had happened to Alva in the desert.

"Fine," she said, terse.

They walked back to the car in silence. She held her crossbody purse against her, and then paused to take a stick of deodorant out of it.

"Sorry, I'm sweating like a donkey's balls in this heat," she admitted.

Lafe snickered. But she wasn't smiling. She put the deodorant back and her hand grazed against the pancake fork trophy. She pushed that back down. That had been a fun moment, a light moment—after their past years of unrequited…something. Now it looked like whatever it was between them was unspooling before her.

They made it to his car, and the sun's angle had moved so that it was not as well shaded. So when she sat in the passenger's seat, she winced from the hot seat. He started the engine and the air conditioner clicked on.

"You okay?" he asked her.

"No."

"Want to tell me why?"

"I'm pissed off."

"About?"

"The goddamn greenhouse!" she sputtered, folding her arms across herself, settling the purse in her lap.

"I'm sorry. Look, I'm a literal guy. I didn't see it. I'm always skeptical. It's not you."

"You don't believe me," she says angrily. "That's hurtful. Do you understand? Why would I make this up?"

"I'm not saying you're making this up. And we've seen a lot of weird shit. I'm just…"

"You're gaslighting me."

He flinched from her piercing stare. They sat as the car whined its little electric hum.

"Fiona."

"Lafe, stop. Maybe I should go home."

"What home?"

"Oh, fuck off."

She almost opened the car door, but he was right. Cheeks ablaze, she turned back to him.

"Now what do we do?"

Lafe sighed and rubbed his face.

"I think we'd better have some dinner. And after that, we'll figure things out."

The red and green neon of Don Rafael's restaurant blinked back and forth in the pattern of a red and green parrot flying. She sipped at her mojito, and he scooted back in his chair, cradling a tall Mexican Coke bottle.

"You could stay over," he said finally.

"I don't know. We—we've not talked about *that*."

Lafe twisted his mouth back and forth, because he knew "that" meant their kiss.

"We don't need to ever again. If that's what you want." He said it with a slightly uplifted tone at the end, as if it were a question. "I never expected it, and I don't expect anything else."

She stared at him. She wanted to feel anger toward him, because it was at least something that made her feel strength, after everything they had been through.

"Thank you," she said, and she lowered her eyes, her cheeks burning.

Lafe paid the check, and they walked out. By now it was twilight. Fireflies began rising from the grasses, their blinking patterns spinning a few feet above the ground. They would work their way up the tree canopies through the night, she knew, their phosphorescent messages dancing.

They communicate better than we do.

"Want to walk in the park?"

Lafe gestured toward an ornate, historic gate, from which extended an old, spiky wrought iron fence in a square around immense old oaks, tulip poplars, dogwoods long out of bloom, and lemon-scented magnolias. It was the kind of park one might see in Savannah or Charleston, minus the hanging moss. And it was deserted.

With its redolent blossoms, the park beckoned, and Fiona liked the thought of immersing herself among the greenery in peace. Thunder rumbled off in the distance, likely over the Smoky Mountains, but she could see some open sky above them and the shivering stars between the clouds.

"It was Gale, back there, in that lab," she said suddenly, and she became hyper aware of the loudness of her voice, so she lowered it quickly, as if on sacred ground in the park. In fact there were some quite ancient tombstones off in one corner, given over to lichen and the etchings of many rains upon their faces.

"It's pretty fucked up, if so," Lafe remarked, grim.

"Look, I—it's soon. You know?" she fumbled the words. She regretted them as quickly as she said them.

"I know."

They paused and stared at each other. She wanted badly to step forward, embrace him, kiss him, sink into the grass despite its dew, there under the stars.

"No, you don't know."

She wondered if she might regret what she was going to say next...but at least she *would* say it. Because she thought, given how fraught and how fragile everything and everyone around her seemed just then, that she might regret never telling him how she felt.

"You don't have to say anything," he said, but his voice betrayed him by quavering.

She took his hands in hers, under a dogwood tree.

"I don't know what I would have done without you, during all this," she said to him, glancing from his eyes to his chin. "And even though it's too soon for anything, I just—maybe after this is all over, we can…well."

Lafe smiled awkwardly.

"Well, what?"

She interlaced her fingers in his.

"I just think that maybe…it might be, I don't know, pretty fucking cool if we dated."

She wanted to sink down into the ground in shock from her own words, but the gasp from Lafe jerked her out of that morose reverie. He traced her chin with his fingers.

"Fiona Hawthorne, yes. It would be fucking cool if we dated."

And he kissed her.

They held hands, kissed, and slowly walked back toward the gate of the park to leave. Fiona felt herself grow hot, wondering what would happen now when they drove off…back to his house, back to the comfort and the acceptance, and she knew for certain now, the love. She kissed him again. They made it to the gate, and as Lafe opened it, he paused, and he stared off to one side of the park.

She followed his gaze, and she clapped her hand over her mouth.

Something quivered there, under a tree, next to the fence. She knew that shape, that movement.

Because she'd seen it in the greenhouse.

She tugged on Lafe, who stood transfixed, staring.

"What is it?"

She pulled at him desperately.

"It's…it's what I saw. In the greenhouse."

Lafe looked down at her, eyes wide, and she could see an avalanche of apology there. She shook her head. There wasn't time for that now.

"Let's get the fuck out of here!"

Lafe pulled the gate slowly behind them, and as it closed it creaked and ground horribly, setting Fiona on edge. It clanged into place.

They ran.

The gate made no more sounds.

Relieved by that, and looking behind them as she ran, Fiona let out a huge sigh at the sight of Lafe's car. Lafe unlocked the car and they looked across the hood at each other. Then he fell with a sickening thud.

"Lafe!" she cried.

Something trembled and swayed where Lafe had stood. It shone and quivered and shook, and there was nothing remotely recognizable or human about it…except for its voice.

It spoke.

"I know you miss your friend Alva."

It spoke in Jack Cordeiro's voice.

"I'll take you to her."

CHAPTER 24
NO NEED TO PANIC

Her thoughts screamed, but her voice cried out again, "Lafe!"

She ran around to face the thing and see what had happened to her friend. The thing had gone: *What?* She'd just seen it…and could not comprehend how it had disappeared, for she'd just been looking at it.

Lafe lay still, and she feared the worst, but she felt his neck, and a pulse met her shaking fingertips. But it was faint. She reached for her phone inside her purse, which she still wore across her body, and then a stinging sensation coursed through her hand to the point that she shouted in pain and dropped it.

She looked up then, up and up, for something pale gold quivered in a gelatinous tower above her, and she fell back onto her hands and gaped in disbelief. It began to fork out, stalks ripping with a rubbery, tearing sound that chilled her, and then she could make out appendages: a head, arms, legs, and it shifted and squirmed. She then opened her mouth wide to scream, but something from that mass shot toward her mouth and hovered there, and she closed her mouth with a clack and groaned with her lips tight, to prevent it from entering her throat.

Oh God! Oh fuck!

Yet she could not stop staring as the mass shifted again and shrank and coiled in a bit, and then settled. She watched as small protuberances emerged from the head region: eyeballs on stalks, and those swiveled down to stare into her own wide eyes. And then teeth, only teeth, slicing through the slimy gel, one by one, until all she could resolve were eyeballs and teeth. It shook and shimmied and then fingernails emerged from what eventually became hands. At that point it reached down and retrieved a duffle bag on the ground and pulled out what looked like gloves in the form of human hands, and it donned those, and began pulling on clothes from the bag as well, as its form shrank again and warped and popped and squelched.

She had a fleeting moment of clarity and thought, *How did he speak without a mouth?* And: *Why does he need gloves, is his entire body a glove?*

That was quickly and horribly answered for her, as the gelatinous portions of the creature solidified into skin, and attractive skin at that.

Why the gloves?

She got no answer for that, but the skin stretched itself over the shape of a face, and soon Jack was grinning down at her with his bright, white smile gleaming in the dim light. He was backlit by a lamppost, and it gave him a halo. But nothing holy emitted from this man-creature, and if Fiona believed in the Devil, surely this being would qualify as one of its ilk.

"What are you?" she managed to wheeze, finding her throat filling with drained snot; only then did she realize she had been terrified to the point of tears, and worried so about Lafe that she had lost the ability to comprehend fully what she was feeling at all.

He—and she was not sure the thing could have any gender, yet still it appeared as Jack, so she thought of it as male—threw back his dark, curly head and laughed. And he did so in as charming a voice as someone might greet a friend and laugh over a joke. Somehow that frightened her most of all, and she hugged herself, pressing her purse into the hollow of her abdomen, using it as a sort of protective shield, or at least something to hold onto. For in that moment she could feel everything else slipping away.

"I'm Jack," and he shrugged nonchalantly.

"You—you aren't Jack Cordeiro," she gasped.

He laughed lightly again, and she shuddered.

If he's not Jack Cordeiro, he's not a person. If he is Jack Cordeiro, and he's been masquerading always as a person...

The thought sent her tumbling into despair.

Alva!

He stuck his hands—covered with flesh-like gloves, and had she not seen him don them she wouldn't even have suspected—into his pants pockets and flared their legs.

"Of course, of *course* I am!" he said, grinning all the time. The image of the teeth forming from the golden gel looped in her mind as she stared at that smile.

"Lafe," she said suddenly. "What did you do to him?"

Jack shrugged again, not even bothering to look over at the unconscious shape of her friend where he lay sprawled on the pavement.

"He's only knocked out for now," answered Jack simply.

"What do you mean, for *now*? What are you going to do to us?"

She felt pathetic and useless for asking it. She knew this was bad, that at any second this thing might kill her. After all, it had killed before…

"What are you worried about, Fiona?" asked Jack, tilting his head.

"I'll scream," she sputtered, but he held up his finger to his mouth.

"Shhh. Shhh." He looked then over at Lafe. "No need to panic! If you scream, I will kill him. So that you can see he is dead. And then I will dispose of you."

Fiona recoiled and shook all over, whimpering now, pleading with her eyes.

"What do you want?" she wailed.

"Shhhh. Quieter, please." In his magnetic smile she could then see a tic at the corner of his mouth, and in his brow a flatness of expression, but it absolutely read as hostile to her.

"We want similar things," he declared, leaning down to look at her. He drew something out of the duffle bag that she could not see.

"Please let us go," she begged. "Please. We won't tell anyone. I promise."

He shook his head, smiling the entire time.

"No, no, Miss Hawthorne. You see, you want Alva! Yes?"

She froze, staring up at him.

"Alva's dead," she whispered.

"But you see, Alva wanted *you*."

She opened her mouth and closed it.

"You'll be reunited at last."

Fiona shook her head.

"You killed Gale," she whispered. "You killed Alva, then, too. And all the others."

Jack clicked his tongue and shook his head disapprovingly.

"Oh, *Fiona*, you're not seeing the bigger picture here!" Yet he kept smiling. "So I'll show it to you."

"What do you mean?" She liked this less and less by the second.

If I scream, would anything happen?

"If you scream, he dies, remember?" Jack answered her aloud.

She felt a nervous shock like a stab of ice. He'd heard her thoughts somehow.

"Why haven't you killed me, then?" she asked, clinging to one last string of hope in that awful moment in the parking lot, where the summer-heated asphalt crumbled beneath her and began to pock her legs, which were starting to go numb from not moving. She shifted about to prevent this, and almost fell onto her back.

Jack then pivoted the object in his glove-hands and said, "I need you."

"You've got me right here," she snapped, her voice rising in pitch.

"No, you don't understand, dear Fiona," he sighed. "I need you *there*."

She blinked up at him.

"Where?" she whispered.

And then things happened fast. In one hand Jack held a small oval piece of fabric, and she just caught a whiff of it: a sickening, cloying, volatile substance. In the other, he held a longer, dark strip of fabric. She tried to stand up, but he caught her in the face with the oval cloth, and she made the mistake of inhaling, and began to feel very drowsy. She stumbled, but he caught her and shoved something in her mouth, small, like a breath mint, and it began to dissolve quickly, bitter yet sweet on the tongue. He then turned her fully around, as she felt her limbs go strangely loose, and he wrapped her mouth and eyes deftly with the fabric. Everything went dark, and she was falling, falling down, falling in her mind, her limbs limp, her knees almost hitting the ground, but he seized her in the darkness. She could see nothing. She could hear her own pulse, but only for a few seconds.

Then in her ear he murmured in a disturbing, musical tone:

"Atacama."

CHAPTER 25
PRETTY BIRD

She woke with a headache so incredible that she dry-heaved, for there was nothing willing to emerge from her mouth otherwise. She was not sure how long she had been unconscious. But now that she was awake, she in some ways wished to return to that state. She blinked: she was in a completely white space, disorienting in its flat pallor, lit from some unknown source, shadowless. *Not the garden.*

Am I dead?

She looked down and found that she sat on…something. She still wore her clothes, still bore her crossbody purse…in fact she clenched it so tightly her knuckles had gone white.

If I am dead, at least I still have my purse.

But she was stiff, taut, sore…and her vision kept blurring in and out of focus. She felt a tug in her left arm and saw a little object sticking out of her hand.

She wanted to say, "*What the fuck is that?*" but she could not seem to find her voice.

She did, however, hear other voices, muffled and shifting in timbre.

"It will last?"

She tensed. That was Jack; she was certain of that at least.

"As we've said, yes, the effects will last. You will have to figure the rest out, I'm afraid."

A woman's voice. Not…Berkeley?

"You'll have the team ready?" Something in Jack's voice confused Fiona. Was he…nervous?

Can a gelatinous man-thing be nervous?

"Everything is in place. Assistance has been procured. You'll have a clean path in and out."

It might be Berkeley. But that woman's voice had been so dull and unremarkable, it could have been anyone's. So Fiona could not be sure.

She closed her eyes for a second to try and quell the light making her head hurt.

She jerked: time had passed.

The light in the room had dimmed, but she was fairly certain it was the same room. She felt something slightly heavy on her hand and looked down. A little bag hung there, attached to her hand, and she realized it was a form of IV drip. She wanted desperately to pull it out but could not move her arms to do so. She could not move her legs, either. She wanted to scream and could not find her voice either. So she tugged against the drowsy-frozen feeling, a waking nightmare, moaning or trying to moan but not quite able. She would thrash if she had the energy, but she did not…and then she closed her eyes again.

She was standing. No, she was walking.

It was morning. Perhaps.

She was unsure. She was walking and then she realized she was walking in a long hallway, not unlike the one underneath the biochemistry building on campus. It was not the university, however. It looked…like a cargo tunnel, perhaps. There were pallets. There were large parcels. She heard a distant roar and whine. Something mechanical. Loud and winding up. She was unsure.

She was walking and she was walking alone. Maybe. She could not tell. She did not understand how she was walking, because she was not doing this herself. But when she turned to look, she could see no one. She could not, however, stop herself from walking.

The IV bag on her hand was gone. Her skin looked clear and unmarked…*Is that makeup?*

She thought this in the span of seconds as she kept walking down the corridor toward a bright light.

Surely I am dead and this is like that tunnel near-death experience people talk about. I'm going toward the light.

Then she was outside, and now she understood what the sound was. Engines. The sound of planes taking off. It was an airport.

It was not a passenger terminal, though. She could see shipping jets on the tarmac, but that was not where she was headed. She walked of her own accord and yet not so, and she blinked. She headed for a sleek private jet, its stairs down.

She paused.

Keep going.

A voice. A voice in her mind.

Jack's voice.

A person in white stepped down out of the jet. She could not discern their gender. They bore an insignia on their lapel. They stood next to the stairs and glanced up into the body of the plane. Then Jack stepped down and faced them.

Fiona wanted to stop walking. But she was propelled. One foot in front of the other, and vaguely, she thought, *Shouldn't I be stumbling?*

Yet she walked as calmly as if on a summer stroll in a park, in the darkness, with fireflies, and someone she cared very much about.

She tried to remember who that was.

But in her mind, she heard, *"Shhhh."*

The sharp tang of jet fuel and the heat of the tarmac made her dizzy.

She walked toward Jack and this individual clad in white. She reached the jet's stairs and stood looking straight ahead. Her eyes struggled, though, and out of her peripheral vision she could guess the shape of the insignia on the person's lapel: CUPRUM.

"Everything is ready," the person in white said flatly, their golden eyes looking only at Jack, and never at her.

Do you not see me? Do you not see I'm being kidnapped?

Jack turned his head slowly to look at her and smile.

"Shhh."

He never opened his mouth to say that; it pressed into her thoughts like an exploring finger, unwelcome, poking deep at something essential. A violation of something sacred.

"Let's go inside, shall we, Fiona?" he asked aloud.

Jack's hands steepled under his chin and he bowed. The CUPRUM agent turned and walked back toward the airport terminal. Fiona's vision swam, but she could see a couple of guards there, and she wanted very much to scream at them, for them to realize she was being taken, she was not in control of her body.

She could feel herself walking up those stairs into the jet and could not control her own legs. Her arms stiffly clutched her purse, and she was pulled upward, and then inside. Jack followed her.

Once in, she blinked in her wrecked vision and tried to take in her surroundings. It was immaculately clean, and sleekly glamorous in a corporate executive fashion. She realized then she had not taken a good look at its livery to try to find any numbers. She had felt too confused. She felt a creeping little flush of anger at herself for being so careless.

Even Hansel and Gretel left crumbs to find.

That thought unnerved her more, when she thought that would not be possible.

Will he bake me and eat me? Is that what she did to Gale? To Alva...

"Shhhh." Again this came from Jack, this time aloud. "Sit there, Fiona." He gestured with one of his hideous glove-hands, and she found herself obeying him, against all her wishes.

Did you roofie me?

"Shhhh." This time he sounded soothing, his eyes approaching a kind affect. He seemed pleased. "What do you think? Nice, yes? One of CUPRUM's. Comfortable for you."

She could feel herself slipping again, and then blinked. It was a very finely appointed private jet.

Pretty bird.

She could hear the whining of the jet engine.

Who's the pilot?

He did not answer her.

Ah. So...no one. A remote. A drone.

She sat in the chair, and it strapped her in automatically, and she stared at Jack as he laid out little plastic parcels of something on a tray near his seat.

The jet was rolling now. She tensed, or tried to: faster and faster it rolled forward.

Can't someone tell I've been kidnapped? Aren't there cameras? How can they just let this happen to me?

The plane ascended, and she felt the pressure build in her sinuses.

Jack glanced at her, unfastened his seatbelt, and approached her. She was stuck here with him, in the air. The slant of sunlight through clouds shone through the windows of the jet, striking her face. He pulled down the window shade next to her. Then he turned to look at her.

She could only stare or blink back, she could not speak.

"There," he murmured, looking most pleased with himself. "Sleep now. When you're awake, we'll be landing."

He walked back to the tray by his chair, retrieved a small packet, and walked back to her.

She could feel her heart race, and then he placed his glove-hand on her chin, but she could not move. He squeezed her lips and her jaw, and she opened her mouth, although she did not want to. He slipped something from the packet in. This was different from before, smaller, and bitter-sour. And then she felt herself go very light, even a bit giddy, as she stared ahead, eyes glazed.

She was trapped now, the world falling beneath her, in the belly of a pretty bird, partnered with a worm within.

CHAPTER 26
THE GHOST SHIP

H er head lolled and she drooled, yet she could not move her body. She opened and closed her eyes. She was vaguely aware from the pressure that something in her environment had changed. She felt heavier, perhaps. Then the first shudder of the jet as turbulence asserted itself. They were descending. And where they descended, the cold of the Pacific met the air currents of the tall Andes, and quite suddenly the plane jolted and shimmied.

She jerked awake, panting. This would not be a comfortable descent.

And whoever's flying this plane isn't here to experience it, to adjust it.

She tried shifting, with every part of her feeling leaden and heavy. She knew she was drugged beyond imagining, that many of her bodily functions had slowed.

If I take a shit anytime soon, it's gonna be concrete.

She wanted to laugh ruefully at her own body's tragic lack of help in her current circumstance. She was a "good girl," or had been; a square. Not one for taking anything illegal. Not one for partying too hard, and she had never been blackout drunk. Until now, perhaps. Or rather she wished she were, now that there was turbulence. Nausea surged within her, but she could do nothing for it.

"Let me tell you a story."

Jack watched her from his seat. He looked pleasant enough, but that pleasant-faced man—or creature—had killed Alva, injured Lafe, and drugged and kidnapped her. How dare he begin telling her a story?

"There is a local legend called the *Caleuche.* A ghost ship that traversed the bays and rivers, making a trade with the merchants for the price of their daughters. It sounds a bit like a fairy tale, yes? But there is more to it. In every folk tale there is some kernel of truth, and yes, some sort of vessel visited the shores, but it was not a schooner or any such thing as that, and its entry was meant to be kinder. So it was that the…sailing was rough, the turbulence, as it were, extraordinary; the sailors themselves injured or killed or buried, scattered in the desert, away from the shore, away from the whale fossils…"

His voice trailed off for a moment.

She hated that she'd found it mesmerizing to listen to, and she realized he had been trying to calm her.

The plane jolted again, and she panted, licking her lips. His brow creased, watching her, and he finally unstrapped, lost his balance momentarily as the drone plane adjusted to the turbulence of the descent, and picked up something off the tray.

Oh good, more drugs, she thought dully.

"You are panicking," he told her. "The tincture is being overridden. They did say this might happen. So another pill for you."

You mean I'm fighting it, fuckface!

She jerked and trembled but again she felt trapped in a dream paralysis, stuck in her seat, unable to move *away*, and so any movement at all seemed a futile endeavor.

"You are nervous. I did not realize! You do not like flying."

The hand-gloves pushed through the additional pill. Her anxiety receded, but her anger did not.

Got a pill for rage, motherfucker?

"Shhh. I will tell you more of a story to calm you."

He slowed his voice down and she realized then the power of Jack Cordeiro's particular charm. For his voice was mellifluous, singsong when he chose it to be. Whatever relic of the man remained, this creature had wisely chosen to collect the most appealing aspects.

Clever fuck.

He shook his head, smiling, and put a finger to his mouth.

The plane jolted, buffeted; the wings extended, and so she knew they must be getting closer to their destination. She wished she could see outside her window.

His voice, lilting, twisting around words and making them seem larger and cloudlike as starlings in murmuration:

"There are glass fields east of the Pampa del Tamarugal. That is where the *Caleuche* sailed its final journey.

"I landed here, and my compatriots met a foul end. It was a quiet time, and in it I slept. I could hear the rumblings of movement, of earthquakes, of industry, of failure and thirst and death.

"Still I slept, and crawled and made my way, avoiding the Chuquicamata. I knew of it and kept away."

The Copper Man. Fiona had forgotten; Alva had been fascinated by the discovered mummy, encased in copper salts, and hoped not-too-secretly she would discover more. It was one of Alva's macabre little quirks that Fiona found endearing.

But after the copper sulfate in the lab, and whatever remained of Gale...

Jack's voice, velvet, spun the tale out in finest thread, and she followed it as he wove her into his mental cocoon:

"There are more mummies beneath the desert than all those who venture across it now, I can tell you. There is glass from impact, spread across the Pampa. I listened to your people's rovers traversing it, as if they could help you on another world. It's an expensive fantasy, or a cheap one, depending on who you ask: that you could comprehend what's out there. It's much more interesting down here, I've discovered."

Would I become one of those mummies?

She felt even more disorientation, trying to parse his words. What was he telling her?

Fiona tried breathing through her nose and out through her mouth, as Lafe had suggested. The plane's recycled air had dried her out already, but what lay beneath her, she knew, would parch her more quickly than anything else on Earth could. She licked her lips and found them dry and cracked. She tried to say something, anything. She tried groaning. What was wrong with her voice?

"Shhhh."

And Jack this time dispensed some sort of hideous green liquid into her mouth through a dropper. She had little time to feel sickened by it, however. She slid off into a pain-free oblivion, yet remained awake.

"Shhhh, shhhh. We can't let too many people look your way: just enough, and so you will smile and nod, smile and nod...A pretty lady in the desert already draws enough attention."

She could not decide which disturbed her more: the fact that she would be forced to perform as a puppet, or the fact that Jack—or whatever he was—considered her at all attractive. How much of it was a remnant of Jack? Was that his thinking, something residual from his personality, stretched like a skin over this creature?

Her thoughts wafted back to *Caleuche*. She imagined a ship, but not so: something shimmering in the night sky, a constellation brought to earth, sailing at striking speed, setting the air alight, into the delta of a river long dead, into floodplains long desiccated, encrusted with the fossils of fleets of beached whales. The waters vanishing in the blink of an eye, or millions of years, where rainfall died, or if it touched the parched earth, it burst expectant extremophile microbes to their doom; too much of a good thing, and it would kill you. She wondered how much she imagined, and how much Jack actually showed her through his thoughts.

"I'm taking you to Alva, remember. I know you want to be with her again."

CHAPTER 27
HALF THE FLESH

S he was pliable as new taffy as he warped and spun her with his
words. The jet bumped and fell and parried with the eddies of
downdraft winds. If she had been more in control of herself, she
would have vomited. All that she could do was sit helpless and rigid.

"We'll be met by a CUPRUM team."

He said that flatly; unusually so, for him. She blinked at him, for
it seemed, for a moment, that he stared off into the distance. Then *he*
blinked, and turned back to her.

"I have a distaste for them; they are a foul amalgam, your kind
and your ill-begotten technology, at best immoral and at worst, a
gloating illegality."

This coming from you? *That's rich.*

"A means to an end, for researchers who are hungry."

There was a shadow of something in his gaze.

Is Jack still in there?

"Grants to fund you. Fountains of cash. From where? Not that it interests me. It interests me more, the effect that source has on you. Yes, even your Doc Bingham, an old buffoon, though a kind one, no doubt. Perhaps he means well, but he escapes their event horizon only by stepping away entirely, and he won't do that."

You're wrong about him. If he knew any of this, he would sever all ties; he would make sure the world knew.

At that, Jack chortled and shook his head. That angered her even more.

"So yes, I dislike them. Yet look at the favor they've done for us: an exchange. To get you here."

Why? Why do you need me?

"For Alva, of course!" The bright, model-perfect smile.

Alva. Is. Dead.

"Alva might not be…recognizable to you"—Fiona shivered—"yet she exists. Because of us. Because of me, as the code my kind left in the soil directed scaffolding—hampered of course by its lack of water. This is not where we had planned to be, hence the slow crawl…at times literally across broken glass, to get to where I needed to be.

"I wanted it to be someplace humid, see if we could succeed elsewhere. The team was perfect: send samples back to Tennessee, try them out. No one knew but Jack, and by that time, it was too late. He was resilient, you see. I could scaffold *with* him; I rearranged things."

So you killed Jack. How did CUPRUM allow this?

"It's all about exchange." He shrugged.

Part of Jack *definitely* remained, and Fiona thought achingly of Alva. What had happened to her? Did she have a doppelgänger? The thought burrowed down into Fiona's psyche, coiled, a snake to bite her should she test it.

"I have knowledge beyond reckoning. CUPRUM wanted it. There is a price for everything with you people! So Jack became our liaison over time. I crawled through his mind inasmuch as I could bear, reorganizing, expunging the parts I found intolerable."

Intolerable? Like his attitudes?

"He was more of an allergen to me. Like the mines themselves, which I avoided. Like the Copper Man.

"Although it gave me the idea for preserving, at least in the lab. The scaffolding worked beyond imagining, too quickly, and the only way to stop it was a dousing of copper sulfate. This is what Gale helped me with."

He smiled then, eyes half-lidded, as if he were recalling a fond memory.

Fiona went ice cold, despite the blazing heat of the desert below, despite any climate control on the jet.

"Yes, of course I knew who she was. She started the *making* in the lab. I knew it was too productive, so I sent her to get the salts, the copper sulfate; copper would kill the process. But she was a witness, so I locked her in with it—so ending them both."

He held his hands out.

"CUPRUM would call it the price of doing business."

CUPRUM doesn't murder people!

He turned to stare at her coldly, and she realized she had surprised him.

"You think they do not? That they have not scraped and scoured lives, and words, and numbers, and money whenever it gave them a chance to do so? I assure you, they have."

And yet we're meeting them in the driest place on Earth, to do what?

"It is an exchange, as I have said. I give them knowledge, I give you Alva."

Why bring me all this way just to see someone who's dead?

He smiled back at her, radiant, even hopeful.

"We were incomplete, we were not as you are; we found material to scaffold, to build, to make. But so many inferior subjects sank into that sand: sank their fortunes and their dreams, even their little songs and shows, even their children, all buried, all blown to dust or rust or to mummification. The unlikelihood of finding someone perfect…I admit I despaired. Until Alva came along."

You killed her! What good is she dead?

"Shhh….Shhh. We will land soon. I should strap in. But stop thinking in terms of your kind being dead. If they can be scaffolded, we both continue. I needed but one perfect unit to make it work, to make it last, one perfect mind…or as close to one as any of you can get. For my own completion. That is worth any exchange with CUPRUM."

But what do you get?

"I get…you."

CHAPTER 28
ADVENT

*W*hy me? What makes me so special, of all the people you've…supposedly come across, from the time of mummies to the boomtowns that went bust? I don't get it.

He smiled and waved her off, and he stepped away to buckle into his seat. He flicked out a tablet chip and spoke into it.

"Final approach. Yes, should be starting soon. I'll get her ready."

He pressed something on the tablet, looked back at Fiona, and put his chin on his hands, grinning at her.

"You'll feel a little strange for a bit, and then we'll be there!"

He sounded excited. She didn't like that at all. But she had little time to dwell on that.

Blackness consumed her vision and then she was falling, slowly falling in a bottomless place, eyes open but not seeing, breathing somehow but with stale air. Occasionally a series of patterns emerged in her vision: radiant swirls and starbursts, the curving scotoma of a migraine, or waving objects that she somehow registered as either tentacles or antennae, but of no physical nature. They were more psychological, and as such, electrical. Something tickled at the innermost parts of her mind, branching, reaching out, and then tugging. Pulling at those thoughts that she kept the deepest: moments of shame and pain, humiliation, rage, despair, and even the little, tiny sparkles of hope that she also hid from the world. Something reached for all these things, the very gossamer fabric of her soul, and pulled at it like hooks.

This was something *other*. She knew it on a fundamental level: there was no human with her, there was no animal; there was no plant or fungus or protist or bacteria or virus. This was *other* and it preyed upon the stilled waters of her psyche.

More lights, more swirls, and finally something resembling true light, as though she looked up at the top of a water column, seeing sunlight through its shifting barrier, and without hesitation, every part of her sprang for that light.

She jerked. Drool snaked its way out of her mouth, and she blinked. Her head sagged against a hard, plastic surface: the window. She heard the distinct whine of the jet's engines. She tried moving, but for several moments she could not. She could not turn her head; she at first could not even turn her eyes. But by and by, just as her sight—albeit somewhat blurred, her eyes like sawdust—returned, so did her ability to move her eyes. And then, slowly, her head.

She swallowed, her throat raging in pain, the lack of moisture in her mouth telling her she'd had it agape for a long period of time. But no, more than that…the irritation in her throat. She knew that feeling.

I was intubated at some point.

Sensation returned throughout her, terrifying her with small moments of realization.

Little sparks of panic jolted through her body, and she realized, too, that her legs were bound. By what, she at first could not fathom. But she knew, again from hospitalization, what she was feeling. She had little pumps on her legs, squeezing and releasing, over and over.

So I didn't get blood clots.

Then she pushed herself into an upright position, instantly straining her neck, but that blade of pain only momentarily distracted her from the growing remembrance that she was not in a hospital. She was, indeed, still on the plane. The shade had been opened and she looked out the window and could see only blue sky above.

She looked at a seat adjacent to her and blinked. There sat her purse, and an unfamiliar, oblong wallet with a bit of paperwork sticking out. She reached down to unbuckle herself from her seat, and then found she could not completely control her arms. Yet still, more feeling coursed through them than she had felt since this ordeal began.

She was alone.

Where is he?

At that moment, a curtained area up the aisle opened. Out stepped Jack, smiling broadly with such white teeth that he could have been a toothpaste ad. He stretched out his arms wide and then clapped his hands together.

"Good!" he exclaimed. "You're awake. Quite the view, isn't it?"

She licked her lips, and he nodded, and opened a mini fridge. Inside it, she could barely see a few bottles of champagne, mineral water, and beers. He found a bottle of flat water, unscrewed the lid, and brought it to her. She wanted to take it but could not yet move her arms.

"Ah, ah!" he cautioned, holding the bottle to her lips.

Without hesitation, she slurped at it, and he stood, grinning, as she sipped it down. She was too thirsty to resist, but still on edge. A fair bit of the water spilled down her chin and onto her blouse, which she now felt soaked with sweat. She could smell herself and she recoiled.

"I," she began, and then she coughed, and suddenly could not stop coughing. It hurt; everything hurt, her throat, her lungs, her ribs, her somehow restrained arms.

"Everything with you always starts with 'I,'" whispered Jack. "Every single one of you. So strange."

She blinked up at him, and he smiled again. Her sense of smell returned, and she breathed in the scent of him: new, fresh clothing and a bit too much cologne, something expensive. His perfect dark blue jeans and crisp white shirt, his designer belt and boots…everything reeked of newness, of money, and of something indefinable to her that she could not quite figure out. All the scents…they *masked* him, she realized. They were a glamor for all to see and think: *success*. Unapproachable and yet somehow relatable.

"I—can't," she started again. "Move—my—arms." It was effort to speak. She gasped. Her throat railed. She swallowed and it was agony. But she was glad to *have* her voice again, despite this.

"Oh!" said Jack brightly. "Well, good thing you don't have to." He beamed. "It's safer that you stay put, for now."

"I've—been. Staying. Put."

It exhausted her, the attempt to speak.

She fought a shudder. Whatever was happening, she did not want to come unhinged. Not yet. She was a woman of science. She needed more data.

She had many questions crowding to the surface of her mind from those strange depths she'd experienced earlier, but one thought quite quickly asserted itself over all others.

"I"— another agonized swallow—"need—to—pee."

Jack tilted his head and barely drooped his energetic eyebrows.

Then he laughed.

"Of course! Of course. I had hoped you could sleep the entire way, but your thoughts were quite active. We slowed everything down until we could get you here."

He leaned down toward her. She felt self-conscious of her own smell, and that angered her.

Why should I give a fuck about how I smell *when I've been* kidnapped?

She pushed herself back into her seat. He unbuckled her, and then he placed his gloved hands firmly on her shoulders.

Is he going to take me to the toilet himself?

She felt a warm tingle travel from his hands into her shoulders. Then she felt the discomfort of many tingles throughout her arms, as all the feeling came back to them. She winced from the pain.

I could swing at him.

He giggled. He shook his head.

He knows I can't do a thing. What happens? I swing, weak as a new calf, I miss…he knocks me out. I can't even stand yet.

He unfastened the compressors from her legs.

"It's a small plane," he said. "But there are two bathrooms. One at the front, one at the rear."

She pushed with all her might and stood before he could try to stop her, and she immediately stumbled.

"Shit."

He pulled her up by her underarms, which she knew stank, and she felt completely helpless. But still, she pushed away from him, holding on to her seat back.

"No," she insisted. She took deep breaths in and out. She swallowed, and her ears popped. The pain of that made her blanch. She steadied her breathing and her voice. "I will go—on my own."

He then stepped away from her and shrugged. He stood and watched her struggle, and she felt his eyes on her always. Her body temperature vacillated wildly as she worked hard to remain on her feet. One moment she felt frigid, the next she felt ablaze. She gripped her seat and wobbled, braced herself, panted, and lurched step by excruciating step toward the bathroom. Her bladder hurt, and it took all her strength not only to walk but to avoid pissing herself.

She pulled open the little door. So great was her fatigue that she stumbled against the toilet cover. She shut and locked the door, testing the lock twice, for she did not want him coming in there. She clung to the sink as the plane began the final approach to…wherever they would be landing, presumably not in the middle of the desert, but she had no idea what CUPRUM had planned, let alone Jack. She lifted the toilet lid and pulled her sweat-soaked pants down and sat so hard on the seat that it took her breath away.

Peeing hurt, and she winced; her bladder was quite full. This made her angry, and yet she felt vast relief.

Thank God, he didn't catheterize me.

That thought unsettled her.

He could have done so; he'd applied the leg pressure cuffs, after all. He'd drugged her. He could have done more…She shuddered.

It felt good to shudder; it meant she had *some* command of her body, albeit that perhaps of a tottering fawn.

But he's letting me walk now. Sort of. Probably not for long.

Relieved of her full bladder, she washed her hands and gripped the sink as the plane whined.

"Strap in!" called Jack.

For once, she appreciated his advice.

She hung onto the door of the bathroom and then gripped her way across the floor of the jet, and tried to avoid falling into her seat. Instinctively, she grabbed her purse, and noted again something sticking out of it. She threw the purse over her body and the seatbelt fastened itself over her.

"What is this?" she asked, tugging at the wallet.

"In case anyone asks questions," he answered nonchalantly. "They won't, don't worry."

Oh, I'm absolutely going to worry.

The rapid descent was followed by a quick *KA-THUNK* as the wheels hit, presumably, a tarmac. That was some relief then; they weren't landing in a salt bed. It was some kind of runway. She hoped it was a proper airport; at least then, she might have a chance for running, for escape.

Jack said nothing, but he did tilt his head back at her and catch her eye with a bemused expression.

She loathed him with every part of her, and yet she still felt a sense of guilt and shame, that somehow, she'd allowed this to happen. That was stupid: he'd kidnapped her, he'd murdered others.

Why would you want me if I can't even escape you? How am I superior in any way to anyone else? Fucking bullshit.

The plane taxied and then halted at last with a slight lurch.

Despite everything that had happened, she was glad to be on solid ground.

Jack unbuckled and stepped over to her, about to do the same for her, but she quickly unfastened the belt herself, defiant, furious. He shrugged and put his hands in his pockets; a platinum watch glistened at the edge of one pocket from where he'd snapped it onto his wrist.

The door to the jet opened and its stairs extended downward, and in that moment a gust of desert wind funneled through and into the cabin of the jet. The light from that open door pierced her, and she then realized that all the windows of the jet had been shielded somewhat, and that nothing could prepare her for that unyielding brightness. Her headache returned with a vengeance. Jack glanced back at her, outlined in the brilliant light, and then he pulled something from his left pocket: a pair of sunglasses. He approached her, set them on her face, and where she stood, he stepped back, appraising, adjusting her collar, nodding. As if he were a fashion designer, preparing her for a runway walk.

"Remember: smile and nod, smile and nod. Pretend"—he giggled—"pretend you're a Royal."

The thought struck her as gauche, but so did everything about him, and all of this, outside the horror of it.

"Will you give me a choice?" Her raw throat raged in pain at her speech, but at least it was hers, for now.

"You will put on a show, the likes of which the desert has not seen since its Copper Boom; the perfect pantomime," he said, his voice low and quiet and cold. "Come. They're waiting."

CHAPTER 29
THE HAND AND THE GLOVE

She teetered, rebalanced, and caught herself, and took each step down carefully, as a fine grit billowed up and crept into every crevice. She could feel the arid air siphoning off every bit of humidity around and within her, and she craved the bottle of water she'd left on the plane. Blinking, shielding her eyes despite the sunglasses, she could make out a vehicle: a white, large SUV, with black, tinted windows. A Range Rover, older, but in mint condition, with a copper-colored infinity symbol on its side, but no words. She did not need to know whose it was, for the people who stepped out told her that.

Three people emerged, all dressed in white all with black sunglasses, their hair slicked back. One was a woman: Berkeley.

So they flew down here as well.

Fiona scowled.

"Smile and nod," Jack told her from behind. He stepped down beside her, donning his own sunglasses, looking chic and cool, whereas she was now stained with old sweat; the only part of her not so blemished was her purse, and she held it and the large wallet poking out of it carefully.

"Why?" she hissed. "They know who I am."

"Make it look good." In his voice, she heard a sinister tone.

What would you do if I didn't?

He shot her a look over his sunglasses, even as he grinned.

"Do you want to know, Fiona?"

She swallowed.

"No."

"Good! Then let's meet them."

She looked around and found that this must be a private airfield; another private jet, a couple of smaller drones parked in a solar cell-covered hangar, and a few old Cessnas, one of which was covered with a silver tarp that billowed and glittered in the bright sun.

"Where are we?" she whispered.

Jack cleared his throat, nudged her elbow, and gestured forward. "Walk."

She did not want to be forced, so she walked toward Berkeley, who met them halfway between the jet and the Range Rover. Berkeley gazed up and down Fiona.

She's looking at me like I'm a ham at the grocery store.

"Well, the desert does preserve," said Jack quietly.

She shivered in the warping heat.

They seemed to be in a valley, with the brilliant salt beds to the south and distant mountains to the north and east. She had no idea where they might be, and felt a pang of missing Alva, who probably could have prattled off all manner of information about where they were, what the soil type was like, what the cline was, if there was any at all; and yet here she was alone, with no friends for thousands of miles. No one that she knew except for a plastic, corporate shill and a monster gloved as a man.

"Miss Hawthorne," Berkeley met her with a clipped tone, disapproving, her blandly pretty face sneering. She'd taken in Fiona's sweat-stained underarms in one glance. Fiona then wondered if perhaps at some point in her flight she *had* pissed herself.

"Miss Berkeley," returned Fiona, her teeth gritting.

Jack cleared his throat again and said, "Thank you for meeting us!"

"I trust the flight was satisfactory?" Berkeley inquired, perfunctory, obviously not really interested.

"Satisfactory?" blurted out Fiona. "Is that what you call—"

And then she felt very tired and heavy, as if a hand pressed down on her head, pushing her down; she felt her knees start to buckle and she let out a hiccup of shock and stared at Jack.

"Smile. And. Nod."

His voice, penetrating again, without moving his mouth. The voice and the unseen hand, pushing. What else could he do with his mind? She did not want to know, because she had already seen and heard enough.

Message received, asshole.

Her cheeks went hot, and her eyes prickled with the pain of unshed tears. She squeezed them shut and two tears escaped, only to be swept away in the wind, to add to the humidity on the most minuscule level, and then to turn to salt again, just as everything around her, stretching in a great white bowl meeting fangs of mountains, jutting into a bleached azure sky. She felt then the sensation of being inside a mouth: its jaw unhinged, with her in the back of its throat, ready to be swallowed, her last view of free sky perhaps forever.

"*Smile. And. Nod.*"

And so she did, a proper marionette. She decided she would be a good girl; an even better puppet.

I'll show you how well I can sing and dance.

Jack blinked at her and looked back to Berkeley.

"The flight was perfect. Thank you." He closed his hands together in a prayer pose and bowed.

Berkeley lifted her head.

"We should proceed to the facility." She turned on her heel and walked back toward the vehicle.

Fiona watched, fascinated, as Jack twisted his face a bit, and then hurried forward, away from her, toward Berkeley.

"We had an agreement. An exchange."

The woman turned and Fiona watched Jack face her down. Something seemed to sing in the air between them, some fizzing sound, or it could be that the sinus pressure Fiona felt from the flight had aggravated her tinnitus. Either way, it was an odd moment, full of charge, and if Fiona could choose a vibe from it all, it would be one of deep hostility.

There was no love between these two. It was a business transaction, whatever it was they'd agreed upon. Fiona wondered who would benefit more. She already knew she would benefit not at all; no matter who won between those two, she lost.

"You can have what you need after we get what *we* need," Berkeley said, quietly but firmly enough that Fiona could hear despite the whipping wind.

A breeze caught the ivory silk scarf around the woman's neck and sent it streaming behind her like the crest of a great bird, and in turn, Jack seemed to grow in height.

What is happening?

It was a display, she realized: one of dominance, perhaps. Certainly not one of mating, and even the thought of that sickened Fiona and she hated herself for thinking it. And yet it wasn't entirely inaccurate either. These two had built some sort of strange partnership, each of them not who they appeared to be, and half of that Fiona already knew. But Berkeley? She couldn't decipher the chilly woman or her bland-cheeked lackeys.

Money is a helluva drug.

And so was power, and for the moment, Berkeley seemed to have the upper hand there: she had the vehicle, the goons, and something Jack wanted. But what was that?

The three goons soon let her know. They approached her, their eyes covered in sunglasses, so she could not see their expressions. But this was no welcome mat they extended. They came for her, and she glanced wildly around, tempted to run, tempted to try her hand at survival in the desert. But she noticed then they bore implements on their belts: Billy stick, stun gun…actual guns too. God knew what else.

I'm damned.

"Smile. And. Nod."

She lifted her chin.

Not much point with these douchebags. Keep your smile to yourself. Is this what you wanted?

Jack watched with a furrowed brow as the three enclosed her with their large forms; she found herself staring up at one of them, who wore an implanted earring that winked and flashed in a dark blue crystal on their earlobe. That person was enormous, easily seven feet tall, a brick of a person, with a thick, ruddy neck and shaved head.

Fiona stood stock still, holding her purse, gritting her teeth.

"Miss Hawthorne," called Berkeley. "They're only here to escort you to the vehicle."

"Is this necessary?" Jack's voice, acidic, dripping with distaste.

Berkeley regarded him.

"Perhaps you do not take security seriously, Dr. Cordeiro," she told him, her eyebrows arched, "but we do. Take her wallet, Mr. Wold, and have it ready."

"Why?" Jack demanded. "You assured safe passage."

"We can only assure safe passage if we have what we need to *make* it. Do you trust her to hand over paperwork with a lucid and agreeable mind? No? I didn't think so. We'll handle that. *You* keep her in line, however you wish to do so. We have more supplements, should you need those."

"That won't be necessary," snapped Jack.

She felt…grateful? And hated herself for feeling it. For the moment, she would not be drugged, so long as she cooperated. But she already knew that he could easily control her behavior. She was his action figure, to bend and twist at his will, and he knew that she knew it. So his gaze told her, dark and calculating, but also alert for whatever Berkeley and her cadre might want.

"We get past the checkpoint, and at that point it's eyes only," Berkeley said then.

What does that *mean?*

But she soon figured it out, for she saw one of the goons, shorter and with broader shoulders, pull forth a black cloth.

Oh, goddammit. They're gonna blindfold me.

"Won't that look suspicious?" she called out. Silence met her for a moment, and Jack took off his sunglasses and squinted at her.

Berkeley half-smiled, truly a nasty sight; Fiona would prefer she frowned, for that smile smacked of venom.

"We'll not raise any suspicions. You'll be the perfect passenger. You'll ride up front with me! Jack can sit behind you." She smirked at him. "Pull your strings. But once we're beyond the checkpoint, we don't need you to see where we're going."

"Why, it's not like I can—"

"Insurance." The cold spike of a word shot from the woman's mouth. "Get in."

Fiona sighed, and walked of her own accord, though with a few trips and almost-falls, and stepped up into the Range Rover. Her skin had turned pink even in the few minutes outside. Inside the voluminous vehicle, the air conditioning blasted full on, cold at the vents, but struggling to battle the sun's power even though the ceiling of the SUV was thick. Nothing was stopping the strength of the desert sun in that brilliant, reflective bowl.

She buckled herself in, aware again of her body odor, but strangely, in this dry air, it was not so prominent. Berkeley set the car driving then, and they rode in quiet but for classical music chiming through the stereos. No one spoke, and as they continued across the bumpy access road, Fiona began to discern shapes in the distance. It was a town, she realized, shimmering there, a bit of fata morgana at play, making the colorful buildings look like ships atop a wavering sea. *Ghost ships.* She saw a sign at a traffic stop that read "Yungay," and she realized she'd heard the name before, from Alva.

"We drove from Antofagasta after a beach trip and stopped in Yungay."

It had not been Alva's favorite place, although she had loved the food. It was one of the towns on the road back to San Pedro, their base of operations. She had been glad it was not so far from the dig as to be completely removed from civilization. Fiona felt a twinge of wonder, for surely Alva must have driven on the main road into that town, the B-55, and not so long ago. Alva, alive, just doing her thing, going to get a bite to eat, or more supplies, or to stay in town overnight. It seemed so normal. And yet here Fiona was, hostage, unable to explore that same town, and unable to see her friend, because she had been killed by the creature behind her masquerading as an already detestable man; so he had been in Alva's eyes. And Fiona wondered if that girl's dark eyes had seen him coming for her. She shivered.

"Smile. And. Nod."

Fuck. Right. Off.

The road rolled on beneath them and she at one point jerked herself awake, and she could see the light begin to change; she must have been asleep for an hour, at least.

She shifted in her seat.

"I need to pee," she murmured.

"What?" Berkeley asked, tone flat yet harsh at the same time; again, perfunctory.

"I need to take a piss," said Fiona more loudly.

Berkeley turned her head back to glare at Jack. "She didn't go on the plane?"

"I did," grumbled Fiona, jaw tense. "I need to go again. Unless you want me to piss on the fine leather upholstery. Right here, right now."

Berkeley's nostrils flared and Fiona watched a flush creep up the woman's neck.

"We'll stop for gas," she snapped. "Wold, see to it she doesn't go running out the back."

Wold nodded his nearly neckless head and they pulled into a gas station. It looked nice enough, fully equipped, clean. Berkeley pulled the car up to a pump and snapped at one of her other goons to get out and pump the gas. Fiona tumbled out and shuffled toward the gas station doors, Wold close in tow. She felt Jack's eyes following her the whole way.

The scent of fuel and the metallic salt air of the desert met Fiona's dry nose; she was aware then that it was encrusted, and she needed to blow it.

Lovely.

The door to the gas station opened with a *SHLICK*, and Wold held it for her.

"Well, aren't you the gentleman," she sniped.

Wold said nothing; his face read nothing.

She rolled her eyes and strolled past candy bars and a freezer full of paletas. She could smell something on a spit in the deli section of the store. Her stomach audibly growled. The station attendant grinned at her.

He was young: perhaps a few years younger than she, but she could not tell. His hair was full of twisted, teal green dreadlocks. His skin was rich brown, and his left eyebrow bore a little scar. His ears were pierced with simple, thick silver rings. He wore a vintage T-shirt with IRON MAIDEN emblazoned across it.

"Hola," she said, and then cringed. "Um. ¿Hablas inglés?"

"Sí," said the young man. "I do."

She was not sure, but she thought she heard Wold huff his breath out.

"Thank you," she said to the young man. "Do I need a bathroom key?"

He grinned and handed a long rod to her; very old school, she thought, despite the otherwise modern gas station.

She heard another man's voice say, "¿Es esa otra turista?"

"Sí," called the cashier. "Pero ella es una bonita."

The other voice laughed. "Buena suerte."

The cashier snorted.

Fiona beamed at the cashier, and he winked back at her. She smirked.

She walked on and unlocked the bathroom door. It smelled mostly of bleach with an undercurrent of lavender. It was clean but aged, as if the bathroom were far older than the station itself. The mirror bore a metal frame that was scratched from people etching their names along it. She sat on a folded piece of toilet tissue, relieving herself, and she shuffled in her purse.

"Oh for god's sake," she muttered, finding the pancake prize fork and shoving it aside. She dug out a pen and stuck it behind her ear. Then she flushed and washed her hands. She dried them with paper towels, and then she took a fresh one of them and folded it over. She thought for a second and then scribbled to get her pen going. She then wrote a number on the paper. She tucked the pen back into her purse, patted the bag, and held the paper against her thigh. She walked out of the bathroom, where Wold waited. He watched her but did not seem to notice what she held.

She paused for a moment at the cashier counter and leaned on her elbows.

She heard Wold clear his throat.

"Those paletas sure look good," she said, gazing at the young man dreamily. She read his tag aloud, "Luis," and he smiled. She slid the paper over to him, along with the bathroom key. "Thank you."

She turned then to Wold, scowled, and swiveled to leave.

"Come back soon!" called Luis, and his partner grilled him mercilessly and cackled at him. She didn't understand what was being said, but she knew a roasting when she heard one.

She broke into a sweat then and emerged outside; the sweat vanished quickly, and Jack stared at her with every step she took back to the waiting vehicle, where Wold opened the door.

She willed her thoughts to be very, very quiet, choosing to focus on what she saw. She would not think of him, she would not think of him…only of Alva.

She tilted her head back and could see Jack smiling. He approved of *those* thoughts. Everything else she pushed down.

And after some time, she spied something in the distance.

"Is that the Hand of the Desert?" she asked, pointing.

She thought then of Alva's hand, reaching skyward for help, and she swallowed. Behind her sat a glove over a hand of evil.

"It is," replied Berkeley. "And this is where we blindfold you, Miss Hawthorne."

Before she could say anything, a band of black fell over her eyes, and she sucked in a breath. Only darkness remained.

CHAPTER 30
DESICCATION

She had no sense for time, exactly. Someone had handed her a power bar, some vague fruit flavor like dried apple, which tasted stale to her; she wondered how old it was, or if the aridity had made it go stale more quickly. She had eaten it gratefully still, and choked down some bottled water, which mercifully was kept cool somehow; they must have had a small cooler in the vehicle. She had felt the vehicle come to stops and take turns. She wished someone could see her, blindfolded as she was, but no one stopped them, and she knew the windows bore a dark tint.

No one spoke much, though occasionally Berkeley's lackeys would ask seemingly benign questions of the woman, and she would reply with clipped "Yes" or "No" or, most intriguingly, "We'll discuss it upon arrival."

Arrival *where?*

Fiona's thoughts wavered between despair at her situation and still some lingering hope that, whatever horror lay before her, she hadn't arrived at it yet, and presumably the CUPRUM contingent wanted no harm to come to her while they traveled. She thought the blindfold was silly; who would she tell where she was? She had no working phone; she could not escape them. She dared not think of her act in the gas station again, for fear Jack would pick up her thoughts. She wasn't sure, but she suspected that the walls of the building had shielded her somewhat. She preferred not testing that theory by thinking of anything overt.

She was jolted hard and then felt her body lean to the right, so she surmised they had taken a left off the main road, and now traveled on far more rustic pavement. She did not enjoy that prospect, because the farther into the desert they were, the lower her chances for escape, or for anyone to find her.

Well, of course. They have something in the middle of nowhere.

Yet she wished she could see. Alva had spoken of the road to San Pedro as being long, and at one point branching north. But Fiona could not remember much else about the conversation, just that it had been a long day trip, typical for a desert road excursion; sparse towns, rustic establishments; ghost towns galore, the old *salitreras* from saltpeter mining days, some of which Fiona knew were protected as heritage sites. She would have loved to have seen them.

But on they went, bumping, and for once she praised the idea of a high-end SUV, for at least its shocks bore some of the road's ruts well. She knew they would not be there because of any rain, but from wear, and then she wondered how many vehicles might go out this strange, unseen road, and why. Why would a global company maintain a presence in such a remote place, away from the major towns, and indeed away from the landing strip for their private jets?

It unsettled her anew to think along these lines. But gradually the Range Rover slowed, and at one point, it rolled over something with a *CLANG!* They had crossed over some kind of barrier. She heard a slow grinding sound and speculated it must be a gate. Berkeley drove forward and muttered something to someone; Fiona could not tell who, someone in the car, or someone on a phone.

And then the vehicle stopped, with the crunch of some kind of gravel beneath its tires signaling a different surface than the road they'd just been on. Doors began opening; voices met Berkeley as she stepped out. And finally she felt a rubbery sensation as hands— gloved hands—removed her blindfold. She blinked and rubbed her eyes and found herself staring directly into Jack's eyes. She slid out of her seat and onto the gravel, wobbled for a moment, and steadied herself. She turned this way and that, and found the sky had taken on a softer palette. It arched in a rainbow of pastels as the sun dipped, with mountains in the distance glowing maroon, or other radiant colors in bands. Beneath her feet, the pebbles were white, like ice pellets, many about the size of marbles. The heat of the desert wafted up from the gravel through her shoes and up her legs, in addition to the incredible air, sucking all liquid away quickly.

She beheld then a low series of buildings, resembling an artistic adobe style, pale, quite as if they were enormous pebbles themselves; they blended with the environment, and she guessed that from the air they might be difficult to see. And indeed someone came and drove the Range Rover down into a garage below them. Two of Berkeley's assistants walked off to one of the buildings and entered a door that at first, she could not distinguish from the rest of the building. It was all cleverly camouflaged. No one would see vehicles from above; but a fence, a gate, maybe? She wasn't sure of that either, for she could not see one when she turned to look back up the gravel drive.

Then it struck her: what could they possibly need this nearly invisible place for, in the middle of the Atacama Desert? They were not so close to Alva's site here, surely. But she had no sense for that, because she had been blindfolded. She looked again at the mountains and thought back to Alva's photos. No, Alva had been closer to those mountains than they were here. *"Thrust upward like knives,"* she had written to Fiona. It might not have been a drastic difference, but being a mountain-raised girl herself, Fiona understood those kinds of distances, and the spaces in between, which could be subtle and tricky, adding more time for travel than one might originally suspect. Even in lush Appalachia, which at this point, she felt might as well be on another planet.

Now I see why they trained for Mars out here.

It was harsh and savage yet stunning and haunting, the fading daylight painting the desert mystical hues, colors her watercolors back home could never achieve. There was no life here, in this stretch. No plants. Salts aplenty; spheres of it, in fact, scattered upon the earth here and there.

Jack watched her.

"What do you think of it?" His hands in his pockets, pushing them out again, as was his habit.

"I think it's beautiful," she said slowly, her face blank, neutral; she fought against thinking of Lafe, and wondering how he was doing, and if, in another life, they could have traveled here together under other circumstances. "But it's old and silent and full of ghosts. I don't belong here."

She thought of her father as well. His favorite movie was *Lawrence of Arabia*, and she knew that he had visited Chile, but not the Atacama. She wondered what he might think of this place; she felt a pang of missing him and her mother, despite their tendency to argue.

What will Mom and Dad think if I don't call them?

"*Shhhh.*" Jack grinned and silently goaded her to still her thoughts. Aloud, he said, "I think you belong here."

She trembled a little, tried not to think of the implications of his statement, and realized then how hungry she was.

"Right," Berkeley called, breaking the moment. "I've asked for dinner, and then we can discuss plans."

Fiona and Jack followed her and her assistants up to one of the "invisible" doors, which glowed softly where a doorknob might be. Berkeley swiped her hand across it and it opened, rather blended outward instead of making a sharp entrance.

Fiona wondered then if it were all a mirage; if there were no door, if it, like so much else in the desert, were fata morgana; an illusion, a fever dream, a hallucination, a forgotten tale whirled away in sands and in desiccated hopes.

She followed through that door and instantly felt moisture in the air, and blinking, beheld something of an oasis; the ceiling was translucent yet present, allowing the sky through, and as they walked down into the structure, a group of palms and cycads surrounded a bubbling mineral spring. All of it encased in this hidden building in the driest place on Earth. She knew there were natural oases in the Atacama, and lakes, of course, but where this facility lay like a cluster of shells upon a large beach, there were no plants. So these had been brought in, and by the look of them, they had been established and protected for many years. There were plants tucked in every corner of the place, and little alcoves, and soft seats blending into the curving, pale walls; some of these changed hues to match the pastel afternoon sky outside, others morphed along cool pinks and purples and teals.

It was a naturally flowing style, yet nothing natural other than the plants existed in it. Everyone she could see, a dozen or so employees walking to and from different areas, some carrying small, clear tablets, others wearing thin visors, still others wearing gems on their earlobes, muttering, discussing…each struck her as insipid and dull. Attractive yet only in the dullest fashion; symmetrical of face, some of them, or with hair scooped back, or under small caps; all of their clothes looked more or less alike, except some of them bore different stitching around the embroidered name CUPRUM on their lapels.

The place gave her the creeps. She was put in mind of a special spa she'd gone to as a bridesmaid once, for a friend's wedding in college; a rich friend, who could afford to host all her several bridesmaids for massages and facials. She had felt uncomfortable then, as it was not her sort of place, but she was far more uneasy now. There was no sense for this kind of wealth in such an impoverished region. Fiona found it offensive. And she wondered again what it could all possibly be for, and what kind of people would want to do this?

"Welcome to the Lab," announced Berkeley suddenly. "You can have your dollar tour after dinner," she sneered, and then she gestured toward another room.

Entering the room, Fiona found a long table, everything brightly lit; harshly so. It looked clinical. The ceiling, however, again showed her the sky outside, yet they were all protected from the elements in here. She thought it must be around 45 percent humidity; dry for Tennessee, but moist compared to the desert; an ideal humidity for clean air, and to prevent allergies (so her allergist had told her years ago).

As she sat in a curved, white, acrylic seat at the long, white table, she asked, "What is this place?"

"This," Berkeley answered, taking a sip of an offered glass of sparkling water, in which bobbed a slice of fresh cucumber, "is our artifact facility."

Artifact facility?

"Why is it in the middle of nowhere?" Fiona stared at her, aware again that everyone looked immaculate except for her. She shifted her purse onto her lap, under the table. She did not want to let it go. "Like, what kind of artifacts?"

"Well, as your Professor Bingham knows, we study botany; specifically, xeric botany, as well as survivability in harsh environments. Since the age-old notion of the desert being lifeless was long ago proven false. We also develop new technologies."

She glanced briefly at Jack, who held onto his water glass but did not drink it.

A server brought in small bowls of chilled, green soup with some sort of herb sprinkled on top.

"Of course, we were limited in scope and scale here, thanks to the heritage site." And Berkeley's voice took on an edge of...disgust? Fiona was unsure. "So we helped fund academic research, such as Dr. Bingham's and your own.

"There are different waypoints around the globe that contain archaeological artifacts no one understands, recently found at roughly the same time a year prior, which have been kept closely guarded by various governments. Dr. Gilden's research team which went to the desert was unaware that they were inadvertently looking for an artifact. Jim Chao knew, and your friend Alva knew, but the other team did not. It's unclear whether Rian knew. That study was funded with our money."

Fiona sat dumbfounded.

"I...never knew," she admitted.

"Well, why would you? Your studies are tangential to our main cause."

"Which is...?"

Berkeley dabbed the corners of her mouth and set her soup spoon down with a clink.

"CUPRUM has injected more money into the Atacama's older populations than any local governments ever could have. In turn, we do research; we gather resources from the desert, we test nanotech processes; it's unfettered access, it's got a clean environment, and there's great signal clarity from here."

That confused Fiona. "How could there be great signal from here, in the middle of nowhere?"

Berkeley smirked over her glass at Jack.

"It depends upon the *kind* of signal."

What?

Jack looked uncomfortable; his face twisted into a frown, and she had rarely seen that expression on his face. It disturbed her more than his treacly smiles.

"We just need certain...*instructions* for our current endeavors to work."

Fiona mulled over the words she'd just heard.

"So...the Gilden team was working on something entirely different than—than they knew about?" she said slowly.

"Well, it was in tandem with their other research; mutually beneficial," added Berkeley.

The soup course was replaced with an elaborate salad full of some nebulous protein, berries, greens, dressing, and what looked like quinoa. Fiona pecked at hers.

"So you put them all at risk."

Berkeley blinked. "There is always risk with field research."

"They're *dead*. Did you think that was part of their research?" Fiona's voice rose.

"Enough," came Jack's mental command, but she brushed it off.

She grew hot.

"Alva was my best friend. There's no way—no fucking way she'd sign up to do something that wasn't aligned with her research, not for some shady, hidden company."

"Miss Hawthorne," Berkeley said, her voice much louder then, and everyone at the table halted their eating to turn and stare at the two women. "We gave you all funding when no one else would. *We* kept the clothes on your backs and the lights on in your homes because we knew how important this project was; it was the least we could do."

"To do what? Clear your conscience of their murders?" She was shouting now. She pointed at Jack. "By *him?*"

"You're ridiculous. Wold!" she called into a commlink watch. The door to the dining room opened. "Escort Miss Hawthorne out and put her in one of the labs. Doesn't matter which. She can eat later."

Jack stood abruptly then.

"She stays with me," he declared.

Berkeley eyed him lazily. "Then Wold can add you to the same lab. In fact, why don't we accelerate things? We've some more artifacts to test. Show us the scaffolding tech. On *her.*" She glanced at Fiona. "Give us answers: about your kind, your technology, your methods. Otherwise we don't need either of you." She dabbed the corners of her mouth. "It's clear we don't have an agreement."

"You said," bellowed Jack, "that we had a deal. That I would give you the tech, and you would give me Fiona."

"*Give* me to *you?*" Fiona echoed. "You kidnapped me: both of you. You forced me out of the country and to…wherever this place is!"

Berkeley laughed, hollow, cold. "Wold," she commanded again.

And then the plates on the table went flying in a crash, as something pale yellow and quivering shot across it and seized

Berkeley by the throat. Her hands flew to it, but it lifted her up. Fiona turned to stare and found that an appendage had erupted from Jack's abdomen, and now it coiled itself around Berkeley's neck.

"Jack!" she shrieked. "Don't!"

The other workers screamed and ran for the door, but another appendage shot out from Jack, and it blocked the doorway.

Wold burst in, and that shuddering, creeping thing caught him and squeezed, and his eyes bulged, and then the man screamed as his features began to collapse in on themselves. He let out one final gurgling yell, and then he fell. His flesh slid off his bones, and all of his organic material began to slough off into piles.

This is what happened to Gale, oh God…this is what happened to Alva.

She sat perfectly still, watching in horror as Berkeley gagged and began to turn blue-purple.

"Jack, please, no!"

But it was too late, and a wrenching, shuddering crack sounded, and the woman fell face first onto the table, and she began to dissolve as well. The screams that erupted then reverberated in Fiona's ears, and she wept and covered her head on the table; one by one, the gurgling, squelching noises ceased the screams, and the smell of feces and vomit and blood and something else, elemental and stark, filled the air.

An alarm had sounded by then, but nothing was getting through that door.

Jack then shuddered, and his two extra appendages snapped into his abdomen again with slurping and snapping noises. He tucked his shirt in and tidied his collar, and brushed his hair back with his hand-gloves.

He then stared at Fiona.

"We will go now."

Shaking, she gasped, "Where?"

"To the cave."

CHAPTER 31
LA CAVERNA DE LOS SUSURROS

The alarms shrieked, and the pair ran. Past confused workers in the hall who, one by one, realized something had gone very wrong indeed, and they fled. Three security guards barreled into the main salon, facing off Fiona and Jack at the oasis: gunshots rang, and Fiona bounded to the floor and covered her head and cried out. The bullets, however, slid right through Jack, and in retaliation, he sent forth cables of himself: golden threads flying around the necks of the guards, snapping them: each collapsed dead and began to dissolve in sheets.

"We'll take the truck," he said matter-of-factly, as though he presented her with a Sunday drive.

She could stay behind, call for help; she felt terrible for everyone there, but she also knew beyond any doubt that this man-creature would stop at nothing, he would not let her go. He wanted her, and still she did not understand why.

"Jack," she said hoarsely, as they ran out into the gravel drive, where the instant dryness and the encroaching chill of the desert night struck her immediately, "Jack, stop."

"No," he urged. "We need to get out of here, get you safe."

"Jack, how do we get the truck? How are we going to get anywhere? Don't you think they've called authorities?"

Jack tilted his head at her, and glancing out of the corner of his eye, he saw another guard approach, gun drawn. Casually, he opened the collar of his shirt and a new stalk erupted from his skin and whipped outward, seizing the gun from the guard's hand, and then used it to smash the man's face in.

"Stop!" Fiona cried. "These people are innocent. Leave them be!"

"They are not innocent," thundered Jack. "They are complicit in every death; they brought it upon themselves, just as they brought it upon your friends, and who knows who else in the desert."

She stared at him, but he seized her hand and pulled her in the direction of the garage.

"But *you* killed them!"

"I didn't!" he roared.

"You killed Alva." She said this quietly, in a soft voice. She felt helpless, like a little child.

He halted their running then and looked down at her.

"I did not destroy Alva," he told her, staring her directly in the eyes, as if he believed the lie himself. "You will see."

The awfulness of the prospect of seeing her friend dead, in the manner in which Jack had killed Berkeley and Wold and the others, was too much to bear, and she wept, but he pulled her on anyway. And ultimately, she decided, what could she do? Stay there? And he might finally be persuaded to kill her as well? If she had one last chance at survival, and it meant going with Jack, she had to take it, no matter how much she hated and feared the idea.

They arrived at the garage door, and it was as well-concealed as all the other doors. Jack puzzled over it for a moment.

"Keypad," she said breathlessly. "There must be…a keypad, or secure lock. We don't have access—"

"I have what I need," he said in a self-assured tone. "I took it from Berkeley myself."

Fiona shuddered, watching him; he placed his hand against the curving adobe-like structure, and she watched in awe as the garage opened. Another guard met him, and Jack picked the man up bodily and threw him against the ground, where he sputtered and then fell unconscious.

"No more," cried Fiona. "No more deaths!"

He wheeled on her, feet skidding on the slick, artistic pavement of the garage floor. "If anyone tries to stop us, I'm taking them out. Now come with me."

She slipped and slid along the garage, and they found several vehicles: HUM-Vs, Range Rovers, bespoke electric vehicles, a tow truck, a half dozen vans…it stretched down into the darkness, dimly lit by overhead lights. But the only one Jack sought was the Range Rover Berkeley had driven, and soon he found it. The key sat in the ignition, as the facility itself had been secured, so all the keys remained in their vehicles. And so they scrambled inside, and Jack turned the ignition, and they hurtled up and out of the facility.

Myriad stars speckled the twilit sky, and they roared out into the night, sending showers of gravel spinning into the air. The gate barely opened in time to let them out; Fiona heard the scraping of metal on the side of the SUV. And off they traveled on the road.

"We won't have long," he declared, as they bumped along the rutted road.

"Where are we going?" she asked.

"To the cave, like I said."

"What cave?"

"La Caverna de Los Susurros," he answered.

She mulled over the words. "The Cavern of Whispers," she said slowly.

She shivered. She rolled the passenger window down and let the wind take her hair and splay it out, although part of it was matted, and all of it was filthy. Still, she wanted freedom; wind gave her some semblance of it when nothing else could at that moment. Jack did not seem to mind. For where could she go? She could jump from the vehicle, but he would come after her. She could try to wander off into the desert at some random opportunity, but he would find her. She was in his thrall now with no way out.

She would see it through to the end. If that meant her end, then at least maybe she could say goodbye to Alva, while she was at it.

The wind funneled down from the mountains, cold and hollow yet also full of secrets and the hints of some redolent bloom from far away, beyond these salt-encrusted valleys and pits. The stars and the sickle moon trembled in indigo twilight, the last glimpse of sunset to the west copper-gold on the horizon, the sun long gone. In her mouth, she tasted salt. Her eyelashes were stuck together with it, from her tears or from the very air, she was not sure. Her lips were cracked, her nose caked with dried blood. Yet that cool wind flowed over her, baptized her with unknowable power. She was at the mercy of so many things beyond her control. Somehow the wind eased her fear, and she slipped into a calm state.

Then Jack turned off the headlights and pulled off the main road.

"What are you doing?" she asked.

"Hiding. They have drones, and we may as well not give them more opportunity than they need to find us. The cave is down this road."

"I hope you know it well."

"Oh, I know it, Fiona. I have crawled above and below it for longer than your kind has walked the Earth."

Darkness welled up and poured down simultaneously, land and sky blending, only the stars—stars beyond fathoming, clusters of them, constellations with which she was not familiar, in the southern hemisphere—coursing slowly in the ceiling above the Atacama.

The vehicle bobbed and thumped and scraped along the abandoned desert road. Old foundations poked up from the sands, remnants of settlements, from old mines. The settlers had dug deep, exhausted one supply, and moved onto the next. The same was true all across the desert, from the sea to the base of the Andes themselves. Pockmarks of boom times, of greed, of ignorance, of debauchery, of glory, of forgotten towns, of families come and gone, and yet above it all that firmament wheeled, and below it all, something had crept unknown, patiently, waiting, watching. And now it had found what it was looking for.

It had found *her.*

She was too tired to question why anymore.

She felt at peace for the moment, in that manner that only starlight can bestow. That she was one speck of countless many, and now she knew for certain, the many included something *other*, something that took on the shapes of people…of animals, too? She wondered. Of ghost ships and chupacabras and legends and friends and enemies, maybe. And whatever these creatures were, they could afford to wait. But what they wanted, she was not sure. To take over the world? Take over part of the world? Survive? In that they had so much in common, and yet their approach differed.

In the darkness, Jack looked askance at her.

"Do you not see what your kind has wrought upon your world? Look around you. Ruins of towns. Craters where forests used to be. Your dead layered upon each other like the sediments of those mountains out there. And yet you see me as *monster*."

"I—I don't—"

"You do. I can see it in your face, and even without pushing I can sense it in your mind."

"Why do you look like us?"

"It's easy, isn't it? I can walk among you, protected for a time. I can understand."

"Understand what?"

"What I'm up against."

"Are there more of you?"

"There are always more of me."

She shivered in her seat.

"But there are always more of your kind too. Just…none special. You alone."

"Why me?"

"Soon, Fiona, soon."

Her lower lip trembled, and she looked up again at the stars, wondering how many more up there hosted something like Jack…or something like herself, spinning on those distant worlds, looking back down at her from the heavens, listening, watching, waiting. She felt so very small then, an infant among ancients.

The vehicle slowed, and she flicked the tears from the corners of her eyes, and settled into a feeling of dread, chilled from within and from the rapidly cooling desert without. Jack put the SUV in park and set the parking brake.

"We're here."

He opened his door, and then he opened hers, and she slid off into soft sand, pale as snow. It was mixed with salt, she knew, and it drifted in ripples. But she could see a bit of a badland, an ancient wash, and Jack stood at the opening of this small canyon and beckoned.

"Come, and listen to the whispers."

He shouldered a small bag.

"To what whispers?"

"In the cave. Come."

Staggering along, completely exhausted, parched, tossing back swigs from a water bottle, her purse bumping on her hip, she followed. She shuffled among the sand until her shoes, now partially filled with that sand, met harder earth, and darker: the sandstone of the canyon. They began to descend.

They walked for a good quarter of a mile, and occasionally Jack would glance back. Sometimes he would stop, and they would watch lights high overhead. Planes, maybe, or they could have been drones, she supposed. She caught sight of an old satellite streaking above; another time, a late Perseid meteor, green upon entry. The desert was quiet except for the wind, which whirled in its own music, a sound garden howling and whistling, and among the sandstone cliffs, moaning and wailing too, and finally, at the mouth of a cave, they stood: and then she heard the whispers.

She shook from head to toe, listening, listening: voices, were they? It sounded like soft murmurings, those whispers: a reverberating set of forgotten messages uttered from lips long shuttered. They spun out of the cave and met her, and they echoed back in, as if alive.

Jack pulled a flashlight from his bag.

"I've got lanterns down in," he told her.

Now why would you do that? She wondered.

Ever the puzzle, this monster-man.

The smell of the cave, which stretched over Jack's head, was that of salt, like sea air. The whispers even reminded her a little of the distant pounding of surf. Descending further into the cave, she listened, and was reminded of holding a seashell to her ear as a child, "So that you can hear the ocean!" her mother had told her. The rushing of sound had been an auditory illusion, and this cave was no different, an illusion just like everything else in the desert.

She began to wonder if she was her own form of illusion to someone, or to the desert itself.

I do not belong here.

"Yes, you do," murmured Jack.

They stopped, and she found herself in a vaulted portion of the cave. A small shaft several feet above revealed the smear of stars shining feebly through, yet that gave her hope. For down here, she was alone with the beast at last, far from anyone who could ever help her again.

She thought of the cave paintings at Lascaux, that she had learned about her freshman year at the university where she would eventually work. In the lab where her life would intersect with Jack Cordeiro, or what remained of him. All of civilization emerged from caves, or from trees, or some combination of both. There were no trees here, but something dwelt in this cave, some forgotten entity. Did it belong there?

"You can sleep under the stars," he said quietly. "That is a fitting spot."

She eyed him. He lit his lanterns, and all about them she found small enclaves, and a few blankets and baskets, some of them quite old. She wondered how old. There was another chamber off to one end, shrouded in darkness, beyond the reach of the lanterns.

"For how long?" she said aloud, and the whispers of the cave swept around her and made her feel quite sleepy then.

"As long as it takes."

Oh, I do not like the sound of that.

"Why did you bring me here?"

Jack beamed, the lantern shadows on his face awful; the tautness of his skin-mask had begun to shrivel, and it aged and warped him. It made him look distinctly other, despite the humanoid features he wore.

"This is where I emerged," he told her. He shone the flashlight all around them.

"As I said, we crashed here, ages ago, long before your ancestors marched across the savannas. Most of us didn't survive the high copper ore deposits here; some of us burrowed deep, and we dwelt in pockets deep underground, trapped…the miners did not know this, when they began to dig. But chiefly, they stuck to copper, so few of them found us. It did not go well for those who did, but that is where some of the legends of the desert began. Still, we slept long, and we crawled, and we dragged ourselves further, but in the end, we were trapped. Until core samples began.

"CUPRUM bartered mine owners; there is a lot of nefarious activity in the Atacama surrounding that, just as there is legitimate. Land upon which no one is technically allowed to mine anymore, much less perform research on. Everything hush-hush; CUPRUM excels at that sort of thing."

"What could they want to be here, though? What kind of tech?" She turned in place and held her hands up to the sky. "There's nothing here."

"Oh, but there is," and Jack smiled, and his body quavered. She feared he might send his gelatinous stalks at her, but he simply trembled, and then she heard a shiver and a hiss of gravel, and then something began to emerge from the ground.

It pieced itself together in a kind of framework.

"The scaffold," she breathed, and she froze in terror. "What is it?"

"In this case, it is something old. Watch."

He worked like a conductor, moving his hands to and fro, and the teetering form that emerged all around them grew to huge size, enveloping the entire cave. She saw long curves, rows up on rows of them…

"Bones?" she whispered, eyeing the shape. "Whale bones. Like the fossils!"

"Ah, but they can live again," he murmured. "Remade."

"Wait, are you…are you bringing it back to life?"

"I could. But it would not be quite as it was. Alive in a different sense. Scaffolded, rebuilt."

She shook her head vigorously. This was wrong: this was an abomination.

"I don't want to see it. Don't bring it back. Not here, not in the desert: that's cruel. There is no water here, in this particular spot. There hasn't been in millennia."

He lowered his hands, and the scaffolding collapsed.

"It is difficult without water. Slower, harder to maintain. Such boundaries here, and yet such openness and purity."

She faced him in the flickering lantern light.

"Why, why do you have me here?"

"You are remarkable."

He eyed her face, and framed it with his hands, but did not touch her.

"I'm not. I'm not even remotely remarkable! I'm not talented beyond sketches, I never get pay raises, my grades aren't awesome. I'm just…I'm *unremarkable*."

"You were remarkable to *her*."

"To…"

"Alva," answered Jack. "I have the imprints of her thoughts in my own mind. So I know you, Fiona. I have known you for some time. Through Alva."

Fiona let out a small whine.

"Where is she? What did you do with her?"

Jack smiled, his teeth glowing in the dim light of the cave. He gestured to the other chamber.

"Let's visit her, shall we?"

And as Fiona followed him, her heart pounding, nausea rollicking through her, she heard whispers again…only this time, she heard *Alva's* voice.

"Wait until you see this, Fiona. You won't believe it!"

Was that Alva now? But no: Fiona paused. It was a memory. It was Alva's voice, yes…but from a phone call. Months prior.

Alva spoke again, sometimes at a pitch that Fiona could make out, other items in the faintest voice, a distant signal poorly received. Fiona wept as she followed Jack along. They entered the chamber. The whispers encircled Fiona, encircled her very memories.

"Here you are at last, reunited," murmured Jack.

And he slowly angled his flashlight onto the floor of the cavern, as the whispers rose like a wind all about Fiona. There on the floor of the cave lay a congealed mass.

The mass that used to be Alva.

Fiona let out a clipped cry. She wanted to vomit but could not.

Jack merely grinned at her, looking from the mass to her face and back again.

"You see, I knew you through her. You fascinate me, Fiona. I could not discover anyone else quite like you, who had so imprinted upon someone's mind the way you had upon Alva's. I'm glad I've collected you. I can unmake you now too. Here at the source where I emerged."

Her mouth went dry, parched as the walls around her, and she realized she'd dropped her water bottle somewhere.

I'm going to die in here, then.

Her lips cracked and the encrusted stress hives on her neck throbbed. She had felt continually at his mercy, forced to perform as a functional person under his puppetry, yet trapped in her agony, for her mind remained intact. Barely. Here she was at the terminus of her own life, and the beginning of his, on Earth.

Jack traced his thumb, gloved as it was with the mimic of flesh, down the middle of her forehead. "It's something in here. And you're not letting me in. But you are remarkable despite what you say. I knew her mind. Her thoughts so lucid in the final moments of her life and floating through her flickering mind after her heart stopped. She reached out to *you* because you were special to her. I see it, almost. If I were to open you up, I might clarify it."

She trembled. At this point, she wished he would just end things. Hearing him talk so casually, while smiling with his radiant white teeth, in his fashionable clothing, sent waves of ice down her spine.

"But if I open you up," he went on, pulling his thumb away and looking at it, as if he had extracted something from her skin—*Maybe he did*, she thought—"then it might disrupt what made you special. A quandary. I've unmade them, but I think unmaking you might ruin you."

Ya think?

"I think, then, you are to be the template."

"Template?" she echoed hoarsely. "Template for what?"

"What is unmade can be made anew," he said, beaming at the rows of quivering death on the floor. "And made with you."

She recoiled and jerked away from him, and he ignored her to walk over and stand over Alva's remains. He held his hand above them and they began to rise up in long, glistening yellow cables.

Oh god.

"We are makers. We improve. We work to craft betterment."

"What. Are. You?" she whispered.

"We are the scaffold of the universe, Fiona." Jack's voice sounded reverent. "What perfect rails upon which to build, with someone like you. Treasured by others, loved, respected, revered. You will be our scaffold now."

"No!" cried Fiona, but he walked casually over to her, held his hand in front of her face, and she could feel her skin tugging. She knew instinctively that he could rip her very skin from her body, but instead he pulled it into a different position, into an unwilling smile.

"That's better," he sighed. "You should smile more."

So she smiled even as horror-tears pooled in her dry eyes from abject fear.

"You see," said the not-Jack being, or whatever it was. He shone like melting wax then, catching the light in pits of his face where wrinkles might normally fall, "I held Alva's impression of you in my head all the way back to your home. But this is so much better, isn't it? For you to be here. For you to make all of this"—and he swept his hands into a wide arc—"happen. For us all."

She wanted to talk then but could only smile. She felt him pull at her skin, but also felt her very thoughts pulled as well, try as she might to keep them hidden. He was a magnet for everything private in her mind; he drew it forward. She sensed that he could yank it out with violence, and shred her physically as well, or melt her...or whatever he had done to poor Alva and the others.

The bodies in the desert were fake.

She realized that now. He'd disposed of anything remaining of Alva's research team. But he'd kept her…enshrined her, even.

So he would easily produce some facsimile of Fiona as well. He could manufacture any tale he wished: that she had fled the country, that she had gone in search of her friend, that she had been an accomplice somehow. This was her paranoia bubbling to the surface of her mind, and he knew it, and he played her thoughts like broken piano keys in a strange and lonely melody from which she had no escape.

My friendship damned me.

Not-Jack began to laugh then, not in a wicked tone, but one of pure delight.

"Is that what you really think, then?"

He advanced on her and marched around her, massaging her thoughts with his powerful manipulation, forcing the smile again. But then he raised his hand and her face fell, relaxed, exhausted. Her jaw muscles ached.

"I would say," he said slowly, curling his hands so that he looked at his fingernails, which looked again too perfect, too manufactured to be human, "your friendship *liberated* you. No one else on your planet was deemed worthy for this. No one! You are free of them. Free of that simpering worm, Graham, who rifled through your private belongings and your emails and would your very thoughts, if he could."

Fiona's cheeks burned with hot rage intermixed with sorrowful remembrance. Graham had not been a perfect partner, but he was not…not-Jack. And Jack's "your planet" chilled her back to reality.

"What was so special about that creature, Lafe, however?" pondered Jack, steepling his fingers under his immaculate chin. "Troublesome, trembling, gawking, skinny ape."

Fiona tried desperately to say something, but she remained locked in a paralysis of a sort. So she could only breathe forcefully, and that made her dizzy. She tried not to think of Lafe overly much, for she felt deep down he would be killed if she did, and she simply did not have the capacity to cope with that potential just now…or ever.

"Don't strain, Fiona," murmured Jack, approaching her again and leaning down. She could smell his—its—breath again, sweet and sickly yet a tad singed, syrupy and metallic at the same time. It was the least human thing about him, she now realized. He did not exist the same way that she did.

What do you really *look like? Beyond the skin, beyond the gelatin? What more is there?*

That thought shot out of her like a dart despite her attempt to stop it.

"I can show you," he whispered, hazel eyes fixed on her green ones. "I can show you everything we do, and everywhere we are. It won't help you to fight. You couldn't fight us all."

CHAPTER 32
THE LOST SALT CONGEALS

Jack looked comfortable, casual, nonchalant, even as he threatened her life.

"Bridget Gilden's team breached a barrier in her dig, and asked Jack Cordeiro to investigate. He fell in here, and they only pulled him out several hours later. *Remade.*

"He'd found a dome of material, like a hardened bubble. He pressed on it, and released me. So I remade him. I scaffolded; he was perfect, you see. And then I visited the team in his guise, and I teased out their thoughts, working my way through each mind, and remaking as I went."

Fiona stood shaking, crying in silence.

"The funny thing is, Cordeiro was associated with a NASA researcher, closer to San Pedro, to the northeast. They were training for Mars, of course. And for finding potential life there. The irony of it!"

He smiled through Jack's visage:

"You know, it was most fortunate for us, but not for him, that he should be the one to fall. The one to find us. The perfect host, a master manipulator. Perfect in all ways except for one: he lacked empathy. He was self-centered. In the short term, that worked well, but we realized we needed someone more convincing. Someone inherently good, yet unassuming. We found that person in Alva's thoughts: we found *you*.

"You are perfect for us. Caring, convincing, steadfast, a perfect friend. You are the template."

"The template for what?"

"The template for which we will unmake your kind, and build ourselves anew."

A template. So, Eve. They want me to be an Eve.

"How trite! No, this is not a story of the fall of humanity. It is about the bridge back to our world. A planet full of you. You do not become a mother of us. You become a god for them."

She shook her head.

"I don't want this."

"You don't have a choice. It's already begun. We've warped your mind at the neural level; there is no stopping us. You are the Unmaker and the Maker."

"No!"

"Shhh. Shhh. You cannot stop us. Don't fight. Just lie back and let it happen."

"I never wanted this! You can't do this!"

"We already did. The moment we shook your hand, we began."

She thought back to that moment in Doc's office. She leaned over and dry heaved.

A handshake, one handshake, and I destroy humanity. No. I really am Eve in this. There is no winning. There is only death.

"You won't die. We will keep you going forever; an endless supply of your very essence, repeated over and over and over again. Your legacy. Not your death."

"No, not my death."

She reached into her purse and seized…something. Long, slender, poky.

She grasped it and held it up.

She closed her eyes for a moment.

Alva. For Alva.

The Jack-thing laughed.

"*Your* death!" she shouted.

She thrust it into his left eye and twisted, and the laugh became a shriek, and then a low, horrible moan, and sparks formed from the tips of the fork. The being flung back and flailed and began to bubble all over.

"Whawawwahwhawaat did you dooooooooo?" it screamed.

She shook violently, watching the shapes on the floor bubble also and spew long strands of yellow slime in all directions, splashing her. She chattered and sputtered and flung it off her.

"You—you didn't like the company," she gasped. "CUPRUM. Copper miners. But there was no copper in this dig. That—that's what made it unusual. Right? No copper. So you survived. When none of your other…travelers did upon crashing here. But this spot: no copper. You lived. Until now. This fork. Is made of bronze, so…copper."

Blue sparks coursed through the creature. It could not operate its arms, and so could not dislodge the fork. But just to be sure, she stepped on its arms; the gloves slipped off. The arms collapsed beneath her feet in crunching slime like honeycomb. Fighting the urge to vomit, she stared down into the gaping maw of what once looked like Jack Cordeiro's head, his dark hair oozing off the scalp, a gale of wheezes escaping his chest, which began to fold in on itself. Long ropes of pale-gold slime lashed her, and she shoved the fork deeper. The blobs below her wailed, and she thought for a moment she even heard Alva's voice, but she shoved that down and dug in deep with the fork. She stabbed repeatedly and shouted through gritted teeth, "For Alva!"

Then Jack's skull collapsed, and its eyes rolled out and fizzed and ruptured on the cave floor. Blood and honey-like slime remained and then a final bright, blue arc of light cracked through the air, and all the blobs dissolved and turned into golden dust.

She staggered onto her side and gasped and coughed, her lungs full of death, and she looked up at the tiny shaft of light, quiet starlight, and she began to weep.

CHAPTER 33
UPDRAFT

S he ran then. She ran, she pumped her legs until they burned, and she did not look back. She doubled over at one point, fell upon her knees, and gasped and gulped the cold desert night air. She stumbled and stood, and she ran again, flailing, all the way back to the SUV.

She flung open the doors and she threw herself inside, and for good measure, she locked herself in.

And then she screamed.

She screamed and wailed and wept and gripped the steering wheel and yelled more. And then she took in gulps of air, shook her hair out of her face, turned the key.

"Oh, thank fuck," she whispered to herself.

But before she put the car in drive, she stared back the way she had run.

"I'm sorry, Alva. I'm so sorry."

And then she drove.

It took some time before she could figure out where she was, but she kept the headlights on, and hoped against hope she wouldn't be pulled over. She drove like a fiend, barreling along, glancing over her shoulder as though something might emerge behind her. She emerged from the dirt road onto the road she felt certain Berkeley had driven her down; she glanced at the dark mountains and made a judgment call. She turned right and hoped for the best.

Her decision proved to be the correct one, and she drove in the darkness until at one point, nausea overtook her, and she pulled off the road, opened the car door, and leaned out to vomit.

Then she wept again, and shook her head, wiped her eyes, shut the door, and continued on. The sky grew flatter with the approach of dawn, shielded by the enormous mountains to the east. Oncoming car headlights streaked by her in the other lane, and her head raged with the beginning of a migraine. She let any drivers behind her pass by, again hoping no police pulled her over.

By and by the traffic gradually increased, and she could see the winking shimmer of a town in the distance. She gasped: there was the gas station. She pulled in.

It was open, but there was another cashier. She gulped and looked all around the store.

She gestured for the bathroom key, and the cashier, an older woman with long, plaited black hair streaked with white and reddish-brown skin, slid it over to her. The woman examined her for a moment, and set her mouth in a line, and nodded toward the bathroom.

After Fiona emerged, she cast her eyes desperately around the shop. Luis was not there.

"Luis," she said to the woman at the counter, her tired eyes questioning.

"Is not working today," came the woman's answer in a thick accent.

Fiona nodded. "Okay. Okay. If—if he comes in, tell him Fiona dropped by and—if he hasn't already—tell him to call me."

She hoped the woman understood.

In her exhausted stupor she walked back outside and climbed into her vehicle.

She sat there for a moment, then leaned over and opened the glove compartment. In it, power bars sat unopened. She tore one of them open, gnawed it, and thought.

Where the fuck is that air strip.

She would drive back to Antofagasta and hope for the best.

As she did so, she wept by turns, and at other moments, she swerved a bit. She would give anything to sleep. Dawn broke, and she eyed the land all around her. She could smell sea air in the distance. She must be close. She eyed the land, and found flat areas, and she watched the skies. Then she could see, off in the distance, a low structure as she drove. She found a side road, and tired out of her mind, she propelled herself forward.

There it was: the airstrip, the shimmering Cessna cover. She let out a wail of relief.

And there sat the pretty bird: the CUPRUM private jet she'd arrived in.

A security guard saw her vehicle and waved her through.

Does he really think I'm Berkeley, or one of those goons?

But then again, why would he suspect otherwise? Berkeley had not and could not have given him any warning Fiona would be there. It was a company car with a security pass. It was a small airstrip, and who knew what kinds of activity went on there. Probably, she realized, the guard wouldn't want any more attention there than necessary. CUPRUM was one of many secretive outfits that did business in that land, she had learned.

She walked toward the jet. Would it work? Would it open?

And it did, and she glanced behind her, uneasily. Was she being watched? Who might record this? Someone surely was.

Yet the jet extended its stairs, and she climbed in, and breathed in the polished scent of the thing. Its engines began to whine.

A musical voice chimed, "Welcome! Tell us your destination. We'll get you there; we're CUPRUM Air!"

"Um," she muttered. "Knoxville. Tennessee. USA. Wherever…wherever you took off from, I guess"

"Wonderful!" the robotic voice chimed. "Do you have your appropriate documentation?"

Fiona gulped and padded her purse. The thick wallet Berkeley had given her was shoved down in.

"Yes," she answered, running her tongue across her cracked lips.

"Help yourself to our bar and have a seat. We'll be flying shortly!"

It was all so polite and cheerful and disorienting. But Fiona sat gratefully. She eyed the tray where Jack had kept the medicines, and she considered.

"Well," she said aloud, "should I?"

"Should you what? How can we help you?" the robot voice asked.

She groaned. "Never mind, pretty bird."

"Very well. Sit back and enjoy your flight!"

She could drug herself. She could sleep off everything. But it was too much. She was too tired, even to sleep. And besides, she'd missed the view before. She wanted to see it now. She wanted to see herself leave that place for good.

She leaned back in her seat, and it fastened her in its belt. She leaned against its cushioned headrest and looked out the window. The jet spun up, began rolling down the tarmac, and sped faster and faster. Finally it lifted up, thumping as its wheels folded in, and she watched the Atacama fall below her, and felt the updrafts from the Andes buffet the jet.

Yet try as she might, she could not stay awake. She slid off and dreamed of a sailing ship made of stars.

CHAPTER 34
EMERGENT PROPERTIES

Turbulence woke her, and she wiped the drool from her mouth. She needed to pee. She could tell she had been asleep for hours, and now the plane began altering course. She looked out at the ocean beneath her, and tall cumulus clouds, and a distant, swirling mass: a hurricane. She unstrapped, walked to the toilet, and relieved herself.

She walked back into the cabin and gazed all around her.

"I've got my own plane," she murmured.

"How can I help you?" the plane asked then. "Would you like to watch a show or a movie? Can I interest you in some champagne from our bar?"

Fiona snorted. And then she laughed. She laughed for several minutes, doubled over, and then she stopped, and she sat on the floor of the plane. She crawled to the bar and found a bottle of Chilean red wine.

"I may regret this," she murmured. She opened the bottle and lifted it up and said, "To Alva," and she took a swig.

For a long time she sat there, and finally she said with a long sigh, "Hey, Pretty Bird, play me something. Cartoons, maybe. Yeah. Cartoons."

And so she crawled back to her seat, strapped in, tried to ignore the turbulence, and the plane shot her northward toward her home.

When it came time to descend, she pressed her face against the window, heart in her mouth, tears in her eyes: green. So much green! Green mountains, green valleys, verdant and undulating, full of life, full of trees and vines and butterflies and blue jays and cardinals, all the things that she loved so much. And then she could spy the university, sprawled below, through the broken clouds.

Home.

When the plane halted on the tarmac, she broke into a sweat. She opened her purse and pulled out her phone. It was predictably dead. She had no way to get in touch with anyone. As it turned out, she didn't have to.

The moment the stairs opened, a CUPRUM agent met her.

A lanky fellow, with medium brown skin and close-cropped dark hair, chiseled cheekbones, and the sleek, white attire of CUPRUM corporate staff, he said to her, "Welcome back, Miss Hawthorne."

She stared at him, pressing her purse against herself.

Would she be arrested? What did this person know?

"If you'll come with me," he said, and he offered his hand to help her step down.

Bewildered, she took it. He held onto her elbow.

"Do you need assistance?" he asked, and not unkindly, she noted.

"No—no thank you," she stammered.

"Come with me, then. We need to debrief you."

Well, here it comes, I guess.

She took a deep breath, then slowly exhaled, knowing she must face something unpleasant. The man led her down the industrial hallway, and at the end of it, he gestured to a door, unremarkable, with a silver knob. He turned it and held it open for her.

Inside, she met Dr. Bingham and with him, Lafe.

With a shout, she was in Lafe's arms, crying, burrowing her face in his shoulder, and he winced and yowled. She pulled herself away from him and gazed at Doc Bingham.

He took her hands in his, and he stared her up and down. He glanced at the CUPRUM worker.

"Dorfman, thank you. We'll take it from here."

The man nodded, bowed lightly to Fiona, and turned and left.

She gaped.

"What…was that?" she asked.

Doc Bingham shook his head. "They're not all terrible. Now come. Let's get you fed, cleaned up, and all sorted."

Lafe squeezed her hand and looked into her eyes.

"I got a phone call," he told her. "Someone in Chile. God, Fiona…they took you all the way down there? And who was the guy?"

She blushed. "Oh, that was Luis."

"Luis?"

"I'll tell you all about it. But first, pie. A lot of it. And coffee. And a shower."

Lafe laughed, and Bingham said, "I'm buying."

"Good," gasped Fiona. "I feel like I've fallen apart. I need putting back together again."

But not remade.

She shuddered.

"You're more than the sum of your parts, Fiona," Doc Bingham shook his head.

"Are you saying I have emergent properties?" she grinned, even though the effort hurt her cracked lips.

He rolled his eyes.

"Get this lady some pie, Lambert, before she tries any more terrible puns on us."

"It's a date," Lafe agreed.

CHAPTER 35
MESSAGES

Lafe drove her back to her parked car. Full of pie and jittery from coffee, Fiona checked the messages on her fully charged phone. Graham had left her one message. Sighing, she listened to it.

"Listen, I was concerned about you, heard you'd gone missing. Hope you're okay."

"Yeah, so concerned that you didn't think once to try and find me," she said under her breath.

She texted him back: "I'll be by day after tomorrow with a moving truck and some friends to get the rest of my things."

Lafe had her box of items Graham had dropped off, given to him by Doc Bingham, and she dreaded having to deal with all of that mess.

"What's the plan, then?" And though Lafe looked hopeful, the look she gave him made him nod very slowly.

"I think…I'll open a storage unit for now. Crash at friends' pads for a bit, and, well…I don't know. Find a new place to live. I have Alva's photos, too…I'd like to send them to her parents."

"Did you…did you get any closure, down there?" Lafe asked her, tenderly. "Given what happened. You don't have to talk about it. Only if you're ready. We've…maybe we've got a lot to talk about."

She nodded. "Yeah, I think we do."

"Look, I'm sorry," Lafe said. "I…didn't believe you, and I should've. Just…I'm just so glad you're okay."

She threw her arms around him. "I forgive you," she said, and they held each other for a long time then. Then they rubbed noses and kissed briefly.

"We'll always have pancakes," he muttered into her neck.

She laughed through her tears. He pushed her tear-streaked hair back and held her face in his hands.

"Take care of yourself. I'm always here, you know that."

"I know that."

She placed her hands upon his and pulled them away from her cheeks. They stood holding hands. She trembled, and he sighed. The hollows under his eyes told a fraught story.

"Rest up, my friend," she said.

"After you."

And so she walked away from Lafe, back to her car, which sat covered in pollen and splotched with dried raindrops.

"Right," she muttered. "You need a car wash."

She opened the car door with an alarming creak, and sat on the hot car seats. The stale, sealed air escaped her open car door. She turned on the ignition and the air conditioning and let it blast before shutting the door again. The air coming through the vents turned her stomach; she was reminded briefly of the scent in the cave, and she felt dizzy. She breathed in and out slowly several times and recovered as the scent dissipated. She shut the door and buckled her seatbelt.

Her control panel came on and flickered. She blinked. The screen showed a logo, and she felt a crawling chill up and down her spine: "CUPRUM."

"Welcome to CUPRUM Enterprises!" a melodious, neutral voice spoke, with no discernible accent.

"What?" Fiona whispered. "No."

"We are so pleased that you'll be joining us on your new endeavor into exploration and research. Note that all your debts are now cleared, and you will be given a company vehicle within a week."

"What?" she cried, louder. "I'm not part of CUPRUM. What is this?"

"Welcome aboard, Fiona Hawthorne. We've been waiting for you."

The screen flicked off. Fiona sat in cold silence.

THE END

ACKNOWLEDGMENTS

This was a difficult book to write, for although its concept had been long in the making, the circumstances at the writing stage were unforeseen. My mother had fallen ill, three years after my father's passing, and she would not survive to read this book. Because much of *Atacama* is actually set in East Tennessee, where I'm from, the writing process became suddenly poignant. After returning to my hometown in summer 2023, I was able to move forward with it, having found some sense of peace. And I know Mom and Dad would have wanted me to finish what I started.

Atacama is also the result of having worked in academic and non-profit research, of living by the grant, never knowing how long you'll have work. In many ways, scientific research is similar to writing in that regard. It's not for everyone. But you work toward the goal of expanding, not contracting; of growing and not receding. I thank all those in both science and publishing who may never see their names in print, such as in an academic paper, or in a finished book. Your work still and always matters.

I want to thank Sley House Publishing for believing in this book, particularly Editor-in-Chief Jeremy Billingsley, who may have read this faster than any of my books have *ever* been read! And for copyeditor Lillian Ehrhart for excellent edits. Thank you to Chris Panatier for the stunning cover art.

Thank you to my dear family on both sides of the Atlantic: my wonderful children (now taller than I!) for their patience with their geek mother, who's always tapping at the keys or wielding a paintbrush…but always has time to bake them something they love. I love you so much! Thank you to my husband Gareth, who always reads my drafts, and always cheers me on in all things. I love you, babe. Thank you to my three siblings Todd, Greg, and Brenda, for always believing in me.

Thank you to beta readers and friends who have read and supported my work: James Dotson, Pam Magnus, Mya Duong, Richard Czernik, Helen Glynn Jones, Danika (D.K.) Stone, Rowan Hill, Scarlett Algee, Carrie Ancell, Jonathan Maberry, Bonnie Burton, Adrian Tchaikovsky, Tade Thompson, Ryka Aoki, Kelly Varner, Sarah L. Miles, Michael Mulhern, Gloria Thomas, Angela Blackwell, Glori Medina, Bill Dobie, Sharie Hyder, Dean Powell, Damian Kirkland, Rebecca Powell, Huw Powell, and Emma Ireland. Thank you to these marvelous authors, editors, and artists across speculative fiction: Cavan Scott, Cynthia Pelayo, Stark Holborn, Ai Jiang, Paul Cornell, David Quantick, Eugen Bacon, Peter McLean, Ren Hutchings, Renan Bernardo, Greg van Eekhout, Pedro Iniguez, Dennis K. Crosby, , J.L. Worrad, KC Grifant, Antony Johnston, Alice James, Khan Wong, Kali Wallace, Laurel Hightower, T.L. Huchu, Gemma Amor, Jonathan L. Howard, Lizbeth Myles, Rachael Smith, John Wiswell, P.A. Cornell, Rachael K. Jones, Joanne Harris, Alison Sampson, and Laura Bennett.

And many thanks to you, readers, for entering the journey to *Atacama*.

Ad astra per fabulas,
Jendia Gammon

ABOUT THE AUTHOR

JENDIA GAMMON is a Nebula and BSFA Award finalist author of science fiction, fantasy, and horror books and short stories. She has also written as J. Dianne Dotson. Jendia was born in Southern Appalachia, in East Tennessee. She holds a degree in Ecology and Evolutionary Biology and spent several years in academic and non-profit research. Jendia is the CEO and founder of Roaring Spring Productions, LLC, and Editor-in-Chief of Stars and Sabers Publishing. She is also a science writer and artist. Jendia is married to British author Gareth L. Powell. She lives in Los Angeles, California, with her family.

Learn more about Jendia and find links to her social media on her website, https://www.jendiagammon.com.

ALSO FROM SLEY HOUSE

NOVELS

A Mind Full of Scorpions
(Eyes Only, Book One)
JR Billingsley

Ground Control
K.A. Hough

Bad Form
Joe Taylor

Persephone's Escalator
Joe Taylor

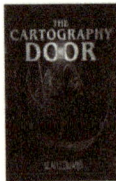

The Cartography Door
Sean Edward

Black Echoes
JB McLaurin

Under the Churchyard in
the Chamber of Bone
JR Billingsley

ANTHOLOGIES

Tales of Sley House 2021

Tales of Sley House 2022

Tales of Sley House 2023

Tales of the Sley Siblings

STORY COLLECTIONS

Melpomene's Garden
Curtis Harrell

Observations and Nightmares:
The Short Fiction of JR Billingsley

JR Billingsley

See more at https://www.sleyhouse.com

www.ingramcontent.com/pod-product-compliance
Ingram Content Group UK Ltd.
Pitfield, Milton Keynes, MK11 3LW, UK
UKHW040843130525
5884UKWH00019B/208